Archon's Wake

By: Daniel Jones

Copyright © 2024 Daniel Jones All rights reserved

The characters and events portrayed in this book are fictitious. Any similarity to real persons, living or dead, is coincidental and not intended by the author.

No part of this book may be reproduced, or stored in a retrieval system, or transmitted in any form or by any means, electronic, mechanical, photocopying, recording, or otherwise, without express written permission of the publisher except in cases of brief quotations embodied in critical articles and reviews.

For more information, please contact Daniel Jones via admin@creatureauthor.com

FIRST EDITION

Library of Congress Data
Library of Congress Control Number: 2024917221
Amazon Identifier
eBook ASIN: B0CS2RHLN1
Paperback ISBN: 9798335423748
Hardcover ISBN: 9798335424981

Cover design by Ivan Zanchetta & Bookcoversart.com
Printed in the United States of America

Archon's Wake is intended for Mature Audiences

You will encounter graphic descriptions of:

Monster Attacks
Blood & Gore
Mutilation
Body Horror
Intense Violence
Strong Language
Recollections of Extreme Abuse

Reader discretion is advised

Not a spicy story

No Generative Artificial Intelligence was used (whole or partial) for the writing, editing, and/or illustrations of this novel.

Strap yourself in and please enjoy the ride!

Journey Checkpoints

0: Emergency On The Harbinger Tundra	1
1: Landing In A Ghost Town, Again	7
2: Next Stop, Certain Death	34
3: Wait, It Gets Worse	63
4: Alive For Now, And It Hurts	101
5: Layers Of The Pain	125
6: Lines That Should Not Be Crossed	151
7: Demons In Plain Sight	182
8: Light Another Fuse, Run Like Hell	212
Aftermath: The Lurking Shadow	241

0: Emergency On The Harbinger Tundra

"I don't know what I can say that hasn't already been said," Rogue Whip says to a young woman, who is holding a pen in one hand and a notepad in the other. "There isn't anything about the Camp Tor incident that I'm hiding."

"You've said that three times now." The woman is trying to be kind; after all, she took a chance to ask Rogue for a quick interview and he set her up with a dinner interview on the spot. This could be the interview that gets her noticed by the Cliffridge Gazette's head editor. But Rogue isn't talking about the famous hydra slaying.

"You've asked the same question three times. Doesn't matter how you word it, phrase it, or what tone you use." Rogue leans back in his chair and looks around the lavish restaurant they're in. Waitresses in sharp dressed uniforms carry bottles of wine and plates of food to anxious patrons, all of whom are comprised of Acinvar's wealthy and elite class. The walls are made with illusionary motion art, soothing water features, and dazzling displays of flame torches.

The young woman nods in defeat. It's clear he won't be talking about it further. If he was going to humiliate her like that, why let her order expensive food on his tab? She wants to sulk and run. "Um-"

He takes a sip of water and sees she's like every other journalist: eager until he shuts them down. But he needs her, or any journalist for that matter, to help him get a different story out. One about his company's new project. "It's all anyone asks me. It's like everyone's forgotten about Rogue Whip the Pilot. No one cares that I can land a dirigible or an airship in the most challenging places or fly through disastrous weather. I miss being famous for my flying skills."

The young woman writes his words down feverishly. If he's going to say something, she might as well write it down and maybe something will happen. "You still fly your own airships? Aren't you, like, the owner of Rogue Whip's Tradewinds Crossing? Why would you waste your time doing a pilot's job?"

"If you want your Rogue Whip article with actual news that no one's ever heard before, that's the side of me you need to focus on," Rogue says, and it's clear that his answer has taken the young woman by surprise. She's looking at him with curiosity. "Yes, I do still own the company, but I love to fly. I personally handle direct shipments of Elvador, Dicrasse, and Othal. When I'm not doing those, I am training a new generation of pilots for the rescue division we opened toward the end of last year."

"A rescue division? Why would you do that? I mean, isn't that what Heart's Mandatory Life Laws are for?" She asks.

He pats the table and smiles. "Now you're getting it. See, that law ensnares too many young and inexperienced pilots who might not be up to the task. Most militaries also don't consider the type of airship they need for such occasions, and while the laws have rescued a few people, not every pilot can steer their airship toward an erupting volcano or a flooded city and be ready for the challenge of those kinds of environments. I'm trying to create a fleet that will be ready to go anywhere, anytime, with people and equipment that are the right choice for the situation. I want to save the lives of the pilots, who shouldn't be forced to sacrifice their aircraft or their lives," Rogue replies.

"Governments have such fleets do they not?" The woman asks, after finishing her notes. This isn't the interview she was expecting, but it's more of a story than she imagined. What a scoop!

"Not many, not enough. Acinvar does not. If you want to continue this at my office, I can give you public records that I obtained when I started the division, showing which governments do and which don't. What's worse, is the ones that do, won't send their untrained pilots to do these rescues, but will hijack a privately owned airship and force its pilot, regardless of their skill, to go do the same thing the government pilot can't do. The result is too often the same. People die."

His passion for this topic is throwing the young woman through a loop. Why hasn't anyone else jumped on this story? In her mind, the big-name news reporters should be setting up daily conferences on this thing. "This topic sounds serious; why hasn't it gotten more attention?"

"That's a good question for the Acinvar Oligarchy." Rogue chuckles. "The Heart Mandatory Life Laws were agreed upon, because of the lack of available equipment. Governments, understandably, can't keep throwing money at it when that money comes from the people. Politics sidesteps the fact that it's created a dangerous situation for too many people over the past sixteen years. There's gotta be a better way. I just need people to stop caring about Rogue Whip the Hydra Slayer for a few weeks and start caring about Rogue Whip's Tradewinds Rescue."

The young woman finishes writing down his words then puts her pen on the table. Every word he's saying feels like gold until he mentions the hydra, and it slaps her in the face. Suddenly she realizes why he's giving her his time like this. "This is amazing. But I think my editor is going to kill this story. He's a hardhead who wants the hydra."

"Your editor and every other in this damn town. But let's try anyway, I'll throw some money at the Cliffridge Gazette if it helps," Rogue chuckles.

"Master Whip, may I join you?" A gentleman interrupts them.

Rogue looks up and sees a well-groomed man, wearing a dark green suit made of the finest wool, adorned with gold trimmings along the seams. He's surprised to see a good friend of his, but one who lives very far away. "Uh, yeah, sure; Miss Avery, this is Cal Sephinoto, Prince of Hurlua on Outer Shell."

"Charmed." Prince Cal offers his hand to her, and she grips it lightly, while giving him a small smile.

It takes her a moment to register what Rogue just said about him. A real prince? Actual royalty? She lowers her notepad and pen to give him a quick curtsy.

Prince Cal keeps his attention on Rogue, completely ignoring the young woman after the obligatory handshake. "I hope you can accept my apology for the intrusion; you were unavailable at your skyport office and the staff said I could find you here. This isn't a personal meal, is it?"

"Media interview, actually. Well, actually, I'm supposed to be at that table where Jessie seems to have everyone eating out of the palm of her hand. I decided to duck out for this lovely young lady. But uh, I always got time for you, my man, what's up?" Rogue replies.

Prince Cal quickly retracts his hand from Avery's, when Rogue says the first few words, and wipes it on his vest. Of all the things he could walk into, this would be the worst. He looks at her like she's a piece of gutter filth. "I see. Journalist?"

Rogue gives her a moment to answer him but she's blushing and speechless. Hurlua has a very tight grip on its media, and their officials despise freedom of the press, such as what Acinvar offers. "Junior journalist, third assignment, potential career maker for her. She's not the bloodthirsty truth warping type." He tries to talk him down.

"Yet," Cal emphasizes. "I am not taking any questions, miss. I do have urgent business with Rogue, however, and it is time sensitive."

Rogue takes a sip from his glass of water. "Oh boy, sounds like you're about to cash in a favor."

Avery scribbles on her notepad.

"Not a word!" Prince Cal points at her.

"Easy. You're in Acinvar, freedom of the press is serious here. You could've waited until I got back to my office if you wanted privacy." Rogue gestures to him to sit down with them.

"No. I couldn't. I need you to evacuate a group of researchers from the Harbinger Tundra immediately," Prince Cal says.

Rogue lays his hands flat on the table. "I'm sorry, what? You gotta warn a guy before you say something like that."

Prince Cal takes the seat and does his best to ignore Avery's noisy scribbling on her notepad. "You are in good spirits today. In all seriousness, there has been a group of researchers on the Harbinger Tundra for some time now, and they have failed to check in, after several missed deadlines. I fear the worst has happened, and I need you to either retrieve the bodies or rescue the survivors."

"There's your headline for your editor." Rogue points to Avery.

Prince Cal rolls his eyes. "Fine, if you must, simply leave my name as Prince Cal; that's my formal title."

Rogue chuckles. "You are an awesome friend. My skills as a pilot have been forgotten, and you're telling me to go fly into no man's land, surrounded by a permanent storm that gives even experienced pilots a run for their money. It's one of the worst conditions a pilot could ever attempt. And you're telling me people are trapped there? This is great! I'll do it!"

Prince Cal is taken aback. "That required so much less convincing than I was ready for."

"Help me out for a sec and describe the Harbinger Tundra to Avery, and why the Ring Storm is a nightmare. Excuse me while I pass a quick word along before I go poof on Jessie." Rogue gets up and walks across the restaurant to a table where his company's CEO, Jessie, is chatting with a few of their business partners.

"That was short! Finished your interview already?" Jessie is surprised he came back already, then gets nervous when she sees the smile on his face like he's about to find a way to weasel his way out of another client meeting.

"What is Prince Cal of Hurlua doing at the table you left?" One of the businessmen gestures over to him.

"Miracles happen when I need them, Rick. Jessie, I need you to get backup pilots on all my routes for the rest of the week and prep them for next week just to be safe. I'm taking a Colossus class from my rescue fleet and heading to Outer Shell; I'll be skyward before you finish up here," Rogue replies.

Jessie stares at him, exasperated. "You can't just up and leave in a three-thousand-foot-long airship with a statement like that."

"It's a rescue operation. Prince Cal came to me with this; it could put my new project on the map, I need to do this, it's happening," Rogue replies.

"Royalty from Shell coming all the way to Heart to ask for your services?" Rick asks. "You keep growing in notoriety by the day."

"Rogue owes Prince Cal a favor. At least tell me where you're going," Jessie says, before she leans close to Rogue's ear. "You may still own the company, but you made me CEO. A little teamwork like the old days would be nice."

"I'll leave a report on your desk and bring two bottles of Grevatto Prime when I come back. No, a whole rundlet, maybe a tierce, if they have one. We're celebrating when this is done," Rogue whispers back, before getting up. "I leave you gentlemen in Jessie's fine hands. Sorry for the abrupt exit, but this is one of those opportunities none of you would pass up if you were me. And I'm not passing it up for anything." He heads back to the table where Prince Cal seems to be having a lively chat with the journalist.

Jessie shakes her head and returns her focus to the men across from her. "Does he always do this to you?"

"It's Rogue, we know his energy." One of the men laughs. "What is this he mentioned about a new project? It sounds interesting."

Rick scratches his head. "Did he even say where he's going?"

Jessie's eye twitches, as she watches Rogue walk out with Cal and the journalist. "Wine shopping apparently. Next time, let's have this meeting at Aurelia's Tavern so I have access to Burbon when he does this."

Rick slaps the table. "Yes. A hundred percent yes. My tab!"

1: Landing In A Ghost Town, Again

Rogue Whip wakes up to find himself on the ground. His entire body is throbbing and his skin feels like it's either on fire or freezing. He groans and rolls onto his back. Above him, the sky is hazy and grey, with large clumps of snow falling all around him. His head is spinning, and he's dizzy, but he can make out that there's a lot of debris around him.

Ugh, again? He closes his eyes and waits for his head to stop spinning. Sensory overload is making the pain worse. When he opens his eyes, he sees trees above him, covered in torn fabric.

What? A forest? That's not, how'd I get-? He rolls onto his side and sees a dirigible crash site. "The Dauntless Crosser? No that's not possible, that was destroyed in-." He pauses when his mind catches up to what he's really seeing.

He closes his eyes and tries to rub them; moving hurts worse than laying still, but he has to figure out what's happening. When he opens his eyes again, he sees a very different scene. A massive airship is destroyed, and he's in a snowy place of some sort. No trees, no mountains, just flat, snow-covered ground as far as the eye can see. The sky is cloudy, blocking out the sun, making it hard to guess the time of day.

Wait a minute, the Tradewinds Goliath. Ugh, how'd this happen? I can't remember anything.

The airship's crash site is compact. Surprising, given how large the airship is. A balloon structure three thousand feet long, with a crew and cargo cabin the size of a large cargo water ship. Most of the balloon structure and fabric are gone. Piles of twisted metal beams scattering the nearby area are all that remains of it, but the cabin structure is still in one piece, for the most part, even if it looks like crushed and twisted metal.

"I see you here. I see you clear," A strange voice echoes around him.

"Who's there?" He rolls onto his stomach and tries to push himself to his hands and knees. When he succeeds, he finds a severed arm near where he landed.

"Whoa!" The sight scares him at first. Then he notices something clutched in the hand, which is curled into a fist. Carefully, he pries the hand open to grab the crumpled piece of paper. A drawing of a gorgeous woman sitting on a park bench.

"I'm always with you Joey, no matter where in Yeraputs you are. Your Hannah." As he reads aloud and realizes whose arm is in front of him, a sense of dread fills him. Joe Duran was the name he knew him by, and he knows Hannah, an enthusiastic young woman who's always one of the first to run out of the family waiting area when an airship with Joe on board lands. She always sprints for him and leaps right into his arms, whether or not he's carrying anything.

Another glance at Joe's arm does little to give him hope that Joe is somehow alive. He pockets the drawing and forces himself to his feet, ignoring the pain. He takes small steps toward the flight deck of the wreckage, which is the only way he sees that he can get inside.

The whole airship cabin appears to be crushed flat. Even if he can get inside, it's going to be hard, if not impossible, to get any further than the hallways connecting the main level decks and quarters. The glass on the flight deck is gone. The snow

Archon's Wake

crunches with the sound of shattered glass as he walks.

Before he gets close enough to crawl onto the deck, he spots a pool of blood under the debris. He looks away and takes a deep breath, preparing himself to find out who it is. When he does bring himself to check, he can't find a body and decides that's probably for the best. His heart is heavy; this is the first time in his company's history that he's lost people on the job. They've had serious crashes, but his crews always survived. Today is clearly a different case.

Getting onto the flight deck isn't difficult, but the sight that greets him when he stands up is. A woman's body dangles from the pipes on the ceiling, one of which is impaled in her chest where her heart would be. He doesn't recognize her face, but the jumpsuit she's wearing is from Hurlua, which makes her one of Prince Cal's people. A look of agony is frozen on her face; the terror in her eyes causes Rogue to look away. At the back of the deck, near the flight controls and navigation console, is another body wearing an impact vest that went off just like the one Rogue has on, but the way it's slumped is unnatural.

Step by step he approaches the corpse and moves some of the ripped airbags away, discovering the man's head is twisted from a broken neck. He walks around the controls and sees a huge wound at the back of his neck, like something tore a bunch of flesh from it. A quick glance up reveals a bent pipe with sharp edges pointing down, there's a bit of torn flesh dangling above the man.

How'd this guy get thrown high enough to hit that? What the hell happened when we went down?

"Skin of heart, skin of cold." A voice whispers from the front of the flight deck; Rogue looks up, but can't see anyone.

"Hey!" He calls out. A chill crawls down his spine and he feels threatened. Something is with him.

"Sense you now, sense your soul." The whispering voice passes him and fades away.

Rogue looks all around him, searching for the source. "Who's there?" A moment passes and he hears no response. "Ugh, must've hit my head harder than expected." He covers the man's face with the airbag. The next thing to do is figure out where he is if he can; the navigation table still has charts and maps clamped down, and after brushing some debris off he's able to see where the last markings were made roughly thirty miles away from their intended destination.

A quick glance out at the tundra and then back down at the map. *There's no way I could walk that far. Not the condition I'm in now. And if anyone else survived this, if they're hurt, how would I be able to get them that far? I gotta do something.*

He grabs his clothes; they're freezing and damp from the snow.

Let's start with getting to my room and getting some new clothes, then see if my ice gear is around and usable. Then I need to check out the cargo hold. There were vehicles on board. Yes, that's right, crawler transports. Coal fueled; steam powered. I know there's a ton of compressed coal on board. If anyone survived, then I can get one fired up and warm. Then search for survivors and get the hell out of here. Ok, I have a basic plan; assuming the ship didn't go too far off course in the crash.

He walks to the doorway leading to the central hallway and peeks around the corner. At a glance, the path is clear enough to walk most of the way down the cabin. There's debris all over the place from the personal quarters, pipes from the ceiling, the floor is bent up in a few places, and the walls look crumpled in various spots. However, the noticeable lack of bodies or body parts or blood spatter and pools is something Rogue is thankful for.

There were twenty-three souls on board. Nineteen crew from Acinvar and four from Hurlua. I hope I'm not the only one walking away from this.

"Hey! Can anyone hear me!?" Rogue shouts at the top of his lungs. "Anyone! Sound off, make noise or something! Let me know you're here!"

He takes a few steps deeper in and hears nothing. Only deafening silence, aside from the gentle clanks of his boots stepping on the steel floor. The first room behind the flight deck is coming up on his left. It's the captain's quarters; his quarters. After a short pause he peeks inside the room, anything not bolted down is thrown all over the place. A breeze comes through the wreck, forcing him to shiver from the cold.

Archon's Wake

I need to find my gear before I freeze to death.

The window across from the door is gone, and the freezing air bites at his skin as he searches for dry clothes and his cold weather gear. He decides to just change into new jeans and a shirt just to get out of the wet flight uniform. As he changes, he notices the frostbite on most of his chest and legs is mild; luckily, not as bad as what his arms look like. He stumbles across a piece of broken mirror on the floor and decides to take a look at his face. His cheeks are beet red, his nose and forehead are bruised black, and his eyes are bloodshot, but not cut or bleeding.

"I've seen better days for sure." He mumbles, after tossing the shard aside.

His cold weather gear is easy to find once he gets the mattress off the ground; his company's signature dark green with teal and beige highlights stands out against the stark white of the snow.

"Wool body suit, anti-frost pants, anti-frost jacket, quilted trapper for the head, and ice resistant-" He stops when he hears a soft clang just outside his door.

"You scared the crap out of me." A woman walks into the room and wraps her arms around him, embracing him tight.

Rogue relaxes after her remark startles him. "Kita, you have no idea how happy I am to see you alive."

"I couldn't find you anywhere in the ship. Where were you?" Kita is a shock trauma surgeon, from Air Drop West Hospital in Acinvar, and was on the team that received Rogue and the other survivors of the Camp Tor incident a year prior. Ever since Rogue started the rescue division of his company, he's brought her along as a medical expert for high profile operations.

"I landed outside, impact vest broke my fall. Did anyone else make it?" Rogue asks.

"Just one of the Hurluans. The Te'Yuro guy. He was in the cargo hold when those things attacked." Kita answers heavily, her mind is on another man onboard; Edward, her fiancé. She can't find him, and she's fearing the worst. Seeing Rogue has given her hope more people are maybe alive somehow. "Wren survived the landing in the engine room, after trying to make sure it didn't explode. But he didn't make it long after that. I couldn't save him."

Rogue's heart skips a beat, he turns away and pounds at the wall, he can't make out what he feels in the moment. It's a combination of unpleasant emotions. "I'm sorry Kita. No one deserved this."

"What were those things? Did Prince Cal or any of his people tell you about them?" Kita asks.

Rogue's brain feels a sharp momentary pain, but he recalls what Prince Cal's men told him. "Gigas Archons. I don't remember much, but they downplayed them, for sure. I was thinking elephant big. Not megafauna big."

Kita stops him from putting his jacket on to get a better look at his arms. Her medical instincts are kicking in. "You're lucky that frostbite is mild. We need to get you to the-" Something outside behind him catches her eye. "What is that?"

Something shuffles around a pile of debris outside. Large, mantis-like creatures, with blade like appendages on their arms and stone looking skin. Rogue rushes to get his gear on. "Where's Te'Yuro?"

"In the cargo hold, trying to get a crawler going," Kita answers.

"Let's hope he's almost ready." Rogue grabs her hand and runs to the hallway, almost running into one of the creatures that made its way inside. It has the severed head of the body from the cockpit held up to its jaws.

Kita screams in terror at the sight, startling the mantis enough to drop its meal and scurry away. She screams again when the man's head rolls and stops with his chewed-up face looking right at her.

Rogue tugs on her arm. "Run! Now!"

They run along the hallway until they reach the passenger entrance to the ship. The whole wall in that area is missing and they jump outside. Kita follows him, then screams again, when she sees there are dozens of them all around the wreckage.

"We have to reach the hold! Now, while they're more interested in scavenging for food, instead of hunting us!" Rogue helps her up.

The sound of gunshots coming from the hold causes Kita

to stop, and Rogue to run toward it faster. The shooting continues until the ground shakes. The tremors cause Rogue to stop in his tracks. His heart races and he begins to hyperventilate.

No, not here. There's no way.

Flashbacks of the ground shaking the same way while in an abandoned mining camp flicker through Rogue's mind. Another set of tremors causes him to drop to his knees. But the sound of ice cracking snaps him out of his hallucination. Nearby, a large sheet of ice lifts up from the ground as a giant crab-like creature rises out of it. It uses long pincers to snap at the mantis creatures heading toward the wreck. It's so fast, Rogue can't even see the crab move, one split second the pincer is near the crab's body, then it's outstretched with a helpless mantis trapped in its grip. It brings the mantis to a multi-jointed mouth and shoves the mantis in whole. The mantises scatter and hide amongst the debris.

Rogue can hardly believe his eyes, the crab is the size of a large savannah elephant, and it's colored the same way the mantises are, with a grey stone-like texture and color. The top of its shell is flattened, and the edge is lined with lots of sharp bladelike spines. Its pincers are thin and made of a bony material, but the rest of it is like any land-based crab, only on a larger scale.

The sky darkens for a short moment, causing the crab to retreat under its sheet of ice, which seems to fit into the ground perfectly, as if it was never open to start with.

Rogue and Kita both look up but whatever it was is now out of sight.

Oh, that can't be good. "We need to keep going, now!" Rogue gets back to his feet.

Kita shakes her head with tears in her eyes, too terrified to move. "We're going to die here."

Rogue takes her hand. "Listen, we're not dead yet. We have a chance to get out of here. Ok? We gotta get to the cargo hold and find Te'Yuro. That's first. Then we do what's next, ok?"

Kita stares at him, petrified. "What's next? What is what's next?"

Daniel Jones

Rogue checks around them; the mantises are now completely out of sight. The side of the cargo hold drops down, slamming on the ground with a massive thud. Rogue gestures to it. "We find hope and push forward."

She stares into space, not reacting to the cargo hold. "That's not-"

"The place we were headed to, where those researchers are? It's not far, if we have a crawler. Less than thirty miles bearing forty-eight degrees; give or take a few miles and degrees. We can find it and get help." Rogue tries to reassure her.

Kita can't bring herself to get up, but she squeezes his hand. He pulls her to her feet and helps her walk to the hold.

A man wearing a Hurluan jumpsuit comes out of the cargo hold and waves them down. "Over here!"

"Te'Yuro! You have no idea how happy I am to see you!" Rogue is happy to see the leader of the Hurluan security team they brought.

"Likewise, mate! Little buggers backed off for a moment. Good thing too, ran out of ammo." Te'Yuro is an older man in his fifties, with short, greying hair, in a flat top cut. He has a thin face, with a few small scars on his right cheek. He's been a soldier for his entire adult life in the service of Price Cal, rising through the ranks to become a specialist in helping with matters the prince deems sensitive. He first met Rogue during a politically tense operation to reunite the royal family of a small nation called Darmoro about six months before.

Rogue and Kita finally reach the cargo hold, which is half the size of the entire cabin structure. It's the only part of the wreckage that hasn't suffered any major structural damage. Everything that was tied down by Rogue's ground crew appears to have stayed in place. There are two more members of Rogue's crew standing next to a crawler that's rattling to life.

"You found survivors?" Kita asks Te'Yuro, her face lights up with excitement.

Te'Yuro gestures toward them. "They landed outside and smacked down into the ground with those fancy impact vests."

"Same as me," Rogue comments. "I'm lucky the wreck didn't come down on top of me. Gerrard! Sarah!"

Archon's Wake

Gerrard and Sarah both look up at the sound of Rogue's voice and wave to him.

"There's one more in the back of the crawler; bloke named Perry, according to those two. He's alive, but not awake. I found him before the Scythe Mantises showed up." Te'Yuro grabs Rogue by the shoulder.

"Your people should have told me the truth about those archons. They're a lot bigger than you led me to believe." Rogue grabs Te'Yuro by the shoulder and has half a mind to punch him in the face.

Te'Yuro keeps calm as Rogue gets in his face. He's about to say something when strong winds shake the hold and the area outside darkens again.

"What's doing that?" Gerrard points as the darkness moves across the ground and out of sight.

"Our attacker." Te'Yuro points up as a massive object comes down from the sky. They can't make it out through the snowy fog, but they can see its massive shadow. "I'm sorry mate, I didn't know they got so big. I'd have told you if I knew."

The ground shakes hard, knocking everyone off their feet, and a fierce gust of wind blows snow past the wreck. The open side of the cargo hold is slammed by a wall of snow like an avalanche. Tremors rattle the hold as they come from each footstep the gigas archon takes.

"I didn't get the best look at it when it took us out. Did you?" Rogue glances over at Te'Yuro and Kita who both shake their heads no.

Te'Yuro keeps his eyes on the approaching shadowy mass, it's growing larger and larger with each step. "Has anyone ever seen something so big?"

The look of awe on Te'Yuro's face mimics the one Rogue has, the sheer size of what's coming toward them is difficult to believe. "That's already as the big as the Tor hydra was," Rogue stammers.

"This snow isn't that thick, almost a thousand feet visibility, and we're still seeing nothing more than a shadow." Te'Yuro doesn't hide how nervous he is.

"On a good note, they won't go out of their way to hunt

15

down tiny prey like us," Rogue says, even as he realizes they're inside the cargo hold and the airship could be seen as prey. "The hydra saw us as entertainment, a break from the usual grind. If these archons have that kind of attitude, then I'll panic. Laws of nature apply, right?"

The gigas archon is now close enough for them to make out details. The creature is hundreds of feet tall and appears taller as it approaches. As everyone digs themselves out of the snow in the cargo hold, they get a better look. Its head is like a lion, with a thick bushy mane, on its back are two folded wings, and it has a long, bushy tail. Its legs are thick, stocky, and muscular. Its fur has black and white stripes like a tiger.

"How the hell did you know nothing about them?" Kita asks.

"They can't fly through or above the Ring Storm. They're trapped here until that storm fades, if it ever does." Te'Yuro sounds as terrified as he looks.

"This can't be the same one that tried to attack us in the air," Rogue comments.

"I see you here. I see you clear." A strange voice says inside Rogue's head. In his mind, he sees a glimpse of a man's skeleton with a lion's skull, shrouded in a black foggy haze. "You should not be here."

What the hell was that?

"No, this one is twice the size, easily. I was in the observation deck before it was smashed." Gerrard speaks up because he did catch a good look at the one that took the airship down, and it was enormous, but this one dwarfs the one that attacked them.

Everyone watches anxiously, staying silent and motionless.

The archon lowers its head to sniff the wreckage. Its eyes dart around from one person to the next, taking note of everyone's presence, but stares at Rogue as a green shimmer in its eyes flash at him. When it finishes, the archon rubs its chin against the top of the cargo hold, scratching an itch before walking away a bit. Then it unfolds its wings, raises its hind legs and stretches its front paws out.

"That wingspan is thousands of feet," Te'Yuro mumbles.

"Half a mile, or close to it." Rogue notices the wings are

similar to that of an owl's, which explains why they can fly without being heard.

Te'Yuro watches the claws sticking out of the front paws as it stretches. The claws themselves are nearly twenty feet long; they're also serrated in reinforced layers. It would have no problem tearing into anything man could possibly create, as proven by the one that attacked them and shredded the airship in a matter of seconds.

Another archon roars in the distance, and the one in front of them tenses up, faces the wreck, and roars back. The sound is deafening, causing everyone to cover their ears. A violent infrasound shakes everything around them. Rogue and Te'Yuro drop to their knees; their bones and organs vibrate inside their bodies. Gerrard and Sarah fall to the ground and writhe like they're having seizures. The archon flaps its wings, which produces hurricane force gusts with each flap, and leaps into the air, sustaining its flight and vanishing into the fog going toward the direction of the other roar.

Rogue helps Te'Yuro up. "You know what, I was able to stay mentally focused after the crash, but now I think we're screwed."

Te'Yuro grabs at his heart. "That thing's roar, that bellow, it-" He drops back to his knees and has a coughing fit, spitting out blood several times.

Rogue glances over at Kita, who's lying face down in the snow. Gerrard is unresponsive, with bloodshot eyes that are pointing in two different directions, and blood leaking out of his nose. Sarah is desperately trying to wake him up by shaking him.

Before anyone can tell her to stop, she starts coughing up blood herself.

"Shit. Bad enough we survived the way down. Now we've got serious problems," Te'Yuro says.

"That roar shook my insides. Kita, we need your help." Rogue goes to her side and puts his hand on her shoulder, she groans and rolls over.

"What… happened?" Kita barely manages to say.

Rogue gets to Sarah and Gerrard. Sarah falls over sideways when she tries to stand back up. "He's gone." She curls into a ball and cries. "He's gone, he's gone, he's dead."

"The roar killed him?" Te'Yuro repeats in disbelief. "What the hell are we up against?"

Kita pushes herself up and looks at Gerrard. "It caused a bleed in his brain. That sound, the vibrations, they shook us that hard?"

Rogue and Te'Yuro manage to get Kita and Sarah inside the crawler, where they find Perry dead in the same way Gerrard is. Sarah clambers into a chair, pulls her knees up and buries her head into them while crying. "This can't be happening; this can't be happening."

"How much fuel is in this thing?" Rogue asks Te'Yuro.

"Got enough compressed coal to keep it going for two weeks," Te'Yuro replies.

"We're going to try and get this thing moving. That Ghonda outpost we were supposed to land at is about thirty miles away between forty-five and fifty degrees bearing. If this tundra is as flat that far out as it is here, we will see it and get to that research team. Figure out next steps there." Rogue heads for the cockpit.

Te'Yuro carries Perry's body out of the transport and places him next to Gerrard. "Sorry mates," he says, before going back inside the crawler and closing the rear. The ground shakes again, like it did before.

"Oh no." Kita straps herself into a chair, covers her ears, and closes her eyes.

Sarah whimpers and curls into a tighter ball.

Rogue looks around for any sign of the archon but doesn't see it. "For something as big as it is, it's alarming how quiet it moves." The archon's paw steps down in front of the cargo hold as it steps over the wreckage and walks out to the open tundra. *Ah shit.*

The archon's pace slows, and its already quiet movements become fully silent. Its footsteps don't cause tremors anymore. It lowers itself, as if on the hunt. But there's nothing around, as far as the eye could see. Its wings unfold and rise high into the air and then flap down, right as it leaps into the air. The archon jumps to an incredible height and comes down with its full body weight on its front paws. Its landing smashes through the ice, sending shards in all directions. The ground quakes, shaking the entire wreck and causing the debris to rattle.

The gigas archon's head lifts from the hole with the crab creature from earlier caught in its jaws. The archon shifts its prey around to get the perfect bite down on it. Its teeth pierce through the stone-like armor of the crab and cut it in half.

Rogue watches half of the crab drop, blue blood squirts out, the legs and pincer twitch around until the archon lowers its head to finish its catch in a swift gulp. Te'Yuro and Kita join him in the cockpit to watch what's going on.

The archon sniffs the ground nearby for a short moment, searching for anything left of its meal, then turns its focus to the wreckage while licking its lips clean.

"Why do we have its attention?" Te'Yuro asks Rogue.

"I have no idea. But I don't think it's good," Rogue replies. *It's looking straight at us.*

The archon walks up to the wreckage and starts rubbing its chin against the cargo hold, it grasps the cabin with its immense paws and lays down. Like a colossal cat, it keeps rubbing its head against the rigid edges of whatever part of the cabin will withstand it.

"It's going to knock the hold over!" Kita shouts.

"Oh, don't say that," Te'Yuro gripes.

The archon in the distance roars again. Everyone covers their ears and hides behind the chairs in the cockpit. The archon nearby snarls, kicks at the wreckage and leaps into the air before unleashing its roar. The gusts from its wings flapping blows away loose snow and sends smaller bits of debris flying.

Rogue looks up in time to see snow rippling to the infrasound's vibrations.

"That's absolutely insane. Do you have any idea what kind of sound that thing has to produce to do that?" Te'Yuro points up to the sky.

"I'm still feeling it in my bones from the first time it did that." Rogue jumps into the driver's seat and starts adjusting some levers to get steam pressure into the mechanical system. He's not going to wait around to give the archon a chance to knock the cargo hold over, which will trap them in the crash. "Let's hope we can still move."

Daniel Jones

"That thing came back for a quick bite, so whatever you're doing, you need to-"

"I got this; make sure the boiler didn't take any damage from that thing's damn roar," Rogue cuts Te'Yuro off. "Kita, can you watch the steam pressure gauges over on that panel and let me know when the dials start moving." He points to a panel at the back of the cockpit.

"I see movement from here," she replies. "Everything except the one labeled valve nine."

Rogue glances over at a metal panel above his head that lists the various gauges and systems. "Valve nine? We don't need that."

"What's it for?" she asks.

"A crane arm. It's not important because this thing doesn't have one," Rogue replies, and pulls back on the lever that puts the vehicle in motion. The tracks grind on the metal floor and the transport plows out of the cargo hold, through the snow, and onto the icy ground.

Sarah's cough in the back of the transport sounds worse than before and Kita goes back to check on her. She puts her hand up to stop Kita.

"I need to check you out." Kita dismisses the gesture.

Sarah kicks at her while coughing up blood. "No." She throws a punch at the air. "No. Let me die."

Kita grabs her fist and forces it down. "I can't let you do that. Listen to me, you'll get through this. Alright?"

Sarah spits blood at her face out of anger. "You're lying." She has another serious coughing bout, with mouthfuls of blood coming up until she slumps in the chair with a lifeless look on her face.

Kita searches for a pulse and can't find one. Out of instinct, she lays Sarah's body on the floor and gets ready to perform CPR, when Te'Yuro grabs Kita's shoulder to stop her.

"Let her have her wish. She doesn't deserve to live through more pain," Te'Yuro says.

Kita is astonished by the cold tone of his voice. "No, it's my job. I have to try."

"To what? Bring her back to suffer more? And then what? Wait in pain for the next airship crew to try to rescue everyone or die waiting? No lass, that's not saving a life. Have some mercy," Te'Yuro says forcefully.

Rogue turns his head to look behind him. Sarah's face and chest are covered in blood in a gruesome sight. *Dammit. That roar. Those things. This place. How the hell are we going to get out of here?*

Across the tundra is an entrance to an enormous cave. Massive pillars of ice, gleaming in the sun, line the sides of the opening. Fresh snow sparkles in a dazzling display across the otherwise featureless landscape. Only atop the mouth of the cave is something amiss. Smoke rises from the center of a small campsite that's been destroyed. Tents recently burned away, and there's not much left of any equipment. A large twin rotor aircraft stands alone near a roaring fire.

Several men and women are kneeling in the snow. All of them are tied with their hands behind their back and they've been beaten to within an inch of their life. The blood on their faces is either frozen or dried, and their skin is blue from frostbite where it's not blackened with bruises. Each of them is stripped down to their undergarments and left to take the full brunt of the freezing air. Most of them have broken arms; the bones are sticking out of their skin. One of them has broken ribs poking out of his lower chest and his upper chest appears caved in. The wounds are unaddressed except what's required to keep them alive.

Six men and two women are all that remain in the group that was exploring this part of the tundra for reasons they refuse to disclose. Surrounding them are people in black metal armor, including helmets that don't reveal the wearer's faces. They stand perfectly still, in the same pose at attention with their hands at their sides. Aside from being black and made like plate mail armor, there's nothing that tells their victims about who they are or where they came from.

Nearby is a makeshift fire pit with a roaring fire from coal normally used for fuel. Several victims have already been thrown onto it. Each one burned alive, thrown into the fire only to be allowed to crawl off, kicked and beaten, and thrown back on until they succumbed to their intended demise. On the other side of the fire is a large flying machine, with rotors on the top of wings that tilt. A machine the victims have never seen before.

The leader of these attackers steps out of the vehicle, a woman wearing the same style armor, except hers is unpainted steel. She towers over everyone, standing nearly seven and a half feet tall. If one were to look at her, the only thing that might give her away as a woman is the long red hair flowing from her helmet. She carries a unique gunblade style weapon on her back; it is four feet of tungsten alloy made into a heavy sword, and the hilt is made of a complex revolver that has multiple ammunition wheels.

Next to her is a man, wearing a worn, pale-yellow leather jacket, and heavy-duty canvas pants with pockets for an assortment of tools and equipment. He's taller than an average man, with a fit build, and has a long scar running from the bottom of his cheekbone down his neck, complementing an already rugged and grizzled appearance. A custom-made shotgun is slung around his back and a belt of shells is around his waist. His face is the only one revealed among the people who came off that aircraft and attacked the group.

Each time this man appeared, another person from the group would be taken into the aircraft, screaming would last for what feels like eternity, and the person would be added to the fire. But this is the first time the woman has come out with him.

She raises her hand at the people in black, featureless armor. All of them head for the aircraft without saying a word.

"What? That's it?" One of the women asks, with what little energy she has left.

The woman in the steel armor turns her head to the woman and walks over to her. She takes her helmet off, revealing a thin face with pale skin, almost as white as the snow, pointed almond shaped orange eyes, and a smile of satisfaction that reflects she's gotten what she wanted.

The woman who spoke regrets it immediately and tries to

look away, closing her eyes shut, and hoping whatever fate befalls her is a quick one.

"Sidhia, of the Westloom Sands," the armored woman speaks softly.

Sidhia shudders at hearing her name being spoken and cries.

"You are free to go." She grabs Sidhia by the neck and lifts her up to her eye level. "Your skin was a lovely shade of russet; it matched your olive eyes in a way that glowed with beauty. This death of ice is not so befitting of you."

Before Sidhia can react, the woman forces her into a kiss, sucking the air out of her lungs, using her tongue to keep Sidhia's mouth open. Before the kiss ends, darkness overcomes her, and nothingness follows.

The woman throws Sidhia's severed head into the fire and kicks the rest of her body away. She swings her sword to fling the blood into a straight-line inches away from the rest of the survivors. "Feisty, that one. Her last breath was rather delicious and showed far more life than was deserved," she says to the others, who remain motionless during the act of senseless violence. "Make yourselves more useful than that pathetic woman and at least feed your carcasses to whatever wild animal wants it out here."

"You're a Juman Huntress. I'll bet you savor every murder you commit," one of the men says, as she turns to walk away and retrieve her helmet.

The woman stops in her tracks and turns to the man. Her expression is now one of lust for bloodshed, a smile of twisted intention from ear to ear. It's also clear from the man's face that he's trying to provoke her into giving him a swift death, such as she did to Sidhia. The glimmer of hope that the end of pain and suffering is near, it's seeing that from him so plain and clear that sets a passionate fire in her heart. "Titania, alas no, a Huntress is beneath me. Great guess though, my Mistress would surely applaud you for the attempted deduction. I am a Juman Venator, my dear little prey."

Her reply now has the other survivors looking her way, each of them staring at her in a new and heightened form of terror.

Daniel Jones

"We couldn't find it, not with our best people, and you'll do no better!" the man shouts.

Titania smirks, picks up her helmet, and places her hand under the man's chin, then forces her fingers through the bottom of his mouth until she can reach his tongue, grabs it between her thumb and index finger and rips it out. Using the wound for a handle, she drags the man to the fire, grabs the broken bone sticking out of his leg, and fully rips it out of him. When she's done, she gently places him onto the fire and walks away without saying a word or looking back. Letting his blood drip from her gauntlets.

The man with the shotgun waits for her at the aircraft after everyone else in their group gets on board. "That's a new way to hold one's tongue. Anyway, from this new information, we can locate the actual coordinates of the Ghonda ruins, which is where they've based their operation."

The rotors move as the engines fire up, the pilot looks out the windscreen at them with a thumbs up.

"A different direction and mindset are demanded. No, required! No, ugh; damn, I need a more forceful word. Whatever, you get the point, Mr. Smith. We will report this discovery to my Mistress and allow her to dictate our next steps," Titania says in a cold voice, that fails to hide the excitement she's trying to bury.

Hunter shrugs, and leans against the hull for a second. "You know that journal is a fake, right?"

"Yes, but this impersonator's identity is the key detail. One that is far too interesting. Though, next time, I suggest verifying my speculation the instant it's clear. Lest you wish to join that lot of fodder. It's a long ride back, and I don't want to get bored." Titania puts the tip of her gunblade at his throat. Her movement was so fast he didn't even see it happen. One instant her hand was at her side, then the next her weapon is in hand with her arm fully extended.

"Your point is clear, ma'am," Hunter says, without skipping a beat. "I simply wished to appreciate your flair for the theatric."

Titania chuckles and puts her helmet back on. "Flair for the theatric, or the lust and pleasure of inflicting pain? I do appreciate that you find my taste in amusement to your liking. But, back to business. To your knowledge, has the late Lord Albert Richtoff ever mentioned discovering Dr. Lourcer's laboratory? I heard he often gloated to people while his hands were inside his patients. Oh, how I would've loved to witness a living dissection of his."

"His ramblings were usually about what he could do to the body while he was doing it. But, during the dissections and torturing I witnessed, no, Lourcer is not something he even hinted about."

"Richtoff understood the need for balance. A balance that my Mistress has a distaste for, even if she found ways to tolerate it. Secrets such as the fabled Denwa Lithium mine's location. He destroyed them for the sake of maintaining a balance between powers like Juman, Acinvar, and Solgirus."

"I wouldn't compare Dr. Lourcer's laboratory to a mine that could upend economics. One is clearly more terrifying than the other," Hunter replies.

Titania puts her weapon away. "It's rare to have anyone around to enjoy such insightful conversations, really livens things up. I knew you weren't all silent machismo." She hesitates, before boarding the aircraft, to give him a quick sideways glance, and catches him staring at the open tundra with a surprising amount of attention. "What is it?"

Hunter forces himself to answer her before she loses patience. "Trying to envision Richtoff being out here for any reason at all. This is the kind of place he'd put immense effort into avoiding. Snow and ice and nothing else as far as the eye can see." Hunter follows her into the aircraft. The moment the door closes behind him, he can feel it taking off and takes a seat at the back with the other Juman soldiers.

"Take us to Bluewood Cove with a speed that impresses me." Titania shouts at the pilots. They both respond with a thumbs up and adjust the controls, picking up more speed. After bracing herself to compensate, she reaches into her chest armor, pulls out a leatherbound journal, and opens it. "Mr. Smith, tell me what you've heard of a thing called the Harbinger Weapon?"

Hunter has never heard of it before, a fact that is reflected

Daniel Jones

in his blank expression.

"Not so well informed after all, pity." Titania is amused by his reaction and holds the journal out toward him. "Entertain me; take a shot at using what you know of Lord Richtoff to decipher the laboratory's location."

Hunter takes hold of the journal, but she doesn't let go, instead yanking it out of his grip with a grin. "You thought I'd let you read the full contents. What a silly man. These secrets belong to Juman; secrets that can make soldiers on the battlefield simply vanish without a trace."

Until the moment she started thrashing unarmed and helpless people around, Titania was a cold, silent, and serious person. Every muscle she moved, right down to every breath taken, was precise and dedicated. Now she's animated, vibrant, and full of energy.

Hunter gives his most polite smile. This spontaneous nature of Titania's is coming out of nowhere. And it's terrifying. "That sounds powerful; I can understand the Mistress's interest in such a thing."

Titania puts her hand on his neck and runs her finger along his scar. "I know what made these ripples. Must've taken years to fully heal, micro-serrations from a gritty texture blade. To celebrate our tenth outing together, tell me, which of my sisters did this to you?"

"Liliana; she was a Huntress at the time," Hunter says.

Titania grips his neck and squeezes tight. "How dare you spoil it for me! You gotta tease a lady, make her beg a little, pull her hair, those kinds of things; ugh, you're no fun at all."

Hunter does his best to keep calm, and not react, aside from making eye-contact even though he can't breathe. "She failed to assassinate Lord Richtoff because of me," he manages to say.

Titania sits in the seat next to him and holds him close to her side, walking her fingers up his chest. "You? You stopped Liliana, as a Huntress, before she became Venator? That's hard to believe. Tell me the story, and tell it right this time, we have an awfully long flight."

He does his best to prepare himself for the rest of the flight.

Rogue stops the transport outside a large building that has new equipment all around it. "This must be where they set up." *For ancient ruins, this place looks amazing. The buildings are in perfect condition. Wide streets for massive vehicles. You'd never guess this was abandoned four hundred years ago.*

Te'Yuro jumps out the rear hatch. "It's like stepping through time."

Kita peeks out the hatch to have a look for herself. "I thought the Shiv Empire perished some hundred years ago?"

"Technically the last of it fell two hundred years ago, but in this region, it was wiped out almost four hundred," Te'Yuro elaborates.

The ruins of Ghonda don't look like they're from an empire that fell hundreds of years ago. The buildings are still standing, and appear to be in good condition, as is anything else made of stone, metal, and concrete. Signposts with directions in the Shiv language are still standing in most places.

Te'Yuro walks up to the warehouse's hangar style door, and something catches his eye on the ground behind a wooden crate.

Kita kneels next to a pile of sandbags. "Is this some Hurluan thing?" She holds up some clothes from a pile on the ground.

Te'Yuro rummages through the clothes next to the crate. Belts are all buckled, and tools are secured in the pockets. It's like someone assembled them to fit together and dropped them on the ground. But there several of them all over the ground, most of them are near big objects like crates. "This is not normal."

Rogue looks in the back of the transport at Sarah's body. *I don't know what to say, hardly have any idea what to think. This isn't worth the lives I've lost.* He returns his focus to the controls, releases some steam pressure, and makes his way to the boiler compartment to close the air intake. When he finishes turning the system off, he leaves to join the others.

Daniel Jones

"Rogue, you need to come see this," Te'Yuro says.

Now what? He heads over to Kita and Te'Yuro who both have the same terrified expression as they stand right outside the door. As he gets closer, he notices the clothes on the ground. "What's with the piles of laundry?"

"Rogue, it gets stranger inside," Kita stammers. "I don't like it."

"The only way to describe it is people just vanished. People stopped writing mid-sentence, tools dropped in the middle of use, I've never seen anything like it." Te'Yuro's voice is shaky and subdued.

Rogue eyes the door and takes a deep breath. "You know what, why not? Let's dig around and see if we can't disappear ourselves."

"That's really not funny." Kita barely manages to stop herself from slapping him.

"I'm not being funny; my company's crew are all dead." Rogue storms past her and barges through the warehouse door. Inside looks like an operations center. Freestanding walls with large maps and charts all over the place, desks with stacks of paper, large tables with cartography equipment, it's not far from the few large scale scientific, archaeological, or other research expeditions he's visited to deliver equipment and supplies.

A woman's bloodcurdling scream pierces Rogue's ears, and he looks up and around. But there's no sign of anyone. Goosebumps form over his skin, but not from the cold. He feels like he's on edge in heightened fight or flight mode.

The floor is littered with piles of clothes and dropped tools exactly as Kita and Te'Yuro described. And it's far creepier in person to see it in the limited glow from the high windows and fading oil lamps. Standing in the building makes him feel apprehensive and nervous at first. Those feelings grow into dread and even trepidation.

Ok, this shit is seriously creepy. And it happened recently, whatever it was.

He walks up to the table with a large hand drawn map showing the entire Harbinger Tundra, marking its borders with where the Ring Storm is. Dozens of locations are marked across the tundra, some are names of Shiv ruins, others are caves or caverns or other underground locations, many of which are crossed out. Nearby are notes about penguin colonies, archon territories, and the canyons that sprawl through the southern half of the tundra.

Te'Yuro joins him. "Any ideas?"

"They seemed determined to locate these so-called Harbinger Penguins. Most of the notes I see are pertaining to possible places to find them," Rogue says.

Te'Yuro picks up another map and whistles. "Wow. Geologically, this is scary, check this out. The magma pits beneath Ghonda are essentially a pressure sieve for subterranean volcanic activity. One bad quake could make this place collapse and that would block the magma flow. If these measurements are right, which I seriously doubt, they think this place is sitting on a super volcano."

Rogue walks over and eyes the papers Te'Yuro holds out. "Let's not trigger a quake then. I'd rather not test the theory."

Kita leaves the warehouse and goes to a long building across the way where ice has been cleared from the ground. She peeks inside a window to discover the building has been turned into a barracks. Basic wooden bunk beds lined with thin mattresses covered in blankets and small nightstands are covered in personal items. "How many people were out here?" she mumbles to herself.

Something moves inside, startling her. She screams and sprints back to the warehouse.

Rogue and Te'Yuro investigate the back of the warehouse where there are dozens of strange glass cubes stacked in a pile. All of them are made with panes of frosted glass on the outside and lenticular glass on the inside. Each one is three feet long, wide, and tall with metal edges on all sides and locking latches on the top.

"I wonder what these things were for," Rogue says. "I'd think these would be too delicate for samples of any kind. And I don't know what kind of supplies would come in containers like this."

Te'Yuro turns his attention to the more normal looking crates of supplies further down. "Who knows, maybe if someone shows up you can ask them. I'm more interested in the fact these supplies aren't marked as Hurluan."

Rogue glances over and spots what Te'Yuro is curious about. "What would make that so strange? It's not like you don't outsource for supplies on expeditions like this."

"Except for the fact that all of this is marked with the same crest, and I don't recognize the language."

Rogue comes over to take a closer look. "That's from the desert region of northern Inner Shell."

"The Sandseas? Can you tell which one?"

Rogue pops the top of a crate open, finding a variety of foodstuffs in glass jars. He pulls one out. "Candied cactus leaves; my guess would be the Blooming Sandseas. That, or someone paid more than a few shiny coppers for these. Supposed to be delicious."

Te'Yuro raises an eyebrow as Rogue pops the jar open takes out a yellow green cactus leaf dripping in a pink sticky goo. It smells like a mix of honey, watermelon, and aloe. He takes a leaf out of the jar when Rogue offers him some.

"This stuff is so expensive it rivals Elvador black label teas. And it's rare, because you can only get it during certain times of the year. A jar like this in Acinvar would fetch an easy six figures," Rogue says, before taking a small bite out of the leaf.

Te'Yuro holds the leaf at arm's length before deciding to give it a nibble. It's as sweet as he expected, with a soft fleshy texture, and the aftertaste comes with a hint of a spicy kick. "I wouldn't pay more than a few coppers for this, but it is good."

Rogue finishes the whole leaf in a few quick bites. "Neither would I, but wow, that's full of flavor."

Kita slams the door to the warehouse shut. "There's something out there!"

The men run through the warehouse to her. "What'd you see?"

"Something moved in the bed building across the way!" She keeps her body weight on the door, pushing to keep it closed.

"What was it?" Rogue puts his hand on hers and peels it off the door to get her attention. "Kita, breathe. In. Out. Breathe."

Kita can't calm down and slaps him across the face. "Don't you dare!"

"Easy love, what did you see?" Te'Yuro says.

"I don't know what it was. The building across the way is where these people were living, and I saw something move. After seeing nothing but creepy shit, it freaked me out, alright?!" Kita screams.

Te'Yuro rolls his eyes and waves her off.

"Alright, we'll go take a look," Rogue says.

"Fuck you. I'm not doing anything." Te'Yuro walks off and takes a seat on a nearby table.

"Fine, I will go look, then!" Rogue cuts in as loud as he can. "You two wait here and try not to kill each other."

Rogue helps Kita back to her feet, then opens the door, checks the street, and walks out when he's sure the area is clear.

"Hey, don't die. Please." Kita grabs his arm as he walks out.

"I don't plan on it." Rogue peels her hand off. "I'll be back. There's food in the crates over that way, go grab something to eat, until we can figure out if this place is safe or not." He walks across the street, following her footsteps in the snow to the building she mentioned. The door to its lobby is wide open, and inside it looks like a normal communal living space: chairs and couches, with tables scattered about. *Wow it's hot in here; come to think of it, so was the warehouse. No way small lamps could warm up spaces this much. Makes me wonder where the heat is coming from.*

He enters the large room full of bunks and checks around the doorway. It's quiet; there's nothing moving, no sign of anything out of the ordinary. The beds are made, and personal items are kept on them or the nightstands. Some items are under the beds in a clean-ish fashion. No signs of panic, clearing out, rushed exits, or other problems.

Something leans on his shin without warning. Causing him to jump and yelp.

An orange cat yowls and jumps at his yelp.

"Shit, you scared me to death! You scared Kita too, I bet." Rogue kneels down and offers his hand to the cat, palm up.

Daniel Jones

It purrs while rubbing its chin on his fingers, then he gives it plenty of chin scratches before picking it up. *Calm for a cat; must've been the local mascot or comfort animal or something.*

He looks at the collar hoping to find a nametag on it, but there isn't one. "I know someone who would love to meet you right now."

It rolls out of his arms and lands on the floor, then takes a few steps and meows like it wants him to follow. As he does, it occurs to him that nothing looks like it's in the process of being packed for folks to leave. Rogue was sent here to bring them all back, so why is nothing packed or ready to go?

The cat jumps onto a bed and rubs against the nightstand next to it. On the floor are two bowls. The cat meows louder.

"I see. Alright, hang on, let me have a look." Rogue pets it and then opens the nightstand. "At least your food was easy to find."

Meanwhile, Kita stares at the warehouse door, waiting in silence with her arms wrapped around her legs. She gasps when the door opens, then relaxes when she sees Rogue come through it.

"I found it." Rogue faces her with an orange cat curled up in his arms.

"They brought a cat?" Te'Yuro chuffs.

"Kitty!" Kita rushes to it and snatches it out of his arms. "What's its name?"

"Cinder, according to the food bowl it led me to. Cat food was in the nightstand next to its owner's bed."

Kita sprints past him. "We can't separate a cat from its food! Are you crazy!?"

Te'Yuro chuckles at the stupefied look on Rogue's face. "She's got a point, you know."

"It's warmer in the other building, anyway, has only one way in and out-"

"Found something you might be interested in." Te'Yuro hands him a stack of papers while he follows Kita out.

Rogue looks at the top page. "Harbinger Tundra Bestiary Profiles."

"This place is full of life under the ice. Best we stay on the surface," Te'Yuro says.

Archon's Wake

Rogue thumbs through a few pages, finding handmade drawings along with handwritten notes. He stops when he finds a page that simply reads: GIGAS ARCHON. The next few pages are drawings of them, and finally he comes to one that has notes:

Gigas Archons are the apex predator of the Harbinger, and a megafauna that scales far greater than its habitat would theoretically allow, despite the harbinger tundra being just under two million square miles in size. First impressions are that of awe; its sheer size is difficult to comprehend. They largely share features with the Forest Archons commonly found through Yeraputs. Lion-like heads with horns, and wings protruding from their backs that grant them the gift of flight. We found out most of this the hard way. Is there anything new in here.

He runs his finger along the notes until he comes across some new details. "They are extremely exothermic and rely on the tundra's frigid temperatures to survive. Keeping their distance from the canyons or other places where the volcanically active cave systems are exposed. They migrate across the tundra following the movements of other exothermic creatures like the ice pit crabs. Blah, blah, blah, this isn't all that much of a discovery."

He thumbs through more papers looking for the entry on the penguins that he kept seeing notes for. Finally, he comes across a page that reads: HARBINGER PENGUIN

The following pages are blank, except for the last one, which has a short note:

HARBINGER PENGUINS ARE NOT THE MYTHICAL ANIMAL THEY WERE ONCE THOUGHT TO BE. NEW EVIDENCE SHOWS THEY EXIST, AND THAT THERE IS TRUTH TO THEIR LEGEND. WE WILL FIND THEM, AND WE WILL CHANGE THE FUTURE OF THE HUMANS OF YERAPUTS.

"See what I mean?" Te'Yuro says over Rogue's shoulder, after Rogue tilts his head up from reading the note. "You should take advantage of getting some rest while you can; let's figure out the rest later."

Rogue takes another look around the operations center. "Yeah, out in the middle of nowhere, surrounded by monsters... again."

2: Next Stop, Certain Death

The next day two people, a man and woman, approach the destroyed campsite atop a cave entrance. The man is wearing an exoskeleton with hydraulic parts, thick plating, and heavy gear. The woman is wearing ordinary cold weather gear.

She takes her frosted goggles off to see the carnage for herself. Bodies of her people are hunched over, with their hands and feet tied behind their back. And a heap of ashes with several human skeletons is nearby. "Gods be damned." She's on the verge of crying out in pain and anger. The sight makes her sick to her stomach.

The man walks past the bodies and looks down at the cave, finding the rest of the camp's tents and equipment in a messy pile at the bottom of the entrance. "It appears as though time is running out to accomplish this task of yours."

The woman remains silent, taking a moment to look over each body, giving them a silent prayer.

"Isla, we cannot stay here."

"Have you no respect?" She says, with no emotion.

"I respect the danger you face, and fear for your safety. Far more than you have shown either in recent days," the man retorts.

The woman scoffs at him and returns to her prayers.

"Forgive him, my people. His mind is at no less peace than my own," she whispers.

The man rolls his eyes and grabs a metal pole to poke at the fire. One of the skeletons has a chain around its neck with a few small cylinder objects attached. "Empress, whoever did this has the journal."

That's a remark she can't ignore. "Forgive me," she mutters under her breath, and joins her bodyguard at the firepit.

He holds the chain out to her with a solemn expression on his face. "Don't look too closely. It's clear he was tortured before this happened to him."

"That doesn't narrow down the list of culprits." She takes the chain and wraps it around her hand. Something on the ground catches her eye; a small bronze cylinder. She walks over to it and holds it up. "This, however…"

"Juman." The man's exoskeleton arms open up and reveal rotating machine guns with belt fed ammo.

"They've long left the area. We're fine." Isla tosses the bullet casing aside and looks at the cave. "Hondo, put those things away; there's no danger here."

The guns retreat into the suit and Hondo looks toward the south. "They may have headed to Ghonda; we must assume it is not safe to return."

"They'll already be there. Take me to the Sodkar ruins; we will contact Hurlua for more information. After you allow me a moment of silence to honor my people's sacrifice." She kneels to continue her prayers.

Hondo remains quiet and waits patiently for her to finish.

She stands back up, tears flowing in rivulets down her cheeks. "It's not that I don't fear for my life, Hondo; the fact is, that is the very reason we are here. But every life lost here is a sacrifice. It dishonors them, and my kneeling to pray for their journey beyond is the best I can give them."

"You are Empress of the Blooming Sandseas, Isla Amenaza; every life lost is a sacrifice in your defense. Few deaths come with greater honor." Hondo bangs his chest. "Come, the light of day shines brighter than days prior; archons will be hunting beyond their domain."

Another object on the ground catches Isla's attention: an unused shotgun shell. Made for a custom bore, her heart sinks deep into her chest, and she freezes in fear.

Hondo comes to take a look. "I do not know this one."

"This one is revenge for my crimes," Isla says, as she begins to tremble in pure terror.

"I see you here. I see you clear." A voice shouts above the sound of a guttural roar.

Rogue wakes up drenched in sweat, feeling sore all over.

Kita is sitting next to him. "Take it easy, your body is in bad condition. Stay down." She puts her hand on his chest.

"Tell me something I don't know." Rogue takes her hand off him and sits up.

"You need to let me do my job so that when the time comes for you to do yours, you can." Kita gives him a stern glare. She can't stop him but wishes someone would at least listen to her.

"And I will, but at least let me relieve myself." Rogue starts walking to the far side of the barracks to the lavatories.

"Te'Yuro hasn't come back from the warehouse since he left last night. Man is all kinds of arrogant." Kita looks out the window over at the warehouse.

Rogue gives it a quick glance. "Wouldn't surprise me if he's searching that place high and low for answers. Best to let him do his thing."

Kita shakes her head. "He's got more broken ribs than functioning brain cells." She waits for Rogue to come back from the lavatory. "Come, lay down. Doctor's orders."

Rogue stares at the warehouse. "We should probably check on him."

"I refuse." Kita cuts him off. "Go, if you must, but don't exert yourself!"

"I'll bring some food back, at least." Rogue watches her ignore him and pet Cinder. Outside it's a freezing but sunny day, but at least it's brighter than yesterday's snowstorm.

Te'Yuro looks up from the tundra map when Rogue comes into the warehouse. Something catches his attention above Rogue's head, and he's clearly nervous. "Checking in?"

Rogue shrugs. "Something like that. Find anything interesting?"

"Interesting? Well, sure; Ghonda sits on top of a large cave system that has several openings to magma pits. Heat is funneled into the buildings from there, and melted ice is also collected for the running water, which I'll never figure out how it still works after being abandoned for so long. As far as the researchers go, they are indeed from the Blooming Sandseas. These people collected much information on the area for Hurlua, but that seems to be a cover for something else, probably related to the penguins that are rumored to live here."

"Hang on, I didn't have any coffee yet, and my brain is still mush. Small bites please." Rogue rubs his head as Te'Yuro rattles off all this information.

"How about no. I did find something that might wake you up though. They had two lines of communication, one of them was created and operated in secret." Te'Yuro tosses a small wooden box at him.

Rogue catches it and looks inside. "Telegraph transcripts?"

"To Juman."

Those two words do wake Rogue up, and he tenses up.

"I've never known Juman to strip people naked and force them to leave piles of clothes where they once stood. But they were summoned to come here."

Rogue sets the box on a nearby desk. "If they are on their way, where does Hurlua stand with Juman?"

"Neutral. Fair trade practices are upheld. No public discourse. However, they will know who you are and-"

"Acinvar and Juman are in a cold war, waiting for something to spark real fighting. After being credited with slaying a hydra, I would be a very public figure of interest that Juman won't pass on. Yeah, I know." Rogue holds back from shouting. *Boy, do I know what would happen if they did capture me.*

"That, and the stunt with the Darmoro Royal Family reunion when we first met. You're not a dead man, but that's the scary part."

Daniel Jones

"What are you getting at?"

"I'm just saying it might not be a coincidence that Prince Cal had you come here for an evacuation that these people were clearly not expecting to make. Something is off; it seems Prince Cal is hiding something serious, even from his own people."

Rogue leans against the desk and looks up at the ceiling. "I should've asked more questions."

"It doesn't change anything once the Jumans land. But Ghonda's underground tunnels certainly might. Massive multi layered labyrinth, with countless places to hide? Shiv built this place to hide secrets." Te'Yuro points to a table that's covered in a stack, several inches thick, of large paper sheets.

Rogue checks it out. *Seven stories down, each spanning the size of the surface town. That's pretty big. This place had to house at least five thousand people in the buildings up here.*

"There are eight entrances to the underground across the entire town, including one under the glass crates. Getting down there is simple. But knowing where one is once down there is a different matter. I didn't manage to explore much of anything, before realizing I could get lost for the rest of my life."

Something darkens the windows for a moment, causing Rogue to look at the windows at the back of the warehouse. "We've got incoming."

"Yeah, I saw it coming over the horizon before you walked in," Te'Yuro says, and points up. "Juman airship, about as large as the one you brought."

Rogue turns his head to look out the windows on the front of the warehouse and sure enough, there's a massive red and black airship floating above the town. "Whose side are you on?"

Te'Yuro shrugs and drops his arms to his sides. "That depends on who, aside from me, has interest in letting me live. If that's Juman, well, you're not in a great spot. However, if it's not in Juman's interest to let me live, well then, I'll act on that as we go. Unless of course something serious like a Venator shows up or worse."

Before Rogue can reply, the sound of rotor engines becomes deafening. He looks back to the warehouse door and sees an unusual twin rotor aircraft circling the town.

"I've never seen one of those before." Te'Yuro starts getting a bad feeling about the aircraft as soon as he sees it.

"An osprey," Rogue mumbles. *There's no time. Kita. Shit. I gotta do something. I gotta.* He can see her peeking out the window of the other building with enough time to start looking for somewhere to hide. *She's as good as dead if they search there.*

Te'Yuro watches another osprey take off from the airship's hold. "That's unusual, they're sending small teams instead of landing and showing their full force."

Rogue blocks the door when Te'Yuro starts moving. "I'm not about to let you sell me out."

Te'Yuro raises his fists. "Can't say I blame you, but still."

Rogue throws a quick punch into his face, and follows up with an uppercut that knocks Te'Yuro to the ground. "Fuck off, Hurluan. I'm going to them first, and I'll be sure to put you in a bad spot. Ya know, if it saves mine and Kita's lives." Rogue walks to the door and heads to the middle of the street and waves his arms around.

The osprey hovers above the warehouse where Rogue is standing. "Ma'am, there's a man waving us down! He's not one of ours," the pilot calls out.

Titania stomps her way to the cockpit to take a look. "He's a white man, possibly from the diversity of the Blooming Sandseas. Regardless, I know who I will be having some very intimate fun with first. Mr. Smith, come look at this poor fool. Almost looks defiant, no?"

Hunter rolls his eyes and puts on a fake smile as he makes his way to the cockpit. "As long as you torture the poor bastard in private this ti-, uh oh." He can't believe his eyes when he sees the man standing in the middle of the abandoned street.

Titania gasps like a schoolgirl and takes her helmet off. "Oh my, could it be you know this person? You do, oh my gosh! You simply must introduce me to him! Does he have a preferred method of being tortured? Oh wait, he's not been in Richtoff's lab, has he?"

Hunter ignores her. "Pilot, land with the side door directly in front of him," Hunter says. "Titania, you need to treat this man carefully. Even I fear what your Mistress will do to you if he dies."

Titania is about to scold him for giving orders to her soldiers, much less telling her what to do. But the brazenness and the scared aura all over him only fuels her curiosity. She'll play along, if only for the opportunity to enjoy her own spontaneous nature.

The pilot looks back at them and Titania nods with a hysterical laugh. "Why not? This makes my day far more exciting than I could imagine. Everyone get tactical! We are approaching a V-I-P, let's demonstrate the highest professionalism possible."

"Mistress's craft has taken off, she's making landfall," the copilot calls out.

The smile on Titania's face shrinks and she shrugs. "That will dig into my playtime, so make this quick," she says with a huff.

Hunter stands in front of the door and waits for the vehicle to land.

Titania stands behind him, making sure to be as uncomfortably close as possible, and puts her helmet back on.

These people sure know how to make an entrance. The osprey lands mere feet away from where Rogue's standing, and the side door is directly in front of him. When it opens, he's stunned by the first person he sees. "What the hell?"

"What the actual fuck are you doing here?" Hunter steps off and moves to Rogue's side as Titania straightens up to look as tall as possible before stepping off.

"It's complicated," Rogue replies. "Well, it started simple enough, then things happened." He looks up at the seven-and-a-half-foot tall person stepping out. *Whoa, that guy is huge.*

"Hunter, don't leave a lady waiting," Titania says, in her sweetest voice.

That's a woman? Wait, tall women in thick plate armor. I know what she is. This is bad. Rogue eyes her up and down then gulps. "A Juman Venator." He whispers to himself, intending to think it, but right now, he's terrified. Jumans are bad enough, but their special forces?

Titania gasps at hearing him identify her and takes a deep, excessive bow. "At your service mister..." She offers her hand to him, palm down, like a royal does when presenting a ring for loyalty, and takes her helmet off with the other.

She's strong; that sheet metal doesn't hide how strong she is. She's in a great mood and that can't be good for anyone. Ok, make this easy, show no weakness. She's still a Juman, and there might be rules in play.

"Rogue Whip, at your service," Rogue answers, with the most confidence he can muster, and takes her hand to shake firmly rather than kiss. Her grip tightens; she's crushing his hand, but he squeezes back with all his might. It makes her smile ear to ear; she stops squeezing but keeps her grip tight enough to cut off the circulation in his hand.

"Rogue Whip. What a silly name, Hunter was making you out to be someone-" She stops mid-sentence as her mind catches up to what she's saying. The smile on her face fades away and she gets serious. She looks at his hand and loosens her grip. "Forgive me. I am used to knowing that name by its Lotus Island pronunciation. My, my, let's keep this to little mishap to ourselves. I like the Acinvar ring to it. Rogue, Rogue Whip." She chuckles at her own words.

Rogue matches her chuckle and lets go of her hand. "I get that a lot traveling across the Tradewinds. Please forgive me; I didn't catch your name."

Her smile returns slightly. "Hunter, you missed your chance to announce me. He's so bad at introducing his friends." Titania punches Hunter playfully in the shoulder. "I am Titania, Venator of the Maroon Mistress."

Daniel Jones

Te'Yuro keeps his ear by the door, eavesdropping on the conversation after the engines are turned off. His gut writhes when he hears her introduce herself and he panics, searching around the warehouse for somewhere to hide. "This just became a nightmare."

"I think it's out of respect for you; I can't exactly see him stepping out of line in your presence." Rogue keeps the mood upbeat. "Titania, it is a delight to make your acquaintance. Welcome to the coldest and spookiest abandoned town in all of Yeraputs. The setting hardly befits any lady."

"I dislike frigid, but you've aroused my desire for the spooky." Titania glances around, finding it strange that no one else has made their presence known. If these are the ruins of Ghonda, there should be hundreds of unlucky people around. Unless something has happened, and she doesn't have much time to get that kind of information before her Mistress lands. "This place is Ghonda, no? Where are the researchers who were camping here?"

"Gone. Actually, let me show you, what we found hasn't been moved yet." Rogue offers her his arm like he's offering a lady to go for a stroll.

His gesture genuinely surprises her; no man who knows what she is has dared to offer her so much as a hand to hold, let alone an entire arm. Not that they'd survive doing so in usual circumstances. "Hunter, you could learn much of life's great lessons from this man, he knows how to treat a lady." Titania smiles devilishly and hooks her arm around Rogue's gently. "I am a serious connoisseur of the spooky and grotesque; you've no idea how high my expectations are, Mr. Whip."

"Rogue, please. I was hired by Prince Cal to evacuate the people who were supposed to be here. But as a Gigas Archon would have it, I crashed out on the Tundra. Made my way here and found mysteries all over the place." Rogue takes her to the nearest pile of clothes lying on the ground.

Ok, she's playing along for now and my head is still attached to my body; this is going well. He glances over at the barracks; Kita is hiding, and he hopes she got the hint. *If I can buy her time to get away, that would be for the best.*

Titania looks it over, unamused, looking as though she's been slapped in the face. "What am I looking at?"

"Well, if you lay them out like so, it would appear as though someone was wearing these." He pulls the clothes out to lay flat.

Titania notices how the clothes are assembled as if they were on display. Or to Rogue's observation, being worn. It's not much for spooky, but that detail is important.

"Dozens of them all over the place, where the researchers were likely standing. This warehouse was their base of operations. It's my opinion the people vanished somehow, and this is all that's left of them."

Titania lets go of his arm and looks over at the soldiers lined up at the osprey's door. "Search the warehouse! It's exactly what our Mistress suspects!" she orders, before returning her attention to Rogue. "Vanished by some unknown means; have you observed any wildlife in the town since your arrival?"

"Can't say I have, but these folks, if what I saw in there is any indicator, they're obsessed with the Harbinger Tundra's penguins," Rogue answers.

The second osprey lands right behind them, next to the transport crawler.

"Penguins?" Titania tries to be mysterious but comes off as menacing.

"I don't suppose you'd be willing to fill in a few blanks. Perhaps we can help each other. All I ask for is a ride out of here. And I'll make myself available; Hunter can vouch for my ability to be useful."

Titania puts her finger on his lips when he finishes speaking and lowers herself to his eye level, staring right into his eyes with a gaze full of dark desire. "I find your company amusing for the moment. You're strong, polite, and matching my vibe. Do not cause my mind to wander elsewhere. Hunter can vouch for my ability to become your greatest nightmare," she says, while pressing her face right into his and pecking him on the lips.

Hunter watches Rogue somehow endure her threat without so much as a flinch or twitched muscle. "If I may, ma'am, I can get him up to speed on the Harbinger Penguins while you oversee the premises search?" He interjects himself.

Titania watches the second osprey land. "I have a better idea. You facilitate the search, while I introduce my new friend to my Mistress."

"The Maroon Mistress is here?" Rogue is visibly taken aback. *What kind of serious shit did I get into?*

"Oops, he broke. Don't worry, I won't hold it against you. She has that effect on me as well at times." Titania puts her hand over her heart to match her sarcasm.

Rogue straightens himself out and does his best to hide his panic.

She then leans in close to his ear. "Dear sweetie, you'll have to do better than that. How could the man who murdered Lord Richtoff bend so easily? Please compose yourself. Your offer, a clear play at self-preservation, which I loathe and despise, will depend entirely on your performance with her. Don't ask for such, you were making my heart flutter until your weakness appeared. I offer this only because I adore the shape of the bruise on your cute nose."

Is she always this obnoxious? Poor Hunter. How long has he had to deal with this?

Hunter can tell what Rogue is thinking from the look on his face. "You have no idea, Rogue," he mutters to himself.

Titania's demeanor changes in an instant the moment the door on the second osprey opens. She's completely emotionless and grabs Rogue's arm firmly. "Walk," is all she says, before hastily greeting the other venators.

Rogue jogs to keep up. The other Venators all share the same featureless metal plate mail style armor, stand over seven feet tall, and have the same physique as Titania, causing him to assume they're all women under those helmets. He is forced to a stop a few feet short of where the venators are lined up.

An elderly woman, wearing ornamental maroon robes, steps out in wooden sandals. Her face is thin, with perfectly smooth, wrinkle free skin, but in such a way to avoid hiding her age. At her waist is a long, thin, polished black bamboo sheath adorned with ruby red engravings. Her katana's hilt is featureless and painted blood red. She stands about Rogue's height, with long, straight, dark grey hair, tied into a traditional style bun matching the rest of her presentation. As she walks, he notices how her movements are flawless, direct, and balanced.

The Mistress gazes at Titania with what Rogue deciphers as a level of disapproval or disappointment. *This can't be good. Even Lord Richtoff feared this woman. What the hell am I doing here?* He stifles a gulp when her eyes fall onto him.

"A promise kept." The Mistress raises her arm and flicks her wrist.

Behind her, two more Venators emerge from the aircraft with a man whose hands are shackled together, and his head is covered by a hood. They throw the man at her feet.

Rogue watches in shock when they pull the hood off and reveal Prince Cal. Who looks up at the Mistress with tear filled eyes. "He's alive? Oh, thank goodness."

"You're free to leave." The Mistress steps on his shackles, and they break apart.

He turns his head to see Rogue and the relief on his face fades a little. "I'm sorry, I had no choice."

Rogue's blood boils, but he maintains his composure and keeps his eyes forward. *If we survive this, I swear I'll kill you Cal.*

More soldiers in black armor emerge with a second person, a woman by the look of it. When they remove her hood, Rogue recognizes her as one of Cal's bodyguards.

"He's alive? What becomes of us now?" She asks.

Prince Cal clamors to his feet. "Mistress, I beseech you, release her to me. Please."

"Who would you need protecting from out here?" The Mistress draws her sword and returns it to its sheath. The bodyguard's head falls away from her body.

"No!" Prince Cal screams and breaks down into tears and buries his face into his hands. "No, gods no. How could you!?"

Rogue doesn't see the Mistress's movement; all he hears is a split-second grind of metal and it's done. The cut on the woman's neck is cleaner than any cut he's ever seen, it's flat and straight; the whole sight gives him immediate pause.

"I don't tolerate those who fail under their own strength. To beg is a sin." The Mistress steps over the body and approaches Rogue. "Prince Cal promised me much. You will suffice as his payment." Her eyes meet Rogue's, and they make him feel colder than the air around them.

"I am at your service, Mistress." Rogue replies, with a quick but emphasized bow.

Her expression is different when he straightens up. *Oh shit, I'm about to face some real judgement here. Juman, Juman, Juman, what do I know about Juman's elite and powerful?*

Prince Cal trembles, forming fists with his hands but looks around him. There's nothing he can do. So, he runs away while he can; none of the soldiers or venators give his escape any attention.

The Mistress stands before Rogue and clasps her hands in front of her. "I've watched you for some time. I know the truth of Camp Tor. Who truly detonated your cargo, what Richtoff did in his final hours, and that you murdered him. The resulting chaos of your actions is unwelcome to me. His legacy was to maintain balance in this world. No political entity has been unaffected by his absence. However, I know more than most how survival is the very carnal prime of any being who digs into their core far enough. Strength such as this, I acknowledge and hold in high reverence. We share this accomplishment, which is why you've not met me sooner."

"You are better informed than many. Though I question that man's legacy, given he made the mistake of targeting me over someone else, among other reasons," Rogue replies.

"It is wildly uncharacteristic of him to make such a serious mishap." She blinks and takes a few seconds to gaze up at the sky. After the moment of silence has passed, she unclasps her hands. "You seem comfortable enough to converse with me. What do you know, I wonder?"

The tone she uses for that question makes his blood run colder than ice. *What do I know? What is she after?*

"Mistress, forgive me, I do not wish to come off as uninformed, or worse, arrogant. I wish to demonstrate acceptable conformance to your expectations. I know little of you beyond the hearsay of members in Fire Team Dark. However, I suspect I possess something that you desire greatly." He matches her tone when he speaks.

The smallest of smiles grows on her face, and her eyes appear to give her approval. "You comprehend your situation, then. Very well, let us continue."

Damn, that was ballsy. Counterintuitive, but it worked.

"I do, indeed, require your immunity from the Hydra's Wake hallucinogen. We attempted to acquire it from that mute woman who survived, Crystal. However, Lord Richtoff's prolonged experimentation on her body has caused obstacles that cannot be overcome. You, however, have blood that is free of such challenges. You will give me everything I ask for." She kneels on the ground across from him and beckons him to do the same. When he does, she snaps her fingers, creating a fierce, crisp, cracking noise. "Some tea as we progress."

"You are most generous. I look forward to accommodating you," Rogue says.

"Your blood is a unique down payment that allows you to survive this conversation. After that, the rest will be up to you. We discovered the wreckage of Tradewinds Goliath. I am grateful you escaped that horrid scene." The Mistress gives a gentle, genuine smile.

Soldiers in black armor arrive with a wooden tray, carrying a black ceramic pot with a dragon engraved on it using rubies, with matching cups and saucers. The pot is steaming with fresh tea, and the soldiers are quick to pour the Mistress's cup first, and follow with the one for Rogue, ensuring both are filled to the brim.

Spill one drop and it's over. The heat of the tea is valued. Sip lightly and speak fast. Who knew what Rick taught me of Juman culture would come in handy.

The Mistress holds her cup toward him, and he does the same before they take a sip.

Elvador Black Diamond, I need this right now. The sip of tea is soothing, and the smell calms his mind. The tea itself is designed to stifle high energy emotions in the brain. Exclusively grown for royalty and the wealthiest of the elite, the blend helps keep a person levelheaded in any situation.

"Your etiquette is well studied, Mr. Whip," the Mistress compliments him.

"I set the highest of standards for myself when I dedicate myself to a task," Rogue replies.

She takes a generous sip of tea. "Glaring blemishes in your record do that claim disservice. I find the intent is meritless bravado. Regardless, I must consider if half of what I've heard of you holds true, I will see some form of positive result."

He takes his sip next. "Gigas Archons and people who failed to gather correct information before shooting me down aside, my flying record is well intact as of late. But that's not what concerns you."

She takes a smaller sip. "Gigas Archon? I've heard little about them. Do you mean to tell me that they are responsible for the destruction I witnessed?"

Rogue follows the protocol, taking a sip before speaking. "Yes. They are more enormous than what the outside world is aware of. Hurlua's information on them was wildly off. Fascinating creature from a scientific mindset, but I do hope to never encounter one again."

She smiles before taking her sip. "We shall ensure to inform our pilots to exercise greater caution. Now then, to the task I require you to accomplish."

Rogue eagerly takes his sip. "Of course, how may I be of service?"

She can see his nerves fraying, but he is showing her genuine respect. His awkward word choices stem from fear, but his body reflects no sign of it. He's matching her outward strength and composure and keeping a flawless pace. Many men, Kings and Emperors included, would have crumbled before her by now and breeched Juman etiquette. But this man, a simple business owner and airship pilot, is putting on a show worthy of her attention. "Should be a simple task, really. I require living specimens of harbinger penguins. You will collect some for me."

That's it? How hard can that be? He takes a sip and pauses. A breach of etiquette that does not go unnoticed when the Mistress's eyes pierce his. "Forgive me. I am uninformed on the details of the harbinger penguin. May I ask what makes it such a remarkable animal, worthy of your attention?"

The Mistress sets her cup down and clears her throat, and Rogue follows suit. "They are an animal that was of great interest to the Shiv Empire. When threatened, a harbinger penguin will make the source of its duress vanish in an instant. The penguin's gaze was often used as a test for those who betrayed Shiv; accused traitors were forced to walk across a colony. If their loyalty was pure, they would pass through, unharmed. There are no records of anyone surviving this test. Though superstition eventually gave way to science when a man who studied light particles, Dr. Shoujin Lourcer, managed to study their ability. Shiv's desire to weaponize the ability is easy to understand, though the attempt resulted in the abandonment of this tundra."

She hesitates with a gentle smile toward him. "I risk nothing in telling you that Juman openly seeks to weaponize this ability, as well as the Hydra's Wake, if it can be done at all. And that we possess artifacts suggesting these can be weaponized by mechanical means." She picks her tea back up.

He keeps pace with her on the tea and takes a sip. "I've heard of the myth about Dr. Lourcer's laboratory. And rumors that Lord Richtoff once searched for it himself."

She finishes her tea. "He found it." She pulls a small black leather journal from her robes. "Dr. Lourcer's design for said weapon is in these notes. We're missing the organic components, which come from harbinger penguins, and they have proven difficult to secure. Bring me my specimens, and I will ensure you are generously cared for and returned to Acinvar. You will be free of my attention after that to do as you please."

Rogue gulps the rest of his tea down. "I get the feeling you think I am literally the only person who stands a chance of pulling this off."

"You are the only human in Yeraputs who possesses an immunity to any known paranormal ability that isn't otherwise disabled. You get to test if said immunity is broad or if it's simply reserved for hydras."

Lucky me.

A panel in the barracks floor moves, and Te'Yuro climbs out of the small tunnel underneath. "Kita, are you still here?"

"Yeah," Kita replies, watching from behind one of the bunk beds in a corner, and maintaining a view of the street.

"I hope it's not too late to apologize for my rudeness earlier. But the people outside are extremely dangerous, and it's clear that Rogue is trying to stall them," Te'Yuro says.

Kita crawls through the rows of bunks looking for the source of his voice and him on the other end of the building. She scampers as quick as she can, hesitating only when she reaches him. "I'm not ok with this."

"You don't have to be; you just have to trust that I want to get home as much as you do," Te'Yuro replies.

Kita nods. "I can do that. What's down there?"

"This is a crawlspace that connects all the buildings and follows the heat vents to the deep underground. We'll see if we can find somewhere better to hide until they've gone." Te'Yuro helps her down the hole and repositions the panel in the floor.

The crawlspace is dark, lit by cracks in the floor above them, and the crystal torch Te'Yuro has in his hand. "They're searching the warehouse now. So, I suggest we go in the opposite direction."

"I just saw that old woman slice through a person's neck with an ordinary sword. Just the strength needed to cut through neck bones alone is crazy!"

"Well, I'm glad you realize how dangerous she is, let's go." Te'Yuro taps her arm to get her to move.

The soldiers searching the warehouse with Hunter emerge carrying strange glass boxes.

Archon's Wake

The Mistress walks past Rogue to inspect them.

Hunter snaps to attention. "We found piles of these containers. They're designed like the ones in that notebook, but the types of glass used are different from the ones we tried earlier this morning. It seems there are misleading details in the work itself."

The Mistress gives a soft 'hmm' in acknowledgment. "Titania, Prince Cal's short-lived hopes of escape have persisted long enough, dash them at once. And should you chance upon any desert folk, I need them brought back in good condition."

Rogue catches the hint of annoyance in her voice. *Sounds like she doesn't have all the answers. She's right, though. Why would the Blooming Sandseas want to chase something like the harbinger penguins or Dr. Lourcer's laboratory? They're neutral to all major nations, well-liked, and well-protected. Something's clearly off.*

Titania slams her forearms together and sprints off in the direction Prince Cal went.

She's fast. That strength and speed isn't normal. I've heard Venators are superhuman but seeing it for real is insane.

"Shall we load these into the helo?" Hunter asks.

"Load them into the ground transport. You'll accompany Mr. Whip to the penguin colony and assist with his attempts to fulfill my demand." The Mistress turns her back and approaches the line of Venators who have remained perfectly still since they formed up. "Guariana, you will oversee this operation, and you will act on your predetermined orders."

A Venator steps forward from the line and slams her forearms together. "I do not fail."

"The rest of you, search the town for any signs of survivors. And find out what happened to the penguins that attacked the people here," the Mistress orders.

Rogue looks over at the piles of clothes in front of the warehouse.

"Yes, that was done by harbinger penguins," the Mistress tells Rogue, upon seeing his reaction. "My soldiers fared no better this morning in the colony we discovered."

"I haven't seen any penguins here," Rogue mumbles to himself, as he watches the soldiers take the glass cubes to the

Daniel Jones

back of the transport. They also grab Sarah's body and toss it to the side carelessly, causing him to visibly tense.

Another piercing snap comes from the Mistress. "Come now, we are not animals." The Mistress eyes the two soldiers standing over Sarah's body. They pick the body up and bring it over. She gestures they bring the body onto her osprey.

Rogue closes his eyes and forces himself to ease up.

"She wears your company's green and beige uniform. How we dispose of her depends on my mood." The Mistress speaks with a cold and emotionless voice. "Now come, it is time to collect your payment."

Rogue follows her onto her osprey; inside is like any ordinary military vehicle. It's not modified in any special way to look decorated or function differently, which surprises him a little. *A general who rides in exactly what her soldiers do; don't see that in Acinvar.*

The two black armored soldiers lay Sarah's body on the floor by the cargo ramp in the back.

A soldier in white armor steps up from the with a metal briefcase and hands it to the Mistress.

She opens it and shows Rogue a blood sieve coated in a layer of a mysterious glistening oil, along with dozens of glass vials.

That's a lot of blood, she's going to draw half a liter, easy.

"Take a seat." The soldier demands of Rogue, while gesturing the nearest seat to the door.

Rogue does so and offers his forearm, vein side up.

The Mistress takes the sieve and sticks it into his neck. "Blood straight from the heart is my desire."

Before he can try to come up with some way to retaliate, she opens the first vial and turns the knob on the sieve, letting blood flow from his jugular. The soldier opens the next vial and hands it to her when the first one is almost full, and they work in tandem until every vial is full. She closes the sieve and leaves it in his neck while she takes a foil bag from the kit and opens it, revealing a laceration wrap and a bio foam pump. "Do you have a preference?" the soldier asks.

"Laceration wrap please, and thank you," Rogue answers.

The soldier takes the sieve out of his neck and applies the

wrap serum to close his wound. Then wraps the bandage around his neck.

The Mistress seals the briefcase and takes it to the cockpit. "Your willing cooperation is unexpected, but highly appreciated, Mr. Whip. It's delightful to meet someone who understands the predicament, and the reward. Guariana will see to it you are made comfortable during your time with us."

Her words go unheard by Rogue, who feels lightheaded from the blood loss. He's woozy, dizzy, and it's all he can do to keep himself upright in the chair. A sharp stabbing pain hits his bicep; something is being injected into him. A few seconds later he's able to focus, and the side effects from the Mistress's blood draw subside.

"There, that should assist you in getting through your day," the Mistress says. "A mixture of adrenaline and other agents that will cause your blood cells to replenish what was lost quickly. I require you prepared and capable to perform your task."

"I wish you luck in deciphering what you need from that." Rogue gives her a slight bow before excusing himself and getting off the osprey as fast as he can. When his feet hit the ground, he slips. The adrenaline may help him focus, but his body still needs time to recover.

Guariana approaches Rogue and helps him up. Her grip is not as rough as Titania's. "Watch that step now. We have a busy day ahead of us. You'll want to get that transport running."

He nods and then gives the Mistress a final bow, similar to the one he greeted her with.

Guariana makes sure to match Rogue's pace and keeps by his side. Giving him a quick look over. She was expecting him to be a repulsive typical brutish Acinvar man, but the reality is shattering her preconceptions. "You are unusually cultured for an Acinvar man," Guariana says.

Rogue looks at her helmet. "My company's reputation depends on knowing and demonstrating many forms of respect." He stops at the transport's cockpit and climbs up the side to the door.

She follows him inside and positions herself into the

copilot's seat and makes herself comfortable. "You don't strike me as the dishonest type. Work as you will without fear of me."

Well at least she's outwardly relaxed. Not like that Titania woman; what a psychopath.

Something sharp taps the back of his neck, he turns to see Guariana holding her gunblade with the tip dug into his skin. "Huh, thought you'd be quicker. How'd you of all people best Lord Richtoff?" She's disappointed, why didn't he duck or dodge or make any sort of defensive response? He had to know she would test him.

Rogue grabs the blade with two fingers and gently moves it off his neck. "I'll tell you the whole story on the way to the penguin colony. But first, let me get this transport warmed up and comfortable."

What is that smell? Is she wearing some kind of perfume? Yeah that sweet smell is definitely coming from her. It's not fruity; must be some personal choice or something.

Guariana shifts herself when the chair won't budge, trying to fit in the space that's too small for her. "Damn this tiny machine."

"You ok?" Rogue is watching her struggle to fit in the chair; her bulky armor and tall height are not working well in the small space.

"Don't worry about me, this tiny thing didn't have Venator armor in mind when it was made." She gets herself situated and watches him work in the boiler compartment. The position she's put herself in is not a comfortable one, and she's searching for anything that might move the chair.

Hunter huffs when he sets down a glass container.

"Hunter, how many of those containers are there?" she asks.

"More than fifty" Hunter replies.

"Bring plenty of them. Mr. Whip here gives me the impression that he's an overachiever," Guariana calls out.

"Yes Ma'am," Hunter replies, and talks to one of the black armored soldiers.

Guariana watches the Mistress return to her osprey. Its engines roar to life, and they take off before Rogue finishes

Archon's Wake

getting the boiler system functioning. She gives up on searching for ways to adjust the seat and slides her legs onto the driver's seat just to have space. "Need any help?"

"Pipes are frozen; just making sure I don't burst one while thawing them out," Rogue replies.

"This is steam powered? Hurluan then, intentionally small. I should have brought a book. It'll take time before we get cozy in here." Guariana takes her helmet off and sets it on the floor.

Rogue glances at the gauges in the cockpit and then looks at her face. Her brunette hair is short in the back with longer bangs in the front, dark blue rounded eyes, and a fair face. He finds himself staring longer than he should. *She actually looks like she's from Heart, one of the farmland nations to the south of Acinvar. Damn, she's gorgeous. Wow.*

"Hah, works on every man." Guariana smirks with amusement, it's clear Rogue likes what he sees.

"And you're not from Juman," Rogue can't help saying. "Gotta take a guess at this, Uldren? South Carmico?"

She was expecting an outburst about her appearance or a whistle, or other remark about her beauty. His question catches her off guard and she blushes a little. "No, but not far off. South Carmico is the right continent, but you have the wrong country; try again." She leans forward and rests her chin on her hands, bending them against her chin, and smiles, staring intently at him. If he's as well traveled as he claims, he should be able to get it right this time.

"Double jointed hands, that makes you likely from Kasaka. I'll even go narrower and say the Bronze Plains or Lethoso Basin area?"

She claps her hands and laughs. She's excited he got it right. "Bronze Plains of Kasaka! Have you been?"

"I used to fly out to Bell City on a regular route. Would've guessed somewhere a little more western had you not put your hands up like that."

"Fair enough. I must say, you've earned the curiosity and attention of every Venator who witnessed you just now. Few men, even those who meet with the Mistress on frequent occasions, do not maintain the composure you displayed."

55

Daniel Jones

"Not to mention contradicting her at the start of that conversation. I thought you were a dead man." Hunter pats him on the back. "Everything's loaded up, but the hatch isn't closing."

"Give it a few more minutes; the pipes are frozen solid." Rogue glances at the back of the transport as a few of the soldiers in all black armor are sitting along the sides with the pile of glass containers now strapped together in the middle. "Wow, they work fast."

"They're hypnotized labor," Guariana replies. "They do what they are instructed, free of distractions."

That detail sends a shiver down Rogue's spine. He's heard rumors Juman does this in huge numbers, but never seen it in person. The only time he's seen hypnotized people are servants to royalty, and the occasional consorts of hyper wealthy people in places where chemical hypnosis is not outlawed. *Oh yay. That's totally not concerning at all.*

"Among other things," Hunter grumbles. "Seriously man, how long before we can stop the freezing wind from getting in here?"

"Trust me, this ain't a thing you want to rush. We burst one pipe and the whole pressure system could go. And that's not something I want to have happen with the Mistress above our heads" Rogue retorts. "So chill out alright?"

"Hey, fuck you, asshole."

Rogue brushes off Hunter's remark. "I got conned into this by Prince Cal, to settle whatever issue he had with the Mistress, that much is clear, and I don't even care why anymore. What's your excuse for being here?"

"Not your business." Hunter folds his arms and watches Rogue tend to the coal fire under the boiler. "How about you let me do that so I can defrost my damn hands at least."

"Mr. Smith, why so grumpy?" Guariana starts to wonder if Hunter is going to derail her outstanding orders and prepares to shut him down hard.

Hunter gives her a bewildered glare. "You saw what those penguins did this morning. Why would anyone in their right mind want to drive this thing right into them? It's suicide."

"Oh no it'll be fine. I'm the one who has to do the hard

work, remember? It's not like the next stop is certain death." Rogue moves to let Hunter into the boiler and takes a seat in the driver's chair after Guariana moves her legs. "Keep an eye on this dial up here. Let me know if that needle suddenly drops, then we can panic."

"What if Rogue dies? What do we do then?" Hunter asks Guariana.

After that back and forth, she decides that Hunter is simply afraid. She won't need to act out of sorts. "We report Mr. Whip's failure and allow the Mistress to decide future steps," Guariana replies.

Nevermind, she's a cold steely hearted bitch. Damn. Rogue does his best to avoid looking her way after the way she spoke. He goes to the driver's seat and focuses on the gauges. "Hunter, I've got minimal steam pressure to the auxiliary lines. Try closing the loading hatch now."

"How long before we get moving?" Guariana shifts around to sit sideways, laying her legs on his lap, and trying to get legitimately comfortable. "Pardon the intrusion of my body. This cabin is tiny, and you said you wanted me comfortable. But don't enjoy yourself too much, understand?" She wags her finger in his face.

He glances down at her armor; her legs feel like they weigh over a hundred pounds each. "That's a lot of steel."

"Multiple layered and corrugated. Perfect for stopping most ammunition." Guariana says proudly, while running her hand up her thigh plating. "Like what you see?"

And you ladies wear this all day every day? And somehow still move like lightning and outrun sports champions? Shit, that full suit of armor must weigh six hundred pounds or more. I can already feel my circulation getting cut off.

She can tell her armor is crushing his legs and knows that's going to be a problem. "Still not good enough." She shifts around some more then gets frustrated. She grabs the back of her chair, rips it off, and lays it down as a bridge between the front seat and back seat, so she can spread her legs out. Now, she's comfortable. "There we go."

Rogue chuckles at watching her make herself at home. "I don't envy your tailor."

She huffs and folds her arms. "I wish I had a tailor. Finding nice things to wear is hard. It's not like I chose how tall I'd become, but I'm a woman, and I love to do womanly things. I love wearing dresses, I love ballroom dancing, I love going for strolls in the forest, and enjoying the tranquility of nature. But I don't get to enjoy that often. It's all black scratchy cotton form fitting bodysuits that hide nothing and pure plate tungsten alloy that weighs five times my body weight. I wish I could enjoy halters or wrap dresses more. Maybe have a sharp dressed man to hang my arm around while on a lovely stroll." She sounds like she's daydreaming, but she's speaking directly to Rogue.

Rogue can't help himself but picture it in his mind.

She leans right up to his ear. "There's more to me than being a murder machine. You'd look fantastic in a black suit with beige highlights with me in my ash blue and mauve qui pao." She whispers seductively.

He sees the two of them strolling along the streets of Acinvar in those outfits. *She's putting ideas into my head, and I'm, well damn, if the rest of her body matches the beauty of that face, I'd be a very lucky man to have my arm around her.*

"How long until we're moving?" Hunter interrupts. He knows what she's doing to him, and finds it sickening, but won't dare step out of line out of fear for his life.

Guariana backs up, clearly annoyed by Hunter's presence.

"We'll be on our way in less than five minutes," Rogue replies.

"Your highness, what are you doing out here? I thought you were going to Ghonda?" A man asks, when Isla and Hondo exit the vehicle that pulled up to a small hangar style building.

"Juman executed the team on Fabrico's site. Spared no one, not even the Hurluans," Hondo replied. "We have to assume Ghonda is compromised."

"That might explain why they've fallen silent," man sitting

at a telegraph desk nearby says. "Haven't heard anything from them in two or three days."

"James, where is the Pyrite Nest?" Isla shouts. "Sorry, this is a trying moment for me. Juman has no reason to come into Hurluan territory, much less this tundra, unless they know what we are searching for."

James gestures to a table nearby. "It's alright, your highness, no need to apologize. We garnered a lot of attention coming here. Prince Cal could not keep something like this secret from his neighbor for too long."

Isla shakes her head. "Prince Cal would not dare sell us out."

"What if he had no choice?" the telegraph operator asks.

"How would Juman have proof to pressure him unless they regularly patrol the tundra? Which would be inside Hurluan territory," Hondo cuts in.

"It doesn't matter, they are here. And they are tracking down our people to their exploration sites, leaving nothing behind." Isla stares at the empty wall. "We haven't found the colony. We haven't found the lab. We've nothing to show for our efforts except loss of life."

"We are chasing a myth. There's always a chance that it was always just that. A myth," the telegraph operator comments.

Isla shakes her head. "No, the lab is real. Lord Richtoff found it himself. I was in his captivity during the time he found it. If the lab is real, there is more truth to the myths. And that can only mean the weapon is possibly real, or at the very least, the penguins are real."

Hondo rests his hand on her shoulder to reassure her. "Her highness is right. We've located plenty of old weapons caches from Shiv as it is in the caves beneath the ice. And mentions of Dr. Lourcer not related to Lord Richtoff's evidence. There is something here."

Isla walks deeper into the hangar, away from the others. James follows her. "I'm sorry I doubted you. The Juman showing up proves you were right to fear for your life and take extreme measures."

"I don't blame you or anyone else for wondering why we

suddenly need weapons of great power. It does appear like a gross misuse of resources. How could it not? But it feels as though my options are running thin. Juman will stop at nothing to destroy me and see the Blooming Sandsea burn for my-" She pauses and takes a deep breath.

"You need not justify yourself to us. We'll defend you until the end," James says to her, before leaving to give her some space.

Hondo folds his arms. "Where is everyone else?"

"Searching for the Pyrite Nest. It's possible we've lost it too. At the moment, only Bifo and I are here, as the others are scouting its flight path. Minatra is leading the search," James answers as he returns.

Hondo watches Isla stare at an empty wall, lost in her thoughts. "Perhaps it's for the best that so few people are around to see her like this. How overdue is the airship?" he asks, if only to distract himself.

"It's not just that it's overdue, it's that we cannot locate where it is. The crew have not visited any of the ruins we have been in for some time. For now, we hope it isn't near Ghonda" Bifo answers.

The telegraph starts tapping away with a message.

COLONY FOUND. TUNDRA QUADRANT E.S.4.4. INSIDE CANYON CRATER.

Isla listens to the clicks and rushes to the station, knocking Bifo out of his seat. "The gods are gracing us, finally."

WE INVITE YOU, AMENAZA.

"What?" everyone says at the same time.

Isla is immediately apprehensive. "Juman. Where is the source?"

Bifo looks at the board of wires above the machine. "Ghonda."

"They know where she is? They'll be here soon, if they already aren't on top of us." Hondo rushes to the hangar door.

"I don't think so. All the relays we set up are triggering. They're sending that message to every station across the tundra. They don't know where she is." Bifo points to signals from relays nearby lighting up as the messages come in.

"Ghonda has the location of every camp we've set up,

Archon's Wake

except this one. It's why I came here," Isla replies, and pounds her fist on the desk.

"They know the colony's location? And they don't use the penguins themselves? I wonder why that would be?" James comments.

Bifo looks at a map of the tundra. "That quadrant is south southeast of Ghonda, and surprisingly not far from it; sixty or so miles. And look at this: it's in the direction of any reasonable flight path to Ghonda from Juman's border at the Ring Storm over here. They likely chanced it, once they knew Ghonda's location."

Isla stares at the map in disbelief. Studying it as if it will yield some sort of answer to her predicament.

"We need to leave the tundra, right now. The best chance of protecting you is keeping you in the Shimmering City," Hondo says.

"It won't matter. Not after what I did!" Isla shouts at him, her face red with anger and tears streaming down her face.

Hondo huffs and rubs his forehead. "I've refrained from asking for too long, but what is it exactly that you did to piss off Juman?"

"It's not just Juman. What I did? If Yeraputs knew, there'd be no place on Heart or Shell that I could hide."

"Tell me," Hondo demands.

"Don't tell us. We're sure to be tortured; and if we don't know, they'll never find out from us. Even you aren't so tough shackled to a table under a knife, Hondo," James cuts in.

"Is there an option where we don't die or get tortured?" Bifo asks.

Isla locks up, with fleeting thoughts and half-baked ideas flying around her mind until she has a headache. "We'll go home. And I'll... I don't know yet. But it's clear I need to get everyone home. Get you back to your families, whom you've already missed six weeks with, during this search."

In the distance, the roar of an archon sounds, turning everyone's heads to the hangar door.

Hondo looks at the mechanical armor on his arm for a moment. "That sound will never be far enough away."

"They pass directly overhead, going between hunting

grounds. Families of them. They move in single family groups from what we have observed. At first it was terrifying to know we're in their frequent hunting grounds, but they don't stop here. The rocky surface has nothing they want, so they won't land until they reach the ice sheets," James comments.

Isla walks to the hangar door and looks at the sky, with James and Bifo stepping out onto the paved tarmac, placing their hands over their eyes to block the sun.

"It's a better view from here." James gestures to her. "And relatively safe."

It's a completely clear, cloudless blue sky as far as the eye can see, and there they are four archons in the distance; two bigger ones and two smaller ones. One of the adults is above and ahead of the cubs, which are side by side, with the biggest adult flying below and behind them. Isla walks over to the men and watches the flyby. They're fast and silent. Had the sky been cloudy and snowing, like the day before, there'd be no way to know they were even there. The family continues over the small ruins, pass it without distraction, and head to hunt for more food to the north.

"When you stop and watch them for what they are, they are magnificent creatures," James says, with a small, reassuring smile on his face.

"It is a breathtaking sight, both for its heart stopping terror and for the fact that it is as you imply. A family, living their lives as they should." Bifo heads back to his desk.

Isla sits on the ground and looks up at the sky. "It's so strange not seeing Heart in the sky. We've been here for a while, and it's always bothered me not seeing the planet hovering in the horizon. The sun just shines and shines all day, no eclipses, or breaks in daylight until it is time for true nightfall. How do people on Outer Shell live like this?

3: Wait, It Gets Worse

Titania holds Prince Cal by the neck and dangles him over the railing of the observation deck of her airship floating over Ghonda. The Mistress arrives with several more Venators in toe. "Titan, bring him in."

Titania brings him back over the railing and sets him down on his feet gently.

Prince Cal coughs and rubs his neck. "I keep telling you, I don't know why Isla Amenaza came here. I didn't care about that detail, damnit."

"And unfortunately, I have come to believe this" the Mistress replies. "I, however, cannot fathom why you allowed her to search in the first place."

"Do you realize how long Hurlua has sought to find adventurers and serious, research minded people to study this place?" he shoots back. "We offer opportunities to many, but they always fail and never return. Amenaza came and offered the resources to collect knowledge about the Geography, Geology, and Animalia of the tundra. In exchange, I allow her to keep any specimens of her choice for her land's menagerie. I didn't even know she was after Lourcer's lab until we intercepted that message your spy sent."

The Mistress doesn't hide her anger.

Daniel Jones

Prince Cal laughs at her expression. "Oh dear, I've struck a nerve saying the exact same thing again and again, after you've gone and pumped my brain full of neuritanor. Good! Guess what? It's the same answer! I have been telling you the truth this entire time! But you're crossing the line today. Killing my consort bodyguard! I loved her, damnit! If she was nobility, she'd be my wife! And then threatening my own life after not one, but two torture sessions. How fucking dare you!?"

The Mistress remains quiet for a moment. It's clear he's been overdosed and is therefore unable to control his words or behavior. A most unfortunate detail; his father will now have to be confronted. Preferably before the side effects occur.

"You killed the one woman I love in this life. How fucking dare you!? You know what? You were better off as a shared mindless concubine for the Juman glory council. You know, the pathetic, weak, stupid little hypnotized girl with open legs who didn't ruin anyone's life!"

"Insult me further, and I shall kill you and welcome your father's war!" the Mistress shouts at him. She hasn't shouted at anyone in years, and it surprises her that she lost her composure. It further surprises her that this man knows her past. That is a different matter to address later, though.

The Prince stands up straight and faces her directly. "These aren't insults. These are reactions of your own doing. The hole in my neck from your syringe is proof. And worse, I know I'm going to die. I've got mere days to live, if that. That syringe had maybe eighty CCs in it? Double the lethal dose of Neuritanor! What kind of fate will my father watch me endure in those final hours, as my brain deteriorates, I wonder?"

"Silence!"

"No, you are merely the leading general of a visiting army. I am actual royalty in my own land!"

The Mistress rushes past him, then stops with her arm suddenly outstretched and her katana drawn out of its sheath.

Prince Cal's hand falls off, and he screams at the top of his lungs. "How dare-" The Mistress's katana impales him from the back of his head, the blade sticking out of his open mouth.

"We know less than we did before." Titania tosses Cal's body over the railing. "Not to mention he is right about his father."

"I will reflect on what must be done to avert unwanted aggression. For now, we must concentrate on the larger opportunity." The Mistress turns her attention to the southeast.

"What of Empress Isla Amenaza?" another Venator asks.

"An investigation into her actions is still warranted. Such a thing cannot be done from here unless we locate her. Time to accomplish this is less than reasonable. Let's try some simple methods to force her hand. Send a message to her telegraph network and invite her to the crater." The Mistress returns her weapon to its sheath.

Titania turns her head. "Dr. Lourcer's lab could still be in play. Permission to make my attempt at locating it and bringing its contents to you."

The Mistress at first shakes her head no but stops herself from saying so and thinks it over. The empress's people have scoured the tundra for over a month and failed to locate it, but they have also made as much progress in eliminating possible locations. There's no need to capture penguins when they can investigate the laboratory itself. The lab is a grand prize in comparison to the penguins. And there are no guarantees they can keep the animals alive in captivity long enough to study them appropriately. On top of that, there's no guarantee of success in replicating Lourcer's work from the notes they have. And all of that sidesteps Rogue Whip's immunity, which is the true reason they are here. She's sent Venators to do far less meaningful tasks for extended periods of time before.

"My daughter Titan, you are inviting yourself to a challenge where even I admit my expectation is you will fail. If you insist on having your fun here, search for these desert people, make the Blooming Sandseas a non-issue. Your primary goal should be to locate Isla Amenaza, so I might gain something out of this effort of yours. But feel free to investigate all leads you encounter regarding the lab. We already possess our compensatory reward."

Titania slams her forearms together and goes inside the airship to prepare for her task.

The Mistress waves away her other Venators, staying on

the observation deck alone. "This cold air is refreshing for the soul. It reminds an old one like myself how close death always is."

"It was crazy; no one thought Walker survived," Rogue says, while Guariana laughs.

"Hunter, how did you miss such a thing? Absolutely brilliant on Walker's part, though. By slowing his heart rate down that far, he found the only way to survive. Bravo to the man."

Hunter folds his arms and leans against the wall. "I'm not a medical minded person. He managed to take that drug when I wasn't watching. It's that simple. When he looked dead, I thought he was dead."

"For a man who tracks down intelligence agents, you show a lack of it at times," Guariana says, through her laughter. "And Rogue, you hardly did anything, Acinvar made you out to be some superhero. I love the truth of it though. It humanizes you. I admire that." The whole way over she's been finding herself to enjoy his company more and more. He's a pleasant person, and she finds herself fond of him.

Rogue shrugs. "Cut him some slack. Hunter's skills are as sharp as they need to be. I've seen him at his best. It's easiest to say that Acinvar's narrative didn't have a whole lot of my input."

"I'm not talking to you Whip," Hunter retorts.

"Alright fine; just pretend I'm a figment of your imagination," Rogue says back.

"That's it! You're a dead Figgy!" Hunter reaches forward and wraps his arm around Rogue's neck.

Rogue grabs his arm and pulls it off. Hunter struggles to fight back, but Rogue's strength is overpowering. "Figgy's not so fake, is he?"

Guariana stops laughing and clears her throat. The animosity from Hunter is ruining the otherwise cozy moment. "Boys, please behave. Hunter, get off him. Rogue, keep your hands on the controls. I'd hate to tell Titania or the Mistress that either one of you has been a hinderance."

Hunter sits back down and grunts.

"I gotta say, from the sounds of it, you two made quite the team back then. What changed?" she asks.

"Acinvar treated him poorly in the aftermath of that event and I didn't realize I could do something about it until we worked together to reunite the Darmoro royal family. The missing princess, exiled by the tyrant king, was found in the Underlands. She went to great lengths to hide. Even undergoing transgender surgery to become a man. That was a twist no one saw coming. But events in the Underlands caused us to move faster than planned. And I left Hunter behind. It was the only way we could've gotten out of there alive. Winsacht assassins were catching up to us. An opportunity to escape the country by air came, and I took it. I've already said I'm sorry, and I came back to get you when it was all over."

"You're not sorry enough to cover what I lost!" Hunter shouts.

"I've offered you actual fortunes to try. I know it's not about the money, but the money is all I have, to try to make it better for you going forward!" Rogue shouts back. "At least you got the shotgun I sent. Looks good."

Hunter looks at the shotgun and belts of ammo on the empty seat across from him. "It's a decent weapon. I'd be a fool to pass up a Julius Remmen, handmade to my specs. But it doesn't matter," he mutters under his breath.

Guariana darts her eyes between the two of them, until she's certain that there isn't an actual problem. "Well, that wasn't awkward at all. So, what happened to Crystal Whip?"

"Dumped his ass," Hunter says, without skipping a beat. "Smart woman."

"That's not how it happened, and you know it," Rogue replies. "And shut up. It's not that simple."

Guariana is about to take the question back, after seeing Rogue's charming demeanor falter. He's solemn, serious, and pained.

"So, Crystal... she was in the hospital for the longest out of all of us. Albert's experimentation left a lot of damage to her body; she was emaciated when I found her. Turns out the reason for that was to keep her alive. By feeding her, it triggered her body to heal. And within a week she was coding blue several times a day. When she did make it through, she came to live with me as I promised she could. I bought a house on the lower side of Acinvar by the coast; it's an absolutely beautiful part of the city. Gorgeous, nonexistent crime, and full of kind, gentle people. Not like the kind of people you find in the skyscrapers on the top of the cliffs and the upper city itself. Cost a fortune to move, but the Mining Conglomerate made that easy with what they gave me for freeing up the whole Tor Valley to a year-round operation."

"I didn't see so much as a copper you damn billionaire," Hunter interjects.

"I still have a bank account I opened with your name on it with a hundred and eighty million coppers in it. Just stop by and get the damn key. It's yours," Rogue replies.

Hunter kicks the back of Rogue's seat. "Why can't you just bring it to me and piss off?"

"Do you realize how hard it is to find you? It's a small miracle that shotgun got to you."

Guariana cracks her knuckles. "Boys! Do I have to tie you down and gag you both up to keep you two civil?"

"No ma'am," Hunter says.

Rogue gives her a wink and a smirk that makes her blush. "Anyway, Crystal took her time adjusting to having her own space. When she felt ready to go out in public, we gave the dating thing a shot. It was good... stable. We vibed well and we enjoyed each other. But it took away her focus from her recovery, and that did not go well. Flying took me away, and I wasn't there to support her during a serious panic attack. We agreed to just let it fade. She's got so much trauma to overcome, and she's at a point of her life where that's her priority. And I was already back to work. We were just, too far apart in that regard."

"Hey look, not everything in his world is about him." Hunter can't help himself.

Guariana grabs her gunblade and sets it across her legs, tapping it against her thigh while giving Hunter a finger wag.

"He's right; not everything is about me. There, I said it; happy? In recent days, Crystal has made huge progress. Before I left for this trip, she got herself a job working at the Acinvar Menagerie as a keeper in the herpetology collection. Working with animals is something her therapy team thought would help. They pulled strings to get her the interview, and she made it happen. She's been smiling a lot and showing more of her personality lately."

"She deserves it. I don't know many who've suffered through Albert and managed to get back up like she has. I'm happy for her." Hunter's tone doesn't sound condescending for once.

"She still kicks at Walker though. Last week she was in my office chatting with Jessie, whom she's gotten close with, and he came in to give me some paperwork. She kicked his fake leg clean off at the door," Rogue adds.

"So do you two have plans to get back together?" Guariana asks. She couldn't help it; the question slipped through her lips. She's afraid of the answer almost immediately.

"I can't see it happening. We're in two very different points of our lives, and she's trying to forge her own future her way. I'm probably going to be stuck as a friend for that, which is fine," Rogue answers.

"See, she dumped his ass in the friendzone." Hunter gestures to the back of Rogue's seat.

"Do you do this to Titania?" Guariana asks Hunter. Rogue's answer makes her heart flutter and then this bastard goes and ruins the moment by inserting his rude remarks.

"Nope. It's special treatment reserved for this dumbass." Hunter hits the back of Rogue's seat. "Titania would paint my guts all over this cabin if I stepped out of line."

"She can be a passionate woman when she feels free to express herself." Guariana chuckles.

"That's one word for it," Hunter replies.

Rogue makes some adjustments to the steam valves as they reach the summit of what looks like an icy hill. They're here, and the crater is huge. "Whoa," he mutters. "That's a lot of penguins."

Hunter ducks behind the seat.

"Relax, we're not that close," Guariana says, even though her own voice is shaky, and her face shows how nervous she really is. She only saw the events from the airship this morning, but being here on the ground is a whole different experience.

Rogue brings the crawler to a full stop. "Think this is close enough?"

"This should be an adequate minimum safe distance," Guariana agrees; she sounds unsure herself, but they are still quite a ways from the nearest penguins. "Hunter, help the men get the containers ready."

Hunter jumps from his seat and heads to the back.

Rogue takes a deep breath. *So, this is it. This could be how I die.* He exhales, opens the cockpit door, and jumps out. The ground is covered with obsidian, and the air is warm and humid.

Guariana lands behind him and puts her hand on his shoulder. The fear on his face is upsetting her and it surprises her that she cares about him. "I wouldn't blame you if you ran. And I wouldn't chase you."

Rogue gives a half-hearted laugh. "Your Mistress will."

"It'd be a better death than this."

Rogue looks at her face and sees genuine concern. Like she's trying to warn him. "You look like you want to show me something."

Guariana walks to the back of the transport where the hatch is opening. "You." She points to a random soldier. "There is some Juman equipment in that field. Find it."

Hunter watches in horror as the soldier sprints for the colony of penguins.

The soldier runs right past Rogue, heading straight for the colony. It takes them a few minutes to reach the closest ones. They pass the first few, which scatter away. Then Rogue sees some glowing green dots on the penguin's heads and the soldier's armor drops to the ground in an instant.

Hunter turns away the instant he sees the green.

Guariana walks back to Rogue's side.

"That was quite the demonstration," he tells her. "Was it necessary to kill him?"

They're completely hypnotized, alright. If I saw that once, and got that order, I'd defect in half a heartbeat. Face a firing squad instead.

"You need to know what you're up against, and I'd rather you didn't die here. I'll give you a moment to work out a plan." She takes a few steps back. The idea of watching him vanish is unpleasant. If she could, she'd call the whole thing off.

Rogue shakes his head. "That happened so fast. Can't plan around instant vanishing." He goes to the back of the transport, grabs a container, and pops the top open. The container feels sturdier than he expects from glass.

Hunter gives him a sideways glance. "You're seriously going to try this?"

"Like I have a choice? That guy only got past a handful before they got defensive. This place is huge, and there are hundreds of thousands of them out here. There's so many of them; it might be possible to get close to the thinner clusters, let them come to me out of curiosity. Box one up, run away, go to a different spot, repeat. I'll try not to trigger whatever that glowing green thing was," Rogue says.

"That's not what I mean," Hunter says.

"What do you care? I only see one possible way home right now," Rogue replies. "And I'd like to get there. Until then, I'll put some work into it. The Mistress wants a few murder penguins. I'll deliver some of the finest murder penguins I can pick." He sets the container down to take off his shirt and jacket. He's only been outside for a few minutes and it's already hot enough to make him sweat like he's in a desert.

Guariana eyes him, finding herself unashamedly admiring his physique. His chest and arms are nothing but muscle, and his abs are well formed. She was surprised by his charm, but his body is making him the complete package in her mind. Did the Mistress know she'd become enamored with him when she gave the order to watch him? If so, the feeling is a lot stronger than she expected. She stops Rogue when he walks in front of the crawler. She puts her hand on his chest and runs her fingers from his waist up to the bandage on his neck. All that muscle is iron hard and real. "Twenty-four specimens, per her request. Work quickly but be safe."

"We got more crates than that, thought you wanted to outshine?" he replies with a snarky tone.

She leans down and gives him a long, passionate kiss. If he's going to vanish, she's going to have what little of him she can. "Not at your expense. I've grown fond of you. Very fond, Rogue. Don't keep a lady waiting."

Rogue puts his hand on the back of her head to stop her from moving away, and kisses her back. If he's going to die here, he's going to take what he can. "Don't sell me so short. I'll be done before you know it."

Hunter puts his finger in his mouth in a gagging motion. "Rogue, you do know that when a Venator kisses you, they'll usually kill you."

Rogue waves him off. "Venator's kiss of death, I know. Supposed to take my last breath away. Last act of love before death and all. I know the rumor."

"It's not a rumor, it's tradition; a ritual, even." Guariana whispers in his ear. "In one's finality at the hands of a Venator, a kiss is given to take one's breath away. A final act of passion to gift the victim, so they may die feeling a touch of love."

Oh, that's, all kinds of twisted, dark, and... wow. She says that like she believes that's what she's doing. And here I thought she was being a spontaneous flirt.

She takes hold of his free hand and interlaces her fingers with his and locks her eyes with his She wants him and sees that he wants her back. She trembles slightly. "You'll survive my lips until I'm ordered otherwise. I hope you enjoy my gift, and I'll be here if you come back for more."

Rogue smiles to match her level of crazy. "Can't get enough of me, can you?"

"Do I need to leave the transport to you two for an hour?" Hunter shouts. "Otherwise, the clock's ticking!"

Guariana stands up straight. "Do you have to ruin the moment? This is not about you! It's about him. If he dies, I will cry, I will kill you, and you won't get your kiss."

"He's right, I should hurry this along." Rogue lets go of her hand and continues toward the colony. His heart feels like it's soaring through the sky.

Damn that was the best kiss I've ever had. I can't believe I'm thinking I want more. Is she doing that on purpose or is there more to it? And way we locked eyes just now. She feels something, and I'm sparking like a firework is in my chest. I could run, but the Mistress... I have to survive this first, then maybe I can spend some time with Guariana, find out what's there.

A few minutes later, Rogue is at the edge of the colony. It's loud with penguins braying, chirping, squawking, and all other kinds of penguin noises. The ground is covered in smelly white guano that gets thicker as he gets closer.

The penguins themselves aren't any taller than a few feet; barely knee-high to him. Bright blue feathers stick out above their eyes. The penguins he's seen are black and white, but these are red and white. Their beaks are bright yellow, with matching color feet that are talon-like instead of webbed.

He gets within ten or so feet of the first few, walking slowly. They all watch him as he sets the container down sideways, with the top side open and waits.

"Someone help!" A woman's screaming voice pierces the air.

Rogue looks around him. There's no sign of anyone nearby.

Another scream from a man, crying from a child, screaming from another little girl, and shouting from men. His mind is filled with the sounds of countless voices calling out in pain. The screaming becomes painful to listen to. He sits down on a nearby boulder, trying to keep his focus on the first few penguins curious enough to approach him.

The landscape around him changes. The rocky surface is flooded with a dark murky liquid. He dips his hand into it and discovers it's blood. The sky darkens with heavy storm clouds forming in seconds. Thunder booms around him from lightning striking the edges of the crater. A torrent of blood rains from the sky.

Guariana watches Rogue sitting on the boulder and turning his head in all directions. "Something's wrong."

Daniel Jones

"Yeah, he looks like he's freaking out." Hunter watches through a pair of binoculars. "Rogue!"

"Rogue! Come back!" Guariana shouts. She knows she's about to defy the Mistress's orders, and that will only end with her death, but she could care less. "Damnit, I cannot let this man perish. We must do something; I can't let him die."

"Did I miss something on the ride up? You seem awfully attached to him. Titania wouldn't think twice about leaving me behind." Hunter gives her a sideways glance; he knows what the Mistress ordered him to do, so she could cut the act now. But it doesn't look like an act anymore.

"It is not often that we meet men who survive their first encounter with the Mistress who aren't genuinely bad people. Mr. Smith, we're warriors; that does not make us evil. Good men who have the strength and fortitude that he does are rare."

"Got it; you have a crush on the guy."

"If I'm being honest, it's a stronger feeling than that. Despite what you think. I can't stand by anymore!" Guariana takes her gunblade off her back and sprints toward the colony.

"Hey, no! Don't spook them! He's not getting the green dots yet!" Hunter sprints after her.

Guariana gets halfway to Rogue when she runs into something invisible and is knocked backward.

Hunter stops; he's seen that barrier before. A memory from the Gemstone Mine replays in his mind when he and Ned couldn't get past an invisible barrier of some sort. "No, no, no, no! This can't be happening again!"

Guariana gets back to her feet and runs her hand under her nose. She's bleeding. Ahead of her is a small blotch of her blood floating in midair on whatever she ran into. She pokes at it then puts her hand on the barrier. "What is this?"

"Feels like nothing, but at the same time you can push on it, like a wall." Hunter walks up to her side and puts his hand where hers is and feels the same sensation. "Dimensional barrier. Just like the one at Tor."

Guariana looks back at Rogue. "So, he's probably alright then? He walked through this and has that immunity? So it works here too?"

"I don't know." Hunter shrugs.

"I need you to be more certain than that."

"How the hell can I be? I thought this shit was limited to hydras. I didn't expect to see it happen all the way out here."

The blood flood around Rogue is starting to boil, and all kinds of body parts start rising to the surface around him. Organs, chunks of flesh, even severed arms and legs amongst the bubbling hot blood. Half a brain pops up next to his leg.

"Gyah!" He kicks it away. The splash causes a pair of eyes to float to the top where the brain was. A heart, still beating and squirting blood, casually floats by him.

Rogue puts his hands over his ears to try to stop the screaming, but it doesn't work. "Shut up!" He closes his eyes tight while he hunches over and shouts.

His skin feels drenched and slippery. His pants are fully soaked from the blood rain, which is now coming down in thick, gooey, congealed chunks.

The smell of everything around him makes him sick to his stomach, and the flood is rising fast, now it's up to his waist.

A skinless man rises from the blood in front of him. He's laughs and splashes some of the blood on Rogue. "Skin of Heart, flesh of island. See you clear, see you here. Welcome to my domain. Now I will see what you fear." The man vanishes into a black shadowy puff of smoke that wisps away in a gust of wind.

The voices go from nonstop incoherent screaming, to only being audible every time Rogue's heart beats. Scream, thud, silence, scream, thud, silence, scream, thud, silence. It's agonizing and overwhelming his senses. He drops to the ground, falling beneath the blood level, and it all stops.

When he opens his eyes, he sees a penguin at his feet staring up at him. "What just happened?" He holds his arms out in front of him and checks himself over. He's fine. There's no blood in sight, or random body parts. It's a sunny day with a clear blue sky and the ground looks like a rocky mountainside.

He gawks down at the penguin for a split second. "Uh, hi there little guy." His heart is racing, pounding so hard he's convinced it will burst out of his chest. "Hoo, man, things get crazy around here, don't they?"

What just happened? Did they do that green glowing thing to me? Wait, I'm still here. Right?

He looks over to Guariana and Hunter, who are standing halfway between him and the crawler.

What are they doing that far from the transport? Oh no, did I vanish on them?

He waves his hand around.

"Oh, thank goodness." Guariana waves back, she feels immediate relief in seeing him acknowledge them. "Are you alright!?"

Rogue can see them shouting at him but can't hear a thing over the penguins. They also look like they're pushing on something.

The penguin at his feet waddles to the container and pokes its beak at the glass.

Rogue returns his attention to it. "If you go inside, you'll be the first penguin to travel to new and exciting places."

As if on command, the penguin waddles into the container and Rogue quickly closes the top and turns it right side up to lock the latch.

"He got one." Guariana jumps and spins around in excitement. He can complete his task and he's not vanishing. A wave of relief surges through her.

"Holy shit." Hunter can't believe his eyes. "He got one."

Rogue starts walking toward them with the container in hand and the penguin braying loudly inside.

"Oh, wait, you know what? No! Let's think about this! I don't want to be near that thing." Hunter backs away.

Guariana suddenly realizes he's bringing a penguin toward her in a glass container. What if that container doesn't work to stop the green glow? "Hey Rogue, stop for a minute!"

"What?" Rogue shouts back, unable to hear them.

"Put that thing down, before it can make us disappear!" Hunter shouts, while backing up, but Rogue is visibly confused. "I don't think he can hear us. You better run!"

"I think you're right." She gestures for him to put the container down then come over.

Rogue sets it down and comes up to them. He sees the floating patch of blood from Guariana's nose. "What happened? Thought you guys would be staying by the crawler."

"What happened?" Guariana repeats. "We should be asking you that! It looked like you were freaking out and your body was twisting, and you were-, it looked unnatural."

Hunter comes back. "Seriously, we need to think about safety here."

"Yeah, this place has some serious issues. I had a Wake kind of moment; I don't know what it was, but it was freaky and gory. The whole place became a blood storm."

The color in Hunter's skin drains away and he trembles a little. "I don't want to be anywhere near Wake shit! Not again! Not me! No!"

"How the hell are we going to get the penguins to the Mistress then?" Rogue asks.

"Leave my sorry ass on the side of the road! I'll walk the rest of the way!" Hunter shouts.

"We simply want to make sure we're exercising extreme caution," Guariana replies.

Rogue looks up behind them and points to the sky. "Looks like the Mistress doesn't have any patience."

They turn their heads to see the Juman airship coming toward them in the distance.

Guariana looks over at Rogue. "Ok, this is the spot where I broke my nose on whatever this barrier or wall thing is. Bring the crates here, and our soldiers will pick them up. Hunter, have the empty crates brought here."

"What wall thing?" Rogue asks.

Hunter grabs a shotgun shell from one of his belts and tosses it. It hits something invisible next to Rogue and drops to the ground. "That dimensional wall."

Daniel Jones

"Well, that's freaky," Rogue mumbles. "Alright then; blood splat in the air and this cartridge on the ground are a checkpoint. Got it."

"Just let us back up a bit first before you bring that thing near me." Hunter backs away.

Rogue nods and retrieves the first crate. The penguin is pecking at the glass and braying loudly. As he lifts it up, it tumbles around trying to shake the crate free of his grip. "Feisty little one. I don't blame you though. Sorry, but you're part of my ticket home." He carries the case over to where Guariana is standing and sets it down.

Several of the penguins at the edge of the colony start wandering over.

"You need to get back. I can't enjoy your company if you're gone." Rogue gestures to her.

"Same goes for you. Don't disappoint me, you just raised my hopes." She runs back toward the crawler.

Rogue walks up to the penguins and kneels ahead of them, causing them to stop and watch him. They're agitated and behaving aggressively. And the one in the container sounds distressed. Rogue suddenly feels lightheaded and has a difficult time focusing.

Ugh, this is going to be impossible.

"You are correct dear boy. Impossible is the word. You are never capable of defeating me in a balanced setting." An old man's voice rings through his mind.

Rogue overcomes the sensations and sees the man standing before him in a navy-blue suit with silver trim and adornments in a matching bowler hat. In his right hand is a single blade Urumi with a sapphire adorned pure silver hilt.

"You had a hydra's help, and I still bested you," Rogue says back, finding a rusty short sword on the ground near his feet.

"I was mortally wounded prior to our formal introduction and final meeting. I shall have my revenge." The man flicks his wrist and the Urumi whips into the air.

Rogue doesn't so much as flinch as the tip of the Urumi flies within a few inches of his face. "You don't scare me, Albert."

"Pick that blade up delivery boy. Put on a good show; the ladies are watching," Albert demands.

"You're not real. You've been dead for a year."

"And my presence is still vividly felt upon the whole of society. Heart is on edge and Shell is in full disarray. Yeraputs is falling apart. Rather interesting, what happens when there is no possible way of purchasing another government's secrets," he says, before vanishing.

Rogue watches the penguin colony reappear as Albert disappears. "What the hell are these penguins doing?"

A skeletal hand wraps around his neck and grips tight. "See you here, see you clear. Skin of Heart. Man of the sky. What will it take to make you die?"

Rogue grabs at the air behind him and the skeletal hand vanishes. "Show yourself. What are you?"

"See you here, see them clear. Smell of sweet, smell of fear. One of which, from me he cannot hide. One of which she cannot run," the voice says.

He looks behind him, where Hunter and Guariana should be, but they're gone.

"What did you do to them?" Rogue asks. His head is forced to return his attention to the penguin colony. He struggles with all of his might to stop but whatever is moving him can't be stopped.

"You elude me, you evade me. Quite the mystery," the voice says, before Rogue's head can move normally.

Rogue grabs his neck. *Damn, that was different.*

The penguins in front of him are now around the container with the other penguin, trying to find a way inside.

Nearby is a pile of black armor and another glass container. Another hypnotized soldier who was sent to deliver it.

Rogue sighs; there's no point in trying to stop them from being sacrificed like this. Once at the container, he pops the top open, then grabs one of the penguins and drops it in. It nips at his fingers with its sharp beak and writhes wildly, making the same distress call as the first one. The other penguins stare at him with glowing green eyes.

Rogue can feel his body getting weak. Every muscle in his

body feels drained. The penguins seem alarmed that he isn't vanishing, and waddle back to the colony making new sounds. As they escape, Rogue can feel his body returning to normal. He moves fast to seal the second penguin in the container. As he does, he checks on the airship which is now over the crawler. Hunter and Guariana have reappeared, standing next to the crawler.

Oh thank goodness they're still here. The Mistress wasn't gambling with my life. She knew I'd survive, somehow; she actually knew. Testing a theory, my ass.

The colony of penguins reacts to the new noise from the few scared penguins, and they all waddle away making the same distress calls.

Rogue runs to the next soldier who's already bringing the next empty container, hoping to reach them before they get too close. "Thanks bud." He passes the soldier the container with the penguin and then heads back to the retreating colony with the new empty one.

For small animals, they sure can move fast. Rogue jogs some distance before catching up. When he gets close enough, they stop to confront him; aggressively defending the rest of their colony. All of them with glowing green eyes are lunging at him with their beaks, nipping at him wherever they can. He puts the container down and tries to get a grip on one of them, but they duck out of his hands and slide out of his grip while the others keep pecking, poking, and biting. He can feel them pinching through his thick cold weather pants. He's thankful they're thick enough to protect him. Then one of them jumps up at him between his legs.

Rogue jumps and screams a high pitch note. He hunches over and covers his crotch when he lands while still screaming in pain.

Hunter is watching with binoculars and nearly drops them when he bursts into laughter.

Guariana gasps in surprise and covers her mouth with her

Archon's Wake

hands. She can't believe what just happened. "Oh no, it bit him!"

"He got bit in the nuts! By a jumping penguin! Hahaha!" Hunter slaps his knee and keeps laughing, until Guariana punches him in the arm. "Ouch! Damn, woman!"

"I will kick you hard enough to reverse puberty if you don't show some respect." Guariana towers over him angrily. She's ready to beat him to a pulp.

Hunter squeezes his legs together and scoots away from her. "It's still funny, though."

Rogue spots some bigger penguins from the colony coming toward him with glowing eyes. More and more are gathering to confront him. "Yeah, that makes it easier. Come this way." He raises his fists and enjoys the idea of grabbing a few of them to rough up.

"What the hell is he doing?" Guariana asks.

"I don't know. Doing the whole 'being mysterious and let them inspect' idea was working great," Hunter replies.

"He's being too aggressive; this isn't going to end well."

The sound of tungsten clicking behind Hunter's head makes him turn around. A man wearing a large, obnoxious hat, is aiming a futuristic looking assault rifle at him. He moves his hands to grab his shotgun.

"Ah-ah." The man wags his finger at Hunter. "Tch, tch, tch, tch... you know better."

Hunter's eyes dart to Guariana, but she's nowhere to be seen.

"Taking your eyes off me for even a moment? That's insulting." The man tightens his grip on the rifle and returns his index finger to the trigger.

"Sorry, you still smell like hydra vomit. And that face? It looks like you sat on a bomb." Hunter waves his hand in front of his face and grabs his nose.

"You walked me right into that trap!" Westley screams. "I'm just trying to think of how to get back at you. Every bit of my body was blown to pieces in that hydra's mouth. I'm going to enjoy topping that off."

Hunter rolls his eyes. "Damn, your rambling is more annoying than your obnoxious hat." He says, while still holding his nose. At first, he did that to get under Westley's skin, but now he really can smell the same aroma of decay from that moment.

The veins in Westley's arms and neck start popping and he turns several shades redder. "You're not going to get the easy way out. You do not deserve a quick death."

Guariana notices Hunter facing away from the colony and holding his nose and breath. "What are you doing?"

He doesn't react.

She walks over and waves her arm in front of him. His lips are moving like he's talking, and he's got a serious and daring look in his eye. "Hunter, what the hell is going on?" She tries to grab him, but her hand goes through him like he's not there. She pulls her hand away, gasps in shock, and steps back. "It's like Rogue's story. The wake is real and happening here."

Rogue laughs as he kicks at the penguins and picks up rocks to throw at them and then stops all of a sudden.

What the hell? This place changed my whole personality for a short moment. Where'd that aggression, and enjoying it come from? That was intense. Whoa.

He drops the rocks and tilts the container sideways, letting the penguins nip at him as he backs away to a circle around a few nearby boulders. As he's being chased a few other penguins wander into the container to poke their beaks at it. He gets back to the container and picks it up, being quick to rotate it right side up and close the top side.

An osprey takes off from the airship and makes its way down to the crater and lands near the crawler.

Hunter chuckles when he hears the osprey. "Stick around, I'm sure whoever is on board that will enjoy meeting you." Westley vanishes. "I hate this place."

Guariana breathes in and sighs. "Oh good, you're speaking. Does that mean you're back?" She walks up to him and pokes his arm. "You're back!"

Hunter grabs her shoulders and looks at her, terrified. "We need to get the hell out of here. Now. We're in serious trouble. Not even your Mistress stands a chance at surviving this crap." Hunter keeps his eyes on the osprey, expecting the Mistress to be on it. When it lands, the back loading ramp opens. A Venator rides out on a four wheeled vehicle that uses a gas engine. She steers it toward the colony, and Rogue, and accelerates.

Two more Venators come out and look over at the colony. "It's come to the Mistress' attention that Rogue is experiencing abnormal symptoms. She sent the sprinter to hasten the collection along," one of them says to Guariana.

"The situation is different from this morning. We need to evacuate now" Guariana replies. She knows it changes nothing, but she has to try. Even if it means she'll be punished.

"We don't retreat. Ever. From anything. Have you gone soft?" The second venator gets in Guariana's face.

The Venator in the sprinter stops near the containers and climbs out. "A gift from our Mistress. Do not waste her resources or trust."

Rogue looks the sprinter over. A small two-seated vehicle, with a flat platform on the back and large wheels, on an exposed heavy duty suspension system. Well suited for this kind of environment. "I appreciate the equipment. Tell her I have no intention of letting her down."

The Venator nods and approaches a container with a penguin to inspect it. The penguin inside is flashing its glowing green eyes, which look like green lights through the lenticular and frosted glass panes, but the Venator isn't disappearing. "Can you imagine what it must've taken to figure out that this would work in the first place?"

Rogue shakes his head. "Actually, no I don't think I can fathom that."

"Neither can I. But I'm glad it works." She picks the container up to head back to the osprey.

The Mistress watches from the observation balcony as Rogue drives the sprinter to the colony. He comes to a stop, upon experiencing another phenomenon. A skeletal hand wraps around her neck, she grips her katana, and it vanishes. The being that appears next to her gives her quite a shock, a tall human skeleton with a lion's skull. Its bones are a glistening black material, and it's covered in a dark black haze.

"What are you?" The Mistress can't decide if she should try to fight or run, she's never seen anything in her life that looks like this specter before.

"I see you here. I see you clear. One who sets traps. One who sets motion," a voice says, but the Mistress can only hear it inside her head.

"I'll not ask again, what are you?" The Mistress raises her voice out of concern for herself.

"I am here. Traveler and resident," the Shadow Figure replies.

Archon's Wake

Rogue stops the sprinter near the penguins and climbs out. The ground is squishy and covered in a slimy goo this time.

Another full gore immersion? Oh great.

The goop covering the ground shifts and rises into pillars about his height to form human-like bodies. Made of goopy flesh, covered in a thick, black, oily substance.

"Oh hey, I know what you guys are; hydra victims. Neat! I was wondering what Hunter and Walker kept describing."

"We are victims of you! Tormentor!" The nearest one talks back to him.

Rogue raises his fists, relishing the idea of getting into a fight.

"Your aggression makes you manipulatable."

I'm not normally this aggressive. What the hell is wrong with me?

"I'd argue otherwise." Another man comes out from behind a group of the gooey people. He's a burly, strong looking man, and Rogue recognizes him immediately. "You enjoyed killing me. Thought it was the best damn thrill of your life. Hardly the sign of a man who is not aggressive."

"You did horrible things to Albert's victims."

"That's a matter of opinion. I kept them alive. For as long as possible, anyway. I was all the hope they had." Mack brandishes his revolver and aims at Rogue's head.

Rogue looks down in his hands to see Albert's Urumi.

"How'd you get that?" Mack points to the Urumi with a look of horror on his face.

"What? You don't know? It was me who killed him."

Mack's eyes widen and he lowers the revolver. "Is this true?"

"True enough." A younger version of Albert walks through a gooey person and slurps some of the residue off his hand then spits it out. "I daresay he will fail to best me in my prime however."

"You hallucinations are in my way." Rogue closes his eyes and tries to concentrate on ending it.

Mack aims at Rogue and fires.

A sharp pain tears through his body. The bullet strikes his chest and rips through him. He falls to the ground, screaming.

Albert laughs as he tap dances his way up to him. "Does

85

this look like a fucking hallucination to you?" He stomps on the gunshot wound and twists his foot to make the pain worse.

"You gonna gut him here, boss?" Mack asks.

"He is in delightful physical shape. Very healthy, and all this muscle, low body fat percentage, possibly six or seven percent. Very easy to work with. He was even kind enough to remove his shirt before coming. Oh, the fun I will have, digging around inside this one. What I would not give to get inside his mind. Share it with him, if you will. Truly get inside his head and torment him. But for me? My hands will have to suffice for now." Albert takes his suit jacket off to reveal a bunch of tools, used for dissecting people.

Rogue bites through the pain and throws him off.

"How dare you!?" Albert shouts.

Mack shoots Rogue in the head.

The Mistress can see the same thing Rogue sees, and she's having difficulty believing it. "What is occurring here?"

The Shadow Figure reaches out to her, but something stops it from being able to grab her.

The Mistress relaxes and reaches into her robes, revealing a small metal cube, glowing brightly in a glass bauble on her hidden necklace. "Albert was right," she mutters.

"Of course I was right, Lin. This place should be left alone. The barriers between realities are fractured from the abuse of the very device I sought. We cannot allow ourselves to unleash the greater evils that lie beyond. This is not about war or power. This is far simpler. It is a matter of survival for the human race." Lord Albert Richtoff's echoes subtly.

The Mistress looks down at the bauble and grips it tightly. "I know these words are what you would say to me in this moment, my husband," she whispers.

The Shadow Figure tries again to reach her.

"Your efforts are futile," the Mistress says, defiantly and forcefully. She draws her katana out and points it at the Shadow Figure. "Go back to where you came from."

Rogue wakes up on the ground with penguins pecking at his body. His sudden movement startles them and they back away. His body is covered in small cuts and beak marks. "Damnit!" He grabs the closest penguin with both hands and squeezes it hard as he puts it into the container on the back of the sprinter. He grabs a couple more as they waddle away and puts them into containers.

Stop, stop, stop, what are you doing, Rogue? They need to be in good condition, and it's not their fault you're taking them away! Come on man, get a grip. Where is this anger coming from?

"Our Place will be as one. The bridge is here," the Shadow Figure says. "A vast realm. A vast world. In which there are no bounds."

The Mistress looks over at Rogue and grows concerned.

"His immunity to Hydra's Wake prevents the hydras from taking full control of him. That, however, did not prevent him from entering the hydra's dimension. These wakes relocate beings from one dimension to another. You must remember this, we discovered it together," Richtoff's voice says in her mind.

The Mistress sees his face in her mind, speaking to her. She finishes where he leaves off. "But his immunity will act as a resistance, forcing the being before me to act with greater power. This will strain the barrier between dimensions. What have I done by bringing him here?"

"Evade my grasp, you do. This cannot last." The Shadow Figure sounds angry. "Speaking past death. A device of old. A device you possess. A soul of old. A soul of wrath. A soul who speaks past death."

"I am merely envisioning what he would say to me.

Memories, long suppressed and intentionally hidden, are resurfacing. Nothing more. This does not concern you," the Mistress replies.

Rogue brings the sprinter up to the pile of containers and swaps four full ones for four empty ones.

"Rogue, this has to stop. Now." Guariana pulls him out of the vehicle before he puts his foot down on the pedal. She's going to make sure he doesn't go back out there.

Rogue nods. "I can't keep doing this. My head is playing tricks on me. I'm encountering hallucinations and experiencing paranormal shit. It's even changing my personality." His eyes are bloodshot, his skin is pale, and he's visibly weaker.

"Rest a moment, please. Your look like you're dying." She puts her hand on his forehead and then grabs his arm; his skin is clammy. She doesn't have to grab his wrist to know his heart is beating too fast. She's finding it hard to stay composed.

"That's what? Eight captured so far?" He brushes some sweat off his arms and his skin peels away. "Oh shit."

Guariana watches the look of terror grow on his face. "What's wrong?"

"You don't see that I just skinned my arm?" He sees blood spurting out of his flesh and dripping onto the ground.

"No, I do not. It looks normal. You're ok." She kneels next to him, takes her gauntlets off, and gently grabs his arm to try to comfort him. "Rogue, it's ok to stop."

Rogue feels an intense burning pain from her touch charring his flesh.

She lets go when his face reflects intense pain. She closes her eyes and takes a deep breath. "I forbid you to go back out there." As soon as she speaks, she regrets it. "Forgive me, Mistress; I will fail this time," she mutters under her breath.

Rogue groans and finds a small group of penguins heading their way with glowing green eyes. "Guariana, get out of here!"

She draws her gunblade to fire on them. One by one, the penguins are shot by a bullet big and fast enough to destroy their entire bodies; they appear to explode upon impact.

The other Venators at the transports sprint to her position with weapons in hand, upon hearing the gunfire.

Hunter grabs his shotgun and stays by the crawler. The colony's behavior is changing again. The penguins are clustering together in tight groups and coming their way.

Guariana tries to grab Rogue's arm, but her hand goes through him, like he's not even there. "Rogue, come on, you gotta get up. We gotta go. I can't leave you here."

The penguin colony vanishes into a pale blue mist. In the distance, the mist thickens into a massive cloud. A roar of a different kind comes from the cloud. Rogue recognizes it from Camp Tor. "It's too late."

"It's not too late! Come on, you show so much promise and potential. Don't give it up now!" Guariana pleads.

That look on her face. I've seen it before. Her eyes. Those gorgeous eyes. That's more than fond. I think she actually fell for me.

Rogue gives her a curious glance. "You fall hard at first sight, don't you?"

"Why do you think I've been having second thoughts, here? Damnit man, don't prove me wrong!" she cries.

A shadow figure emerges from the cloud and flies toward Rogue. It stops a few feet away from him with its arm outstretched and a skeletal hand exposed, pointing directly at him.

"It is too late. Something just got here. Something dark, something cold. I don't know where it came from." He gets to his feet and puts himself between it and Guariana.

The Venators stop advancing, fearing they'll get too close. "Guariana, regroup!"

Guariana watches Rogue struggle and fade into a transparency. "What design of the gods are we messing around with?" she mutters.

"Run!" Rogue shouts at her, after finally getting back on his feet. He pushes her.

She's relieved to feel his push, even though he looks like a ghost.

Rogue turns to face the shadow figure and walks right up to it. "You. I don't fear you. I know you can't touch me."

Daniel Jones

It tries to grab him, but its skeletal hand passes through him like he's not there.

He doesn't feel anything and walks through the shadow figure. "If you want me, you're going to leave them alone."

"I see you here, I see you clear. I see your world, I see your home. I see the domain beyond my own." The Figure makes a demonic laughing sound and vanishes.

The Mistress watches Rogue disappear and looks over at the Shadow Figure. "What have you done to him?"

"Skin of heart is mine. Secrets he possesses. Secrets are keys. The bridge is clear, but not so near. Keys are to break realities. I see you here. I see you clear." The Shadow Figure vanishes before her eyes into a dark fog that wisps away in a gust of wind.

The Mistress puts her hand over her heart and pauses before heading inside, where her Venators are waiting. "Send word to the bridge, signal an immediate and full retreat! We are risking too much on this venture."

Guariana watches him vanish before her eyes and screams. "No! Rogue!" She drops down on one knee and punches the ground with all of her might.

Hunter lowers his shotgun and shakes his head. "Damnit. Guariana! Get out of there!"

Guariana reloads her gunblade and shoots at penguins at random. She runs at them but slams into the invisible wall from earlier. She slams her fist at it and tries slashing with the blade. Nothing happens.

"Guariana, I said run!" Rogue's voice calls out.

She looks at the invisible wall and sees a mirror reflection where Rogue is visible. He's pulling on her hand trying to lead her back to the vehicles. "You didn't vanish?"

"No, I'm right here," Rogue replies.

She looks around her and doesn't see anything. "You're invisible."

"I'm not invis-, nevermind, run, now! That sprinter, get in!" Rogue shouts.

Above them, the airship fires several red flares and a booming airhorn sounds.

Rogue grabs her gunblade and yanks it out of her hands. "Here, is this proof enough that I'm by your side?"

She looks at the floating gunblade. "What am I doing? Yes. Running."

"You're a real hardhead, you know that?" Rogue jumps in the sprinter and waits for her to climb in.

Guariana takes her weapon back. "This place is clouding my judgement. Like your aggressive outburst, it is not a normal trait of mine to hesitate."

I don't doubt that at all.

The other Venators are already back at the osprey as its engines roar back to life, preparing to take off. Rogue floors it and the sprinter lurches. The further away from the penguins he gets, the more visible he becomes.

Hunter waves them down from the back of the osprey. "Come on!"

Rogue drives the sprinter into the back of the osprey as it lifts into the air.

Guariana looks at the glass containers with penguins that were loaded already and shudders. "Do we really want these things?" he asks the other Venators.

They all look at the containers. "We should toss them. What if it only took one to wipe out Ghonda?" one of them asks.

"We'd be facing a death sentence from the Mistress," another says.

"She wouldn't have called us back early if she didn't acknowledge the danger they could pose," Guariana adds.

"We do nothing to them. If she sees them as too dangerous, she'll order us to throw them over after we speak with her" the fourth venator replies.

Daniel Jones

"Feel your presence, see your soul. Your evasion is a nuisance, my grasp did not hold. Fortune is mine, for I have a way. A man of no skin will see what he can behold." A strange voice echoes in Rogue's mind.

Rogue shakes his head. "Damnit," he mumbles.

"What's wrong?" Guariana asks.

"Voices in my head. Screams, pleas for help. Now there's one creepy one that feels like it's stalking me," Rogue replies.

The Venators all exchange glances with each other.

"Could the Mistress have drawn too much blood before having him do this?" one of them asks.

"She drew half a liter of blood, at least. It's possible," Guariana replies.

Te'Yuro and Kita walk along the Ghonda streets heading back to the warehouse. It's eerie and silent around them; nothing moves, not even a gust of wind.

Kita hasn't said a word since she started following Te'Yuro, who's been quiet out of pure terror.

"You'd think there'd be an army wandering around here." She needs to break the silence, which causes him to jump.

"We don't know that there isn't. Jumans are thorough, ruthless, and efficient. They don't do rush jobs," Te'Yuro replies. "But I must admit, I'm glad that airship is gone. That's a good sign."

They reach the street where the operations center and barracks are, to find a decapitated body on the ground. The crawler transport is missing.

Kita gasps at the sight and covers her mouth. "Please don't tell me..."

"It's not Rogue." Te'Yuro searches the area for any sign of others, but there's nothing.

They slowly approach the body until Te'Yuro thinks he recognizes it. He runs the rest of the way and stops when his fears are confirmed. "No, So'Mala, no! It can't be you!"

Kita puts her hand over her heart and her other hand on

his shoulder when she catches up. "You know her?"

"She was my partner in boot camp. And in our first unit, before she became Prince Cal's bodyguard, consort even. A great friend, and a shining light in this world. Snuffed by the greatest of evils. I am so sorry." Te'Yuro trembles as he cradles her head in his arms. "I was a coward."

"You couldn't do anything to save her. I'm sorry, Te'Yuro."

"Was it quick?" he asks. "Tell me, did they torture her before they did this?"

Kita looks over her body. "The cut is one of the cleanest I've seen. She didn't feel much pain."

"Well, well, what have we here?" Titania asks, from the top of the barracks building. She jumps down next to them and draws her gunblade.

Te'Yuro drops So'Mala's head and rushes her. "You'll pay for this!"

Titania shoots him between the eyes at point blank range.

Kita watches Te'Yuro's head explode into a bloody pulp as the bullet hisses past her. She falls backwards and puts her hands in the air. "I surrender!"

Titania puts her weapon away and approaches Kita with a sinister smirk, offering her a hand up. "An Acinvar woman, wearing an Air Drop West outfit. Now, I wonder who you came here with. Was it the adorable gentleman I met? What was his name? Raw-gue Wheap? Wait, no, heavens, that's how the Lotus Island people pronounce the name. Rogue Whip brought you here."

"I came on Rogue Whip's ship, but I just got here. We both did," she says, gesturing to the body. "We walked here, following the crawler's tracks. I don't think he knew we survived" she rattles off in terror. "Please, don't kill me!"

Titania grabs her hand and lifts her up to her eye level. "I don't believe that. But it doesn't matter. I was ordered to murder desert people, but I have no standing orders for what to do with people from the enemy nation of Acinvar. I could kill you on that basis, alone. But then, there's your profession to consider. I need medical personnel to heal the wounds of people who frustrate me. I presume you possess some competent skill? Yes?"

"The best," Kita replies. "I'll serve you well, I promise."

Titania rolls her eyes, lifts her up by the neck, throws Kita over her shoulder, and slams her into the ground. "You are a weak-minded woman. Grow a backbone! I've no use for weak beings."

Kita curls into a ball, overwhelmed by the pain throughout whatever she can feel of her body. Her ears are ringing and her head is throbbing from hitting the icy road.

Titania grabs her by her hair and lifts her up again to eye level.

Kita tries to feel the ground with her toes but at Titania's height she's more than two feet off the ground.

"Well, what have you to say?" Titania opens Kita's jacket and runs her hand up under Kita's shirt side until she feels a rib bone and grips around it with the palm of her hand, feeling it move freely. She smiles at realizing the bone is fully fractured. She makes the poor woman scream and squirm, raising her up a little higher. "Some medic you are; you're broken yourself. I prefer working with the strongest tools."

Kita screams louder, as Titania pushes the rib in on one side, making it press against her skin in the front of her chest.

Titania gets a firm hold of the rib and uses her immense strength to yank it out of her body. The bone pierces and tears out of her skin. Blood gushes out and strings of sinewy flesh hang from the bone.

Kita screams at the top of her lungs, louder than she ever has in her life.

The blood curdling scream is a euphoric tune to Titania's ears, and she has to stop herself from indulging further. It's not her desire to slaughter this piece of trash. Not yet, at least. "But there's the question of durability. Let's see you survive this little test." Titania laughs as she jams the rib bone into Kita's leg and tosses her aside. The whole sight is exciting; the combination of shock, pain, fear, and such all over the pretty girl's face. Her blood gushing through her jacket onto her leg in a dazzling bright red display are just the kind of things she wants to see before heading off onto the tundra. She draws her gunblade and swings it at Kita, cutting the bone free of her

Archon's Wake

body's sinew.

Kita grips her side and leg and tries to put pressure on the wounds.

"I'll be back with people who will need your help. If you want to see Acinvar again, you'll be ready. And if you succeed, you will see it again alive. But, should you think of simply letting this be your end, I've a little surprise for you." Titania reaches under her breastplate and pulls out a small glass bauble with a shiny golden beetle skittering around inside.

Kita's eyes widen and she shakes her head no. "I'll be ready, I swear," she pleads, as best as she can muster.

"Huh, not many know of the Juman Weavil Bug. You know what this will do once inside your body, correct?"

"Yes, I do." Kita tries to scoot herself away. "Please, no."

"You want a fair chance to prove your skill is worth my attention?" Titania drops the bauble, letting it break. "I was going to place it on your wound, but I'll let it come to you. See if you can outrun it." Titania laughs and makes her way into the next warehouse where she found Hurluan vehicles and had one prepared. Now that she's had her fun with the suspected rats, she's got work to do.

Kita watches her ride away on a two tracked vehicle and her mind focuses on the supplies she brought. A squeaking noise returns her attention to the beetle scurrying in a jagged line toward her. "No!" She cries, and kicks her leg to scoot further away. Those beetles will keep their victim's brains active beyond a body's normal death, which is useful for extreme forms of torture.

The beetle reaches the first drops of blood on the ground. It stops moving in a jagged line and heads toward her with alarming speed.

Cinder pounces on the beetle before it gets too close. The beetle slips out of his paws and he swats at it, knocking it over on its back and pounces again, squishing the beetle into a splat.

"Good boy!" Kita, relieved, turns her focus to the barracks, and the med kit that could save her life. She crawls with one arm while keeping pressure on her side wound. She's losing an immense amount of blood, but perseveres to the front door. Her bag is in the middle of the foyer. And

Daniel Jones

Te'Yuro's stuff is next to it. Their attacker knew they were here.

She reaches her bag and finds two laceration wraps placed directly on top of all the other supplies. "That bitch planned this out." She takes her jacket and shirt off and prepares to put the laceration wrap on. She can barely grip the foil bag with her blood-soaked hands and blurry vision. Staying alert right now is harder than anything she's ever done before. The serum stings as she tries to put it in her gaping side wound. She's used these thousands of times on patients before, but never once had to use one for herself. The sensations are all new to her. After she uses the serum, she wraps the bandage around her ribcage. There's not enough in the first wrap, so she opens the second one to keep going.

Once she's finished, she stops to take a few breaths, ignoring the bone impaled in her leg so she can adjust to the sensation before going further. The moment of rest makes her disorientation worse. She digs around the bag until she finds a red metal box and opens it. The pills inside fall out and scatter all over the floor. She grabs a few of them and puts them under her tongue, letting them dissolve before swallowing them. Right as she's about to black out, her head starts feeling numb and her vision improves. She dumps the bag's contents onto the floor and grabs a pain wipe.

Rogue wakes up in a hospital style bed. He lifts his hand to block out the bright electric light above him.

"Rogue! My gosh you had me worried." Guariana gives his arm a gentle stroke and takes his hand. "Take it easy, we're taking you out of the Harbinger Tundra to Bluewood Cove in Juman to fully recover. When you're healed, I'll make sure you get back to Black Sand City personally."

"Don't overwhelm my patient." A doctor comes over and smiles down at him.

"At this point, I'll be happy just to get out of the damn tundra," Rogue says.

Archon's Wake

"We all agree on that" the doctor replies. "How are you feeling, Mr. Whip?"

Rogue sits up. "Better than I did when I woke up the first time today."

"You can tell it's the same day?" The doctor glances at his clipboard to make a quick note.

"Well, it won't take an airship like this too long to get to the Ring Storm. Doesn't feel like my ears are trying to pop" Rogue replies.

"We're being cautious. We won't be over the Ring Storm for two more days. In the meantime, I'm going to check your heart rate and blood pressure." The Doctor puts a metal cuff around his arm and tightens it.

Rogue watches the gauges on the pressure cuff reacting to his pulse. After about a minute he looks up. "Seems good to me."

"It is very good; you were not faring so well when we first got you here. Now, allow me to introduce myself. I am Doctor Hestar. You struggled in that crater. Can you provide me with some insight?" Dr. Hestar sets his clipboard to the side and sits in a nearby chair.

"I experienced powerful paranormal activity. On par with effects caused by the Hydra's Wake. I never felt the effects of the Hydra's Wake in Camp Tor, but what I experienced here, and saw, was similar to what other survivors have described to me. I don't know how the Mistress came to know that the Penguins and Hydra's paranormal abilities are linked, but that was an experience from hell. And my immunity to Hydra's Wake was not as effective with these animals." Rogue tries to keep his response objective.

Dr. Hestar smiles and looks at Guariana. "He's your responsibility from here. I won't need anything else from our guest."

"Real quick, because we're still over the tundra, have your pilots adjust altitude to below five hundred feet, it will help avert the attention of the Gigas Archons and make any crashes caused by them survivable if there's a problem," Rogue comments. "That's another experience from here I'd not like to repeat."

Daniel Jones

Dr. Hestar raises an eyebrow. "Gigas Archons? Never heard of them. I think our pilots may want to hear more about this."

One of the crew members in the med bay brings Rogue a fresh set of clothes.

"Thank you." Rogue gets to his feet and takes the metal cuff off. His body feels great; no aches or pains from the crash yesterday or the blood drawn earlier. "What did you guys do to stabilize me? It's incredible."

"It's no secret Juman has superior medical technology to Acinvar. We simply did the basic things," the nurse replies.

Rogue notices that there are no curtains to draw around the bed. "Um, where does one get some privacy to change?" he asks.

"Ah, you'll have to get used to Juman's culture. Specifically, a lack of privacy, for the next few days," the nurse replies.

"Right." Rogue takes his medical gown off and starts to change.

Guariana can't help but watch and blushes brightly. His legs are as thick and sculpted as his arms are. And his skin is clean; not a tattoo in sight anywhere. She likes that about him; personally, she doesn't like them.

He notices her staring but ignores it until he finishes. *I've heard of love at first sight, but she's outright infatuated.* "Uh, ok. Um, thank you, Doctor. I'll rely on Guariana the rest of the way. Unless something urgent comes up, of course."

"Of course I hope you enjoy the truth of Juman hospitality." Dr. Hestar heads to the circular desk at the center of the med bay.

"Here are your assigned quarters." The nurse hands him a piece of paper with a number on it.

Guariana glances at it. "The Venator quarters. I'll show you around."

Rogue follows her out of the med bay to a large hallway on the side of the airship lined with large windows along the cabin's hull. "We're pretty high up." He can't help but notice how they appear to be at least five or six miles up in the sky. The ground is covered in cracks from the large canyon network below.

The Archons avoided the canyons to the south of the tundra, if we're over these, we should be alright. One hell of an amazing view, though.

"Is there a problem?" Guariana watches him stare out the window.

"No, just reflecting on some things I've read. Sorry, you were showing me around." Rogue smiles and offers her his arm the same way he did for Titania earlier.

Guariana wraps her arm around his and strolls along the hallway until they cross to the other side of the airship. "You look fantastic in that crew uniform, I must say. Very pleasing on the eyes. Welcome aboard The Luscious, a six-level, rigid body airship, equipped with observation decks on the topside of the balloon structure and base of the cabin, a hangar for multiple rotor wing aircraft, a world class medical bay which you've already been introduced to, a library containing rare literature hand-picked by the Mistress, and crew space for four hundred and sixty soldiers at full capacity. It serves as the Mistress's home away from home."

"It is a pretty massive airship." Rogue notices how everything is sleek and futuristic looking. No exposed pipes anywhere, and all electric lights. Not an oil lamp or spark crystal in sight.

Guariana brings him around the corner and leads him up a flight of stairs. "Venator's quarters are above the bridge." She gestures all the way down the hallway. "Shall we claim you a bunk?"

"Yeah, let's do that," Rogue replies. "Any idea how long it'll be before I'm summoned?"

"You won't be. She encountered a paranormal event herself and called the retreat. She's left the airship in an alticopter. She tasked Hunter with helping two of my sisters find Titania and have her retreat from the tundra as well. We will have plenty of time get to know each other better." She lowers her head near his, teasing him with her breath.

He pulls her in like before and gives her the most passionate kiss he can. She presses him against the wall and kisses him back.

A few hypnotized soldiers walk past, completely ignoring

Daniel Jones

them.

"I guess we should take this somewhere a little less accessible, in case a regular crewman shows up." Guariana pulls on his collar and leads him along the hallway to a large room at the end. After passing a locked door, they arrive in the Venator's Quarters. The bunks are in cubicles, with shelving for personal items and armor. Everything is arranged in a semicircle grid, matching the hull's shape.

"Which one do you suggest?" Rogue can't see any cubicles that don't already look claimed.

Guariana's about to whisper something suggestive in his ear before spotting something pass the windows outside, making her face get serious.

Rouge turns around after seeing her expression change, and sees a quick shadow block out the sunlight. "Oh no."

"That's enormous." As she speaks, an airhorn alarm goes off.

Both of them slam into the wall when the airship moves sideways and shakes violently. Loud metal bangs, snapping noises deafen them, and the cabin loses air pressure, causing disorientation.

Guariana grabs Rogue's arms when the airship tilts forward and nosedives toward the ground. She pulls him up and wraps her arms around him. "This might hurt a little."

"This will hurt a lot!" Rogue is surprised to see the calm expression on her face. "What are you doing?"

"Assessing how best to protect you," she replies.

"Are there impact vests on board?" Rogue asks.

Huge talons tear through the airship's cabin. The sudden depressurization rips Rogue out of her grip, and he tries to grab anything as he's sucked out through the shattering windows. A large piece of the airship frame snaps off violently, knocking him out and flinging him into the depressurizing balloon structure.

4: Alive For Now, And It Hurts

Rogue wakes up to the sound of creaking metal and whistling wind. As his senses come back to him, he realizes he's looking at a wall made of rock and ice. He squirms and discovers that he's hanging in the air, tangled in a mess of cables. The ground is far below him, and above him is the wreckage of The Luscious. Its flight deck is teetering upside down on the edge of the canyon rim. There's no sign of the balloon structure, aside from some of the gas chamber fabric caught in the cable rigging with him.

He grabs at the cable wrapped around his chest and tries to pull himself right side up. At least enough to relieve the pressure from his head. His arms are numb and feel frostbitten again. The more aware of himself he feels, the more he realizes his body has been exposed to the frigid air for a while. The Juman crew uniform is the only thing he's wearing. Most of his skin is reddish white and where it's not numb it's tingling. Beneath the skin, his muscles are sending a biting pain throughout his body. The pain is worst in his left leg, which is caught in a cable knot, and it's what's primarily holding him up.

He glances at the ground to find the shapes of several bodies amongst the debris at the bottom of the canyon. The bodies are unfamiliar to him, so he assumes they're just crew and soldiers. Any effort to focus makes his head throb. It's all he can do to maintain a firm grip on the cables and prop himself up. *Well, at least Juman won't be getting their hands on those penguins anytime soon. I gotta get myself out of this mess, though.*

"Hey! Is anyone up there!?"

A short moment passes with no reply. *Ok, that's not helpful. There were a lot of people on the ship, I can't be the only one who survived the drop. Then again, I'm not sure if anyone who did would be able to help. Wait, Guariana. I know the name Guariana!* Rogue takes a few slow and deep breaths and forces himself to try climbing up. The skin on the palm of his hand peels off from the frostbite. He's unable to keep a grip and support his body weight.

"Shit!"

Blood squirts out of the broken skin on his hand and rolls down his arm. The pain is severe, so he lets go of the cable and rests his body on the ones holding him up. He tears a strip of cloth off his shirt to wrap around his hands, in hopes of stopping the bleeding. *Damnit. That was dumb! Shit.*

An archon's roar in the distance catches his attention. The sound booms around him and echoes through the canyon.

His body tenses and he forgets his current situation while he searches for the source of the sound. His heart is pounding, he's hyperventilating, and terror overwhelms him.

"No. I don't wanna die like this," he stammers. "No, no! Guariana! Get me out of this!" *Shit, shit, shit.*

He wraps his arm around the cable and tries to pull himself back up. The cable he's using stiffens and makes a loud twang sound, followed by a series of frightening snaps. The overwhelming sense of horror gets worse as the flight deck rocks and shakes. Dust, rocks, and small debris rain around him to the dreadful sound of crunching ice and scraping metal. All he can do is watch, as the wreck shifts further over the canyon rim. Another loud twang comes from another snapping cable, which causes him to drop a few feet.

The metal creaking from the flight deck is deafening. The wreckage is edging into the canyon, moving the cable rigging as it teeters. Rogue fights to loosen the cable wrapped around his chest. As he gets a good grip on the cable, the flight deck tilts down until it gets caught on some protruding rocks as well as some of the rigging above him. The cable snaps out of his hand and tightens around his chest, crushing him and making it impossible to breathe. Several loud twangs pierce the air and a few of the cables holding the flight deck up fray and snap until they can't hold it up anymore.

Rogue closes his eyes as the flight deck comes down more until it gets caught on more rocks and cables. He opens his eyes to find he's almost back inside the wreckage. The pressure from the cable around his chest feels like it's going to slice through him. He sees it's one of the cables the flight deck is resting on. He tries to twist his chest and see if he can unwind himself from the cable, but he can't budge it. More twangs alarm him as cables around him snap. It's a chorus of creaking metal and cracking cables.

Damnit, this can't be how I go out. Not like this. As he braces for the worst, the cable around his chest frays; wire after wire splits off the cable, until it finally breaks. His body swings on the remaining cables for what feels like forever. He brings himself to look around. The ground is still a long way down, and as he glances above, he can see more of the flight deck. Something exciting catches his eye. The cabinet where emergency landing supplies are located is still there, and among them is a bright orange bag with bulging pads.

An impact vest. He glances back down to the ground. *It's one hell of a drop, but if I can get to that vest, it's survivable.* He wraps his arms around a few cables that seem to support his weight, and shimmies toward the back of the flight deck. Every time he moves, the metal creaking gets louder. Another cable snaps, and this time, the wreck breaks apart and the flight deck moves sideways, before plunging further down.

He breathes a sigh of relief when the flight deck gets caught on more rocks between the canyon walls. It's not too far below him, but he still needs to figure out a way to get there. The debris above him appears to be beams holding up most of the cables and another deck from the cabin that's hanging off the edge of the cliff. It tilts down until it slides in, getting jammed between the canyon walls above him. It's a mangled mess of twisted metal, but among the mess he can see the bodies of Juman soldiers. One of them still has their weapon. Rogue looks at the tangle of cables on his leg. "That will get me loose. I think." He studies the debris and cables around him to find a way to it. Slowly, he moves along the cables to get closer. The creaking metal above him gets louder. The debris slides again and drops several feet. Rogue braces himself for it to come down on him. After a few seconds, he looks up to see what's happened. He finds the wreck just over his head and the body further away. He might be able to climb onto the debris. Standing on anything would be nice at the moment. He grabs hold of the nearest metal beam and tests his weight on it. Confident that it will hold him, he climbs and shimmies his way to the body, hanging off the side of the wreck hundreds of feet above the ground.

The soldier's armor is split open like a tin can, and his helmet is gone, revealing the face of a man, still a boy really, far younger than Rogue assumed. "Damn, poor kid," he mumbles to himself, when he sees the look of anguish on the boy's face. He reaches for the gun strapped to the boy's chest; it's wedged between the boy's body and the beam that crushed him. Some wiggling is enough to pull it out. Rogue grabs the tangled cable around his leg and draws it out away from him, being sure to put his weight against the metal he's barely got room to stand on, then puts the end of the gun's barrel on it. He pulls the trigger. Nothing happens.

"What?" Rogue ponders and looks over the gun. He can't figure out how to check for ammunition but spots a dial with a notch by the letter S. "Oh, right; safety is a thing on some of these. I really should take Walker up on his gun lessons."

After moving the dial, he tries again. This time the rifle fires and the cable breaks. The recoil catches him off guard and he loses his footing. He drops the rifle and grabs the beam with his injured hand at full strength. He screams in pain, hanging on for dear life, while blood is pouring from his hand.

The flight deck is directly below him. "Aw, crap." *How the hell am I supposed to get there now? I did not think this through.* After a quick study of his surroundings, he can't find any way down aside from jumping and hoping he sticks the landing.

Rogue lowers himself on the beam to get as far down as he can and drops to the top of the flight deck. His landing is enough to cause it to slide down the canyon a little more. He doesn't see a way into the flight deck until he spots some railing going down the side of the wreckage. It's from the hallway that leads to the Venator's quarters above the bridge. His heart skips a beat when he realizes what he's looking at. *Guariana. No, she's a Venator and I've heard some crazy shit. If an ordinary guy like me survived this, then she absolutely did. I hope she did.*

He walks over to what was once the entrance to the quarters. A piece of Venator armor is wedged into the debris, near where the floor is ripped open, leading down into the flight deck. He slides down the hole and drops to the deck below. Most of the equipment and flight consoles are gone, as is most of the floor. Though thankfully he can reach the emergency supplies. When he opens the panel, half the supplies fall out. He snatches an impact vest and lets the rest of it fall through gaps in the floor. *Alright! Now for the shitty part. This is going to suck.*

Rogue straps the vest on and looks for a good spot to jump from. He can see bits of debris on the ground well over a hundred feet below him. He jumps and curls into a ball and makes sure to land on his back. The impact vest deploys its airbags when he hits the canyon floor, cushioning his fall. "Ow! Oh, yeah that hurt about as much as I expected it to," he groans and rolls over to get off his back.

He turns his attention to a box of medical supplies near him. He crawls over and pops it open, finding Juman's equivalent of things he's familiar with. The cloth around his hand is soaked in blood and not doing him any good, so he takes care of that first. He uses the bandages to wrap his hand properly. Next, he grabs what he assumes is a pain wipe tube and opens it; the syringe inside is broken. He searches around until he finds something labeled for pain. He opens the pouch and finds small pills inside that need to be dissolved under the tongue. "I hate these things." They dissolve quickly and he can feel his whole body getting numb to the sensations of pain and the cold. He stands up and nearly loses his balance.

He looks at the cable knot still around his leg and tries to untie it. "Ok, that's going to require tools. I'll deal with that in a moment." He looks around at the bodies of Juman soldiers, but there is one body that stands out, a Hurluan soldier like Te'Yuro, who's got cold weather gear on. "Well, you don't need that anymore."

He takes the cold weather gear off the soldier and puts it on. There's a small notebook in the jacket pocket, which Rogue looks at out of curiosity. Inside the notes are all written in a foreign language. "Huh, this isn't important to anyone but you, I guess."

Rogue tosses the notebook onto the body and looks for a bag to hold the emergency supplies. More debris falls from the wreck above him. Pipes, metal panels, and small rocks scrape off the canyon walls. He goes to another body that has a backpack and takes it off. He recognizes the body immediately as Dr. Hestar.

"Guariana! Hunter! Can you guys hear me!? Hell, I'll even take the Maroon Mistress at this point!" He shouts, even though he's sure it won't do anything.

The bag is surprisingly heavy, so he opens it to find out why; he finds it packed with emergency food and supplies. "That works; thanks buddy." Rogue heads back to the box of medical supplies and fills whatever space is left in the bag. Above him the second deck comes crashing down onto the flight deck. Rogue tuck into a ball and screams, a few seconds he realizes it's stuck. *Shit, that was lucky. I need to get the hell out of here.*

A large thing lands nearby, but it's not debris. Rogue watches the object writhe. It's alive whatever it is, and it's bigger than a human. He looks back up to find the debris being inspected by dozens of scythe mantises. *How the hell do they show up like that?* The one on the ground rears up on its hind limbs and brandishes its two large, blade-like appendages, while it chews on a man's severed arm. It grabs the arm with its bladed limb and tosses it aside when it decides to approach one of the corpses.

Rogue watches in horror as the beast slices the body apart and picks up sections of flesh to eat. He looks at the weapon near the body he stripped just moments ago and takes a few steps toward it. His movement catches the beast's attention, but it doesn't stop its meal. More of them are coming toward the wreck site, crawling down the canyon walls. He reaches the rifle and picks it up; it's like the one he found on the body pinned to the wreck above. He notices the man has several magazines of ammo on his belt. In the time it takes him to get the belt off and collect the pouches of magazines, the mantis is moving to another body. Another one lands closer to Rogue. This one is keeping its focus on him. Rogue turns the safety off on the rifle and aims; the mantis doesn't react and walks closer.

Rogue slings the belt and ammo around his shoulder and backs away, hoping that it's interested in the body and not him. But as he backs away it doesn't change its gaze. "Shit." Rogue does his best to aim at its head and fires.

The gunshot startles the entire group of mantises and takes Rogue by surprise, it has more recoil than he was ready for. He fires again and misses. "Oh, come on! How hard is it to shoot? Soldiers make this shit look easy!"

He fires again but still can't hit the head. He aims lower where the mantis's body is wider and tries to shoot it there. He hits it on the side and the beast recoils, letting out a shrill noise. The same noise is joined by a call from the other mantises along the canyon walls and in the wreck. But the other one on the ground is now charging at him. Rogue barely has the time to aim before it takes a swing at him with a bladed arm. Rogue holds the trigger down and the rifle fires three shots. All of them find their mark in the beast's head. It drops to the ground and curls up like a dead insect.

Rogue keeps backing away from the wreck, hoping none of them decide to follow him. After a few minutes he turns around to look where he's going. The canyon floor gets wider and deeper further along, but it's the only direction he can go; he intends to put as much distance between him and the wreck as he can.

"I'm sorry Guariana. I can't get to you," he mutters under his breath. *But somehow, I know you're out there. And if I can make a miracle happen for you, I will.*

Guariana groans and pushes a large chunk of metal off her. Daylight blinds her for a quick moment before she forces herself to her feet. The Luscious is a massive wreck in front of her, broken into several sections, and the bodies of soldiers lay scattered around her.

"Rogue!" she calls out and drops to her knees, grabbing at her diaphragm before coughing up blood. "That hurt."

Two crew members run up to her. "We have another one! A Venator! She's alive!"

"How many survivors are there?" Guariana grabs one of them by the shoulders and shakes them. "Did the Acinvar man survive? Where's Rogue Whip?"

"Ma'am, he's unaccounted for," the crewman answers. "We'll make locating him a priority."

She stops shaking him and squeezes his arms until he yelps in pain. "The! You'll make finding him and giving him aid THE priority! Last known location was the Venator's quarters!" she shouts, before dropping to her knees. "He was in my arms! I had him! He slid out of my grip and was gone."

The second crewman points behind her. "That's not good. The bow was torn off with the lower levels and landed at the canyon rim over there. Most of it just fell in. If he's in there, we'll do what we can to recover him."

"Rescue! Damnit!" Guariana reaches for her gunblade, but it's gone. "Organize a team of able-bodied survivors and get on it. He is your top priority."

The crewmen slam their forearms and sprint away.

A booming roar alerts everyone that the gigas archons are flying in their direction and swooping down from the sky. "Everyone, take cover!" Guariana sprints for the hangar from the airship, which is still intact and close enough to reach before an archon lands.

She runs through the door and checks over her shoulder. A powerful gust of air and a quake in the ground knocks her off her feet when the archon lands. It flaps its wings to send another fierce gust of wind across the wreckage before folding them across its back.

Several soldiers and crewmen take up arms and start

Archon's Wake

shooting. Their efforts don't reward them with a reaction from the archon.

"Stop firing!" Guariana shouts. Soldiers around her echo the order until the sound of gunfire stops. "Take cover!" She looks around to see if anything in the hangar is still operational. Flying vehicles are either missing or destroyed, and none of the ground vehicles stayed in their restraints. Most of them are piles of scrap, heaped against the rear wall.

The Archon roars at the crash site. Its infrasound shakes and rattles everything.

Guariana has never felt this kind of disorientation before and grabs at her head as it throbs. Her bones quiver even after the roar ends.

Several soldiers around her drop to their knees and scream in pain; others fall to the ground lifelessly.

Guariana wipes her upper lip and finds her nose bleeding again. "Get away from the open air!" She runs to the wrecked vehicles. While they aren't drivable, the armored ones may offer a degree of protection from the archon roar. Before she can reach them, however, the hangar slides sideways, knocking everyone inside off their feet and shaking the vehicles loose from each other.

The archon swipes at the hangar and watches it slide across the ice, then pounces onto it and bats it further away from the crash site.

It's all Guariana can do to leap from the top of one vehicle to the next while dodging debris. A soldier is smashed by one of the wrecked vehicles, leaving behind a large smear of blood. The hangar lurches sideways and spins around. She ducks under a flying tire and jumps onto the side of an armor-plated artillery vehicle. The hangar jolts again and comes to a sudden stop. Everything inside slams against the walls or slides out of the missing hangar doors.

The Archon has the hangar in its paws and bites on it.

Guariana sees massive claws and teeth puncture the hangar walls and ceiling, as the archon rips the structure apart.

The archon snarls, disappointed that it didn't find anything edible, and moves on. It gives what's left of the building a final swipe before going back to check the rest of the airship's wreckage.

Guariana is thrown out of the hangar and slides across the ice until she slams into a boulder. The rest of the hangar is shredded as it slides away. Everything is turned into unrecognizable bits of twisted metal. Even the bulkiest armored tanks are reduced to hunks of scrap.

The archon moves to the next largest piece of the airship and bites down. It lifts the wreck in its mouth and looks around, as if searching for a special spot to rip it open.

Guariana can't believe her eyes as she watches the archon towering over the wreckage like a victorious hunter deciding what to do with its prey. It throws the piece in its mouth to the side and bats around the wreckage. Gunshots ring out, and the archon's paw digs into some of the wreck and the shooting stops.

The archon rears up on its hind legs and slams down on the ground with its front paws, sending shockwaves across the ground.

As the tremors shake Guariana around, the landscape changes before her eyes. The wreckage and archon vanish. "What? No. Are there penguins around?" It's nothing but flat icy tundra, as far as the eye can see.

Loud cracks echo around her, and jets of steam shoot high into the sky in the distance.

Guariana watches as the jets of steam appear to pop out of ground closer and closer. The steam appears pink then red. When a geyser bursts a few feet away from her, it showers her in thick, oily blood. When the geyser stops, the blood boils on her armor, giving off a burning smell. Her armor is being eaten by acid in the blood.

She starts ripping off her armor before the acid can reach her skin. "Shit!" She stops once she's wearing nothing but a thin, cloth jumpsuit.

The ice beneath her starts to feel warm and watery. She jumps to the side fearing another geyser. The water and blood drain down into a hole forming in the ice, taking her armor with it. She keeps backing away, but the hole is widening as fast as she's moving until she hits another invisible barrier. She tries to find a way to climb up or get through it but can't; the hole is pitch black. More loud cracks in the distance are now joined by huge sheets of ice shooting into the sky; the tundra's ice is fracturing in spectacular form.

Shards of ice rain down around her, some are as large as she is. She leaps sideways to avoid them but keeps running into barriers like a maze, with all paths leading to the growing hole. A barrage of icicles chases her closer; they seem to be raining down on her in a targeted way. She tries to jump to the side, slams into an invisible barrier, and barely dodges the icicle that's twice her size as it hits the ground and shatters. She digs herself out and tries to backtrack to avoid the next one, but a new barrier is in her way. Or was it always there and she came from a different direction?

The ground beneath her is falling into the growing hole and she can't escape anymore; she drops straight down into the darkness.

When Guariana comes to, she finds herself strapped to a metal table in a drab room lit only by a dying oil lamp. Blood stains cover the old porcelain tiles on the walls and ceiling; many are broken and cracked. There doesn't seem to be a door, and the only thing visible is the glass oil lamp dangling from the wall by her head. She's restrained with thick metal cuffs around her wrists, ankles, and waist. Using all her might, she can't break free or even budge. She manages to tilt her head up enough to see some syringes by her side, all of them used.

A huge skeleton shrouded in a dark haze rises next to her. "See you here, see you clear. Soul of strength, soul of life." It wraps its hand around her neck.

The room around her is filled with the screams from her childhood, as Juman doctors flash in and out, injecting her with all sorts of chemicals and taking measurements, blood samples, bone marrow. The pain wracks her body, and she screams at the top of her lungs.

A skinless man emerges from inside the skeleton and walks

Daniel Jones

up to Guariana's side. "Yes, this is the one I witnessed. We'll return her and follow along." He places his hand on her stomach.

Guariana tilts her head up at his touch to find the man's arm become slimy and grow suction cups, like an octopus tentacle. Sharp, serrated spines form along the flat edges of the tentacle; she can feel the tips poking into her and wrapping around her stomach.

She squirms and the oil lamp fades out, causing the room to turn pitch black. The spines all dig deep into her flesh along her sides and pulls away, tearing chunks of flesh from her, then digs into her and starts ripping through her organs. Another tentacle wraps around her face, and the spines gouge out her eyes. The tentacle slides down her mouth and slashes through her tongue and cuts its way out of her throat. She can feel it wrapping its spines around her neck before ripping itself away.

In her mind she can picture her neck and head being severed but can't come up with how she's still conscious. "I'm afraid we can't do more here. She's not connected to us in the way you hoped," the skinless man's voice says.

Guariana opens her eyes to see herself back on the tundra; the crash site has been trampled all over and debris scattered all over the place and her armor is still on her body. She quickly puts her hands to her face, but feels no blood or wounds. There's no sign of the archon anywhere.

"I hate this place." She lies back down and stares up at the sky. "Why would anyone want to come here?"

"We'll return her and follow along." The voice echoes in her head.

"What the hell does that mean!?" she shouts. "Who, or what, are you? Show yourself!"

Nearby there's a clicking, chittering sound; it's coming from a scythe mantis that's attracted to the wreckage.

She scrambles to her feet and starts running toward the crash site to find her weapon. "Damn these things!"

Archon's Wake

Scythe Mantises are all over the place, searching for flesh to eat. Some are fighting over the bodies of crew members and soldiers. The sound of her gunblade firing pierces the air; it sounds close. She makes her way around pieces of scrap and debris and comes across several dead mantises that have been shot. Among them are soldiers' bodies with extreme lacerations and severed limbs. For now, she'll make do with the assault rifle from one of the bodies. Her gunblade fires another shot. It's coming from inside a large piece of intact cabin structure.

As she jogs toward it, she comes across an armored tank that looks drivable, so stops to take a better look. Despite the windows being cracked or missing, it survived being thrown around the hangar.

Guariana shoots her way through the bugs; most of them clear out of her way and scurry away to hide. The ones that don't, she makes sure to take down. When she reaches the cabin, she finds the remnants of a bloodbath. She steps gingerly over dozens of dead mantises to get to the body of the first soldier. "Soldiers! Sound off!"

"Here Ma'am!" A soldier shouts, further in.

Guariana follows along the walkway until she reaches a room that's been turned into a defensive stronghold. Two soldiers are aiming weapons at the doorway; one of them is holding her gunblade, but is quick to offer her the weapon back. "You didn't waste any ammunition, I hope."

"Made every shot count, ma'am." The Soldier salutes her with a bow.

She looks over her weapon and hands him the assault rifle.

"They keep coming," the second soldier chimes in. "These things, they just keep coming."

"There're hundreds more of them outside. We must leave." Guariana gestures them to follow her.

"What?" the second soldier asks.

Guariana is taken aback for a moment. "That wasn't a question, soldier."

"I know, but how are we going to get past these things?" the soldier asks.

She smiles. "That archon's roar has freed your mind; that

Daniel Jones

could be useful."

"Freed my mind?" the soldier asks.

"What's your name?" Guariana asks.

"Peng, why does that matter?" he answers.

Guariana approaches him. "Because I can't re-hypnotize you to follow orders. But if you do as I say and keep your vigilance where it needs to be, you might actually get out of this alive."

"Re hypnotize? I was hypnotized? Is he hypnotized?" Peng looks over at the other soldier, who doesn't react to the conversation. "Holy shit!"

"Stay here and you will die." Guariana checks the walkway to make sure it's clear. "Soldier, take point; Peng, reload that machine gun with a fresh belt and take the center. I'll keep the rear and tell him where to lead us."

Where are we? I can't see nothing!" Peng shouts.

"There is a tank I can use to drive us to safety. So shut up, reload, and get your ass moving." Guariana aims her gunblade at him. "You know what a tank is, right?"

"A tank? Yeah, a tank, that... that sounds like a good idea. Ok, reloading and going." Peng grabs a new box of belt ammunition and feeds it into his weapon.

Guariana fires down the walkway when she sees a mantis walk toward her. The soldier gets ahead of her and walks to the end. Peng finishes and nervously gets in front of her, breathing heavily.

She puts her hand firmly on his shoulder. "You're a Juman soldier. You are in control. You will not fail," she tells him.

The ground shakes and Peng grabs the doorway. "Nope, uh-uh, that felt bad. That's bad, right?"

Guariana secures her weapon on her back. "Get out of the wreckage!"

The walkway jolts sideways, tips over, and rolls, until it's upside down.

Peng screams and hits his head on the wall, knocking him out.

Guariana grabs his weapon and picks him up, tossing him over her shoulder. The soldier ahead of her runs toward the exit. She runs to keep up until the cabin is pushed into a

Archon's Wake

spinning motion. The centrifugal force throws her all the way to the end of the walkway and pins her down until it slows.

Peng's body feels limp; his face was cut open by her gunblade when she was thrown around.

"That might have been for the best," she mumbles, and looks at the other soldier, who's getting back to his feet. The cabin lurches sideways and rolls again, landing right side up. "I'm getting tired of these damn archons!"

The cabin lurches harder and rolls several times until it feels like its falling. Metal clangs and bangs are deafening, as the cabin is ripped apart. The wall next to her peels off and reveals a rocky surface covered in scrape marks and small bits of debris. Everything stops with a crash that knocks her off her feet again.

She groans and crawls to the gaping hole next to her. The archon snarls from the top of the canyon rim and tries to reach the debris with its paw, but its arm isn't long enough to reach it. It unleashes a full-throated roar down the canyon, which intensifies the infrasound vibrations. Her brain feels like it's exploding inside her skull, and she can't see straight, her ears are ringing, and all sense of direction and feeling are gone. the archon roars again, louder, angrier, and with its teeth bared at the wreckage, before it leaps into the air and flies away.

Several minutes pass before Guariana can bring herself to move. Everything hurts, and all she can do is pull herself to the edge, roll out of the walkway, and fall to the ground. She lays there staring up, hoping the pain might subside a little, but it doesn't. Eventually she forces herself to overcome the pain and get to her feet. Her head spins and she's still disoriented. She leans against the rocky canyon wall and waits for her vision to improve.

The whole bow of the airship landed in the canyon. The flight deck is sideways, and a tangled mass of cables is draped around it. "Rogue," she mutters. If he somehow survived this, he might not have survived the roar, or the debris crash.

Not far from the flight deck are a few mantis carcasses; they've been shot. And there's a small trail of blood leading away from the wreck. "That better be you, Rogue. Hold on, I'm coming."

Kita is laying on one of the beds. Her leg, side, and the back of her head are covered in bloody bandages. The sound of one of those helicopter vehicle things woke her up, and now she can't run. All she can do is sit and wait for whoever it is to find her and finish the job of killing her. Cinder is laying at her side, purring, while she strokes the top of his head with her fingers.

The door to the barracks creaks, she turns her head and panics. The man that Juman woman landed with in front of Rogue walks into the barracks.

"Got a survivor in here!" Hunter shouts at the two Venators behind him.

"No, please!" Kita cries and shakes her head. She had prepared herself to die but now she can't give up.

Hunter puts his shotgun down by the door and raises his hands. "It's alright; we're not here to hurt you."

"Yes, you are! You took Rogue! And that other woman, she said she was going to bring others. She'll hurt them and make me heal them!" Kita shrieks.

"Rogue? You are not from the Blooming Sandseas then?" One of the Venators asks.

"On the way to the crater, he mentioned two other people survived his crash. I know her, she's a doctor from Acinvar, her name is Kita. It's alright, we're actually trying to stop anyone else from dying and get everyone out of this place now. Rogue's on his way to Black Sand City as we speak," Hunter explains. "Formalia, can you check her out? It looks like Titania did a number on her."

One of the Venators comes through the doorway and heads to Kita, taking her helmet off. She looks very similar to the one who thrashed her around and ripped her rib out. Kita cowers in terror and Cinder hisses.

"Easy, you need real medical care." Formalia kneels at her side and studies the bandage work.

"I am a trauma lifesaver at Air Drop West," Kita argues.

Archon's Wake

"Yes, I can see that. Can you tell me what happened to you?"

Kita reaches over and holds up her rib bone. "Let's start with this."

Hunter looks away and whistles. "Damn, Titania tore a whole rib out of her," he says to Liliana.

"Nice; that must've hurt like hell. Strong woman to survive that injury." Liliana could care less.

Formalia nods and gently lowers Kita's hand. "Mr. Smith, I need to know what supplies are in our bird. She is stable but moving her will require more than I see here."

Kita knows she's seen him before. And it finally clicks in her head. Hunter Smith, one of the Camp Tor survivors. After taking a hard look at him, she returns her focus to the Venator next to her and points to a small pile of medical supplies that she found in the warehouse. "The Blooming Sandseas brought a lot of stuff. I used laceration wraps first, but they did nothing to help my internal injuries. I dug around and found Aixolo Biofoam and Stemogra Serum. They also had a makeshift medical center, but it's been trashed, likely before we got here."

"How long ago did you apply the foam? And what dose of the serum?" Formalia asks.

"Three hours ago, give or take a few minutes. Hundred and twenty CCs; my weight is one hundred and twelve pounds," Kita answers.

"You do know what you're doing. Then we'll let you rest until you can be moved. Mr. Smith, you and Liliana will continue. I'll tend to the wounded and search for how penguins could get here before we arrived."

"Those glass cubes you took, there were a few of them in the medical ward, shattered open," Kita replies. "Didn't see any penguins though. That other monster, whatever her name is, she headed for one of the marked outposts on the tundra map."

"Easy now, you mustn't strain yourself." Formalia takes her gauntlet off and holds Kita's wrist. "Your heart rate is too slow."

"Diotonic cardio, thirty mils," Kita replies.

"Used in conjunction with the pain wipe we found in the

entrance foyer?" Formalia takes a better look at the bandage on her leg.

"That bone was ripped out by hand. I think you can figure out the effects that had on my body," Kita mumbles. "If I have to fuck my organs raw to survive, so be it."

Formalia runs her hand along Kita's unharmed side. She can feel that nearly every rib is broken.

"All but three ribs are broken, spinal damage, leg impalement, and displaced hip. Both clavicles and scapulas are fractured," Kita adds.

"For now, rest, relax, and breathe. You are safe. I'm a lieutenant of the Venators. Titania answers to me. I will protect you." Formalia stands and looks at the row of warehouses across the street.

Kita nods, tears streaming from her eyes.

Liliana pats Hunter's arm. He grabs his shotgun and follows her out. "Three hours? Titania cannot have gotten that far."

"Won't be able to follow those small cycle tracks in the Helo, and the snow's already turned to ice," Hunter comments.

"Then we find the motor pool and take something faster." Liliana heads for the second warehouse, where the track marks are coming from.

Hunter shoulders his weapon and fires down the street.

Liliana grabs her gunblade, but finds Hunter's shot a penguin.

"We got problems!" Hunter shouts.

"Formalia! Penguin sighted!" Liliana adds.

The penguin wiggles and writhes after lying motionless. Hunter keeps his shotgun aimed at it. The penguin's head pops off its body, shooting toward him and lands at his feet. The body hisses as eight bony limbs covered in mucus goo burst out of the sides.

"Oh, please tell me you're seeing this shit too," Hunter groans.

No one replies and he looks around him. Liliana isn't next to him, and he doesn't see anyone inside the windows.

"Aw, fuck me." Hunter shoots again and the creature drops dead, curling its legs in the air the way a dead spider does. "The hell is that thing?" He steps back, and a string of webbing hits the ground in front of him.

Along the top of the barracks, big spiders made of exposed bones and covered in decaying, rotten flesh make themselves known, shooting strings of webs at him.

He raises his shotgun and takes them out while they come down the side of the building. Each one drops dead as he lines it up, fires, and moves to the next one. All the while he steps out of the path of web strings flying at him.

Liliana tries to grab Hunter's shotgun as she starts shooting at the building. "What the fuck is wrong with you?" Her hand passes through the weapon. She tries again with the same result and looks at her hands in shock before trying to grab Hunter. But she can't, her hands pass through him too. She stops to look at her hands like something's wrong with them but then turns her attention to the barracks as Hunter shoots the building,

Formalia rushes to Kita as Hunter's aim lowers down to the windows, which shatter as he shoots them.

Hunter fires off the last round and starts reloading. When he's ready he aims at a spider twice his size as it reaches the ground and rapid fires until it drops dead.

Formalia does her best to cover Kita as Hunter shoots her armor. "Damn that weapon." She turns around when Hunter stops firing.

Kita screams when she sees her foot was shot. Several toes are missing, and blood is gushing.

"Liliana, take him down! This woman can't take more injuries!" Formalia shouts, as she reaches for the medical supplies.

Hunter backs down the street, shooting in random directions as Liliana chases after him. All he can see are grotesque monsters, made of decaying wriggling flesh, with limbs, tentacles, claws, spines, and multiple mouths with gnarly teeth. A bat-like one with eyes all over its wings and a large pincer on its mouth swoops at him.

He ducks under it, spins around and shoots it down. When he looks up, he finds hundreds more of them. More webs shoot at him, and he dives to the ground to avoid them. The ground feels slippery, squishy, and the sky is getting darker. "I need cover fire! Anyone alive? I need... I need... uh... fuck I gotta find somewhere defendable."

He shoots a window in a nearby building and dives through it. The building is so dark inside, though, that he can't make out where the walls are.

The gurgling snarl of the monsters sounds unnatural and each time he hears it he falls deeper into madness. The monsters' exposed bones start glowing bright green every time the light fades.

Liliana catches up to him and tries to grab his weapon again, getting the same result as before. "Damnit." She tries shooting at him with her gunblade, but the shot goes through him.

A slimy, rope-like tongue wraps around Hunter's neck and pulls him into a large chomping maw with glowing teeth that's too big to get inside the room.

He reaches for a knife from his belt, but another tongue grabs his hand and pulls it away. Hunter tries to jam his feet on anything, but he's sliding along the floor until his arm reaches the monster's mouth, where it bites his hand off. He screams and can see his arm clear as day; the stump is spurting blood and he can the pain like it's real. The tongue wrapped around his neck tugs, inching him closer and closer to the door and the gaping maw.

Liliana watches Hunter's feet pushing against the wall under the window, and his body is somehow levitating off the ground, being tugged by something she can't see. She aims out the window and fires a shot from her gunblade.

Hunter drops to the ground, screaming at the tops of his lungs. He sees Liliana standing over him in a strange room.

She takes her helmet off. "What the hell just happened?"

"I, I, it was like at the crater. No, it was worse. It was a nightmare."

"You shot at all of us, Hunter; I'm going to need a lot more than that!" Liliana puts her blade at his throat. "I'll add another scar if you don't start making sense this fucking instant!"

He can see several of his rounds punched into her chest

Archon's Wake

armor and raises his hands. "Please tell me you saw something. A penguin, a spider, a wriggling mess of flesh and bone with glowing shit."

Liliana yanks his shotgun away from him. "I saw the penguin. Then you went on a shooting spree!"

"This is worse than Hydra's Wake. I could feel myself slipping away. It was like I was easy to scare. That didn't happen in Tor. There I was always myself. But this, whatever is going on here, is robbing us of who we are. There were monsters everywhere, unnatural monsters. Spiders, giant spiders, with rotting flesh. That thing, that mouth, it bit my arm off and tried to eat me through the window!" Hunter says.

Liliana wraps her finger around the trigger with the barrel of her weapon aimed at his chin.

"Put me out of my misery. I can't suffer like this anymore. Not again. I can't do it again. Please," Hunter whimpers and cries.

She puts her weapon away. "No. I don't know enough about what just happened to dispose of you yet. I'll discuss it with Formalia. In the meantime, you're not getting this back." She takes his shotgun away.

Formalia finishes bandaging Kita's foot. "I will get to the bottom of what just happened."

"Thank you, for taking some shots for me. I'd be dead if it weren't for you," Kita says. "And thank you for my foot; you'd make an amazing surgeon."

"Bundle yourself in blankets until I can find a place to move you that isn't being flooded by cold air." Formalia says sternly.

Hunter follows Liliana with his hands tied. "Penguins, nine o'clock!" he shouts.

Liliana glances over and sees a group of them waddling down the road. She uses Hunter's shotgun to take them out before they get too close or scatter away.

Formalia runs up to them with her gunblade in hand.

Liliana lowers the shotgun. "This location is compromised."

"Paranormal activity follows those penguins!" Hunter shouts at the top of his lungs.

Daniel Jones

The Venators look at him with surprise. "Did you have to yell?" Liliana asks.

"What?" Hunter shouts. "Damnit, where is everyone!? NO! Not again!"

"Unbelievable," Liliana says.

Formalia rubs her forehead. "I told you to kill him."

"We don't know a damn thing about what we're up against. We might need him for information," Liliana retorts.

Formalia gives him a quick glance. "As long as he's unarmed, I agree. Secure him in the Helo; I'm going to find a way to move the woman."

Titania walks out of a burning building, dragging a man by his neck. Once she's satisfied with how far out they are, she throws him to the ground and steps on his back, crushing his spine under the weight of her armor. She waves the map in her other hand. "Tell me more of this unmarked location where Amenaza is hiding?"

The man glances behind him at the burning building and listens to the screams of his colleagues trapped inside. "You're a monster."

"I'm worse than the nightmares of monsters. And I am offering you a chance to survive. I'll only ask once more, sweetie; tell me where your empress is!" Titania puts pressure on his spine, causing him to scream.

"It's more Shiv ruins. That's all I know. It's near the easter canyons! Where we can't easily get," the man says. "That all anyone knows."

Titania lets her foot off his back and kicks him over, putting her foot on his stomach and pressing down harder. "That's not what I learned."

"Only her security team knows the location!" the man rephrases. "It's all I was told."

Titania stands on him and wags her finger in front of his face. "I asked you to omit any and all lies. That includes half-truths or iffy statements."

The weight of her armor alone is crushing him, and he can't breathe.

She watches him suffocate for a moment longer until he passes out, then gets off him. "You're not worth my effort."

Rogue runs down the canyon, checking over his shoulder at the snarling beasts behind him.

Wolves covered in a smoky haze with flames burning on their backs and glowing green eyes are chasing him. They leave behind a trail of blood dripping from their skinless bodies.

There's nothing for him to climb up; the canyon walls are too steep. The canyon floor is nothing but thick sand, with no boulders to jump on; nothing to put between him and the wolves since they appeared.

He's out of breath, but digging deep to keep up the relentless sprint. The further he runs, the narrower the canyon becomes. He can see a fork splitting the canyon up ahead. On the right is a thick storm, and he can see more of the wolves lined up at the top. The left is a dead end with a massive wall blocking the way further in the distance, like a dam.

The wolves slow and their snarling turns into howling. The howls are echoed by the wolves all over the right path.

Rogue notices the ones chasing him come to a stop, but he keeps running regardless. When he clears the narrow stretch of canyon, the hallucinations vanish. He hunches over and stops to catch his breath. After a short moment he looks up and sees the canyon has several buildings lining the canyon walls on the left, but the giant wall blocking the way is still there. People are walking around, with three large transport vehicles parked in the middle of the buildings.

The ground ahead of him is rocky and has multiple lines of rail tracks running along. They're old, completely rusted, and the concrete sleepers they're on are crumbling and broken.

"Sir, you can't, they're children!" a man's voice shouts.

"What? What did my wife do? Doctor, this is madness!"

Daniel Jones

another shouts.

A child's earsplitting scream of terror and pain makes Rogue's ears ring.

"Please! No!" a woman cries.

More and more voices, pleas for mercy, help, stop, and begs, drown each other out until it's just screaming noise from countless people.

Rogue covers his ears and drops to his knees.

Then silence for a few seconds.

"You disobeyed orders! These tests are getting out of hand! Stand down, Dr. Lourcer! Or we'll make you answer for your crimes!" another woman shouts, along with the sound of a weapon being drawn and cocked.

An old man laughs. "You misunderstand. I'm done testing. The use of this device is revealing secrets to existences beyond our comprehension. The more I use this, the more I learn; and the further human knowledge goes."

Rogue feels something prick the back of his neck. He blacks out to the sound of a screeching, whining mechanical noise he's never heard before.

Hondo walks up and lifts Rogue by the arm, as his mechanical suit retracts a device back into his shoulder. "It is a very bad day to be you, Juman soldier."

5: Layers Of The Pain

A few hours later, Rogue wakes up, tied to a chair in a dark room.

"Oh-ho, you're awake already?" Hondo chuckles. "Tough son of a bitch, ain't ye? 'Specially for a Juman."

Rogue groans and coughs. "Uh, what happened?"

"He speaks freely? Not a hypnotized soldier then," another man in the room comments.

"I'm not a Juman," Rogue mumbles, and looks around the room. His vision is blurry, and he can't make out anything around him. "What did you drug me with? Who are you?"

"Definitely not hypnotized; very interesting. I'll inform her highness he's awake. Get him ready for interrogation. We'll make this fun." Hondo walks up to Rogue and steadies him against the back of the chair. "Damn, that muscle on you is nice and solid. Good, I like durable people to have fun with. Hehehe." He punches Rogue in the face, breaking his nose and slicing his cheek open.

Rogue can feel his nose is broken, and the pain wipe he took at the crash site has worn off. He waits for the blurry guy making mechanical sounds to leave.

"Easy now," the other man says.

"My name is Rogue Whip; I'm from Acinvar," Rogue

mutters. "I was on an airship that crashed; well, two, actually. First the Tradewinds Goliath, then the Luscious."

The man chuckles. "An Acinvar man on a Juman airship like the Luscious, that's a good one. Hondo would've loved to hear that one. How do you intend to explain that?"

Definitely not friends of the Juman, whoever the hell you people are.

"I was their prisoner. There's something in my blood they wanted. They drew a lot of it, and then they, well, you know what Jumans do to people they don't kill," Rogue says.

The man puts some tools down. "Indeed; that's quite unfortunate. Let's get your eyesight restored." His tone isn't skeptical anymore, in fact, he sounds surprised and serious. "If you are who you say you are, it would open more questions than it answers."

"Got a pain wipe?" Rogue asks. "Or some other nervous system suppressant?"

"The inability to experience pain hinders Hondo's preferred form of interrogation. You've already been introduced."

"Didn't think the Blooming Sandseas tortured people. Good to know," Rogue replies.

"We do not, under normal circumstances," the man replies. "These are not normal circumstances."

"Taking advantage of someone out in no man's land isn't an excuse to do whatever the hell you want," Rogue says.

"You fail to comprehend our situation. I am injecting you with a stimulant that should reverse the effects of the tranquilizer Hondo shot you with." The man shoves a needle into Rogue's arm and pushes down on the plunger, leaving the syringe in.

Rogue doesn't flinch at having his arm jabbed like that. He chuckles. "Air Drop West is hiring; you sure handle a needle like them."

The man snickers at the joke. "I like the view from the Shimmering City. Can't compete with that."

"You ain't lying there. Been to a few feats at the palace. Empress Isla Amenaza sure knows how to throw a party."

"Really? Describe one," the man asks.

If it helps prove I'm not Juman, sure, why not? "First time was

Archon's Wake

four years ago. I was a guest invite from Keith Julian, the CEO of Elvador Teas; it was a sort of a reward for my company's services to him and his company. That was a wild night. Oligarch from Tsundam got super drunk during the meal and tried to make everyone drink from his bottle of whatever the hell that was."

"I remember that; the fat man who jumped on the table and tried to declare himself king over all of Inner Shell and stepped on anyone's plate who disagreed with him."

"That was the funniest thing I've ever seen a royal idiot do," Rogue laughs. "Dude just jumped onto the table, threw his plate at Isla's uncle, the Inemperor, and screamed-"

"Ye lack the law dingy to stap my law dingy!" They both say together, mocking the man's dialect.

"That was the talk of the city for a whole year!" The man laughs so hard he cries and has to wipe tears away.

"I remember this security guard just casually walked up on the table, took his bottle, popped him on the head, threw him down on the salad bowls, and slid him off the side. Dragged him out by the coattails. It was like it was choreographed, smooth and non-chalant," Rogue giggles. "Oh man, I'd have not believed it had I not seen it."

"That was Hondo who did that." The man's laughing becomes a nervous chuckle. "The man who just hit you."

"He does his job well." Rogue tries to stop laughing. "But yeah, no, I'm not a Juman. I am who I say I am."

What the fuck am I drugged with? I'm all kinds of weird and out of sorts. I can't control myself. Why is everything so funny?

"That recollection certainly sows strong doubt regarding the idea of you being a Juman soldier, that's true," the man replies. "My name is Dr. Evan Minatra. I will be sure to take care of you once you prove yourself to Hondo and the interrogator he chooses. Should be a simple task if you tell a story like that; Hondo loves to gloat. How is your eyesight?"

That is great to know. Ok, I got this.

"Improving. Evan Minatra, you're Isla's Cousin, Gordon Minatra's kid." Rogue can start making out details of his surroundings; his vision isn't like he's drunk out of his mind blurry anymore.

"Indeed." Dr. Minatra looks out the window and frowns. He quickly grabs the syringe out of Rogue's arm. He goes to a nearby desk and grabs some gauze and tape, applying the bandage over the injection spot. "Well, luckily for you, this matter will be sorted out rather quick, it seems."

"How so?" Rogue asks.

Dr. Minatra finishes the bandage and puts the used syringe and tape away, then stands to the side at attention.

Hondo returns and stands out of the way as Empress Isla Amenaza enters the room.

"Your highness." Rogue lowers his head to imitate a bow. Her presence shocks him; for a moment he was convinced Evan was the head of the expedition, but to see the actual Empress herself in the flesh? It takes him by surprise.

Isla's face turns pale, she gasps, and then freezes in terror at the sight of him. "That's impossible."

"The Juman soldier in question your highness." Hondo gestures to him, then sees her face. "What's wrong my lady?"

She takes a cautious step forward. "It cannot be. It is simply not possible," she whispers.

Hondo raises an eyebrow in a mix of curiosity and confusion.

"Shall Hondo and I leave the room?" Dr. Minatra says, though from his tone he's really not suggesting, hoping Hondo will take the hint.

"We can't leave her with a dangerous monster like him. Are you out of your goddamned mind Evan?" Hondo shouts.

"Leave us!" Isla screams at the top of her lungs.

Hondo looks like he's somewhere between gob smacked and dumbfounded. "I beg your pardon?"

"Hondo, he is no Juman." Dr. Minatra scoots toward the door and tugs Hondo's arm as he leaves.

"The hell he's not, look at that Juman uniform he's wearing. And I found him with Juman weapons and ammunition and supplies!" Hondo shoves him away and pops a machine gun out of his arm.

Isla turns around and slaps him across the face. Then backhand slaps him. "I will order you to slit your own throat if you do not leave this room Hondo. THIS INSTANT!"

Archon's Wake

Hondo shudders. "Why? What am I-"

"That man is from Acinvar; his name is Rogue Whip." Isla lowers her voice. The fact that Hondo isn't leaving is fueling her anger, fast. "I've no idea if he is friend or foe yet. But this is above you, General Hondo."

Hondo kneels before walking out of the room. He follows Minatra a few steps before grabbing his shoulder. "What the fuck did I miss?"

"I thought you were Grand General of the Empress's security detail," Minatra mutters. "Sorry about the demotion my good friend. But sometimes you really should take my advice and ask basic questions first. Thankfully, I learned who he was." He shrugs off Hondo's hand and walks away.

Hondo looks behind him and finds Isla staring at him through the window. He immediately runs to the center of the canyon floor. "No one gets near that building! Her Highness demands privacy!"

Isla looks away from the window and back at Rogue. The man is covered in bruises and cuts all over his face, neck, arms, and chest with bloody bandages on his hand, shoulder, and has a knotted cable wrapped around his leg. His nose and sliced cheek are bleeding profusely. "Why must Hondo do these things?" She goes to the desk and grabs a cloth to wipe his nose, then searches for a bandage to put on his cheek.

"It's not all him," Rogue replies. "I was on a Juman airship that crashed, assuming it wasn't too far from here. Walked for several hours; it feels like I was knocked out for a few more, so however he brought me here."

Isla drops the cloth and backs away at his mention of the Jumans. "Why were you on board a Juman airship?"

"It's a long story, but give me a chance to tell you. Please."

She takes a seat in a nearby chair. "I have little time; do make it as short as you can."

"It started when I was asked by Prince Cal to come out here and evacuate your people from the Tundra. They said your researchers hadn't checked in for a long time. Cal wanted to have someone come and get everyone out. He said nothing about Jumans, but they got to Ghonda while I was there. And lucky me. I have something they want, so they took me

129

Daniel Jones

prisoner. And then the airship, the Luscious... met a Gigas Archon on the way out," Rogue answers. *Wow, I summed that up nicely. White lie and all.*

Isla remains motionless; her face doesn't reveal anything of what might be on her mind.

"Nothing has gone according to plan on this trip. My airship was taken down by an archon near Ghonda. There were several survivors until we experienced the archon's roar. Only three of us made it. Me, a medic from my crew, and one of Prince Cal's security detail. I don't know what happened to them after I was taken by Juman."

"What does Juman want from you that would stop them from killing you on sight? They have given none of my people such courtesy," Isla demands.

"My blood," Rogue replies. "I survived a crash in the Deep Forest Province last year. Escaped by blowing up a hydra. You might've heard the story. But one thing that's not well known is that I have an immunity to Hydra's Wake, and Juman thinks they can replicate it by studying my blood."

"You have a mark on your neck from a blood sieve. They appear to have obtained what they wanted."

"It was the first thing they did." Rogue nods. "Then they made me go to this crater full of penguins; the ones you're searching for, and they made me try to catch some using my immunity. Did not go the way they thought. Turned out to be too dangerous even for them, so they ran. That might be hard to believe. But it's the truth. They decided to keep me around for their own reasons."

Isla stares into space at the wall across from her. "Why did Prince Cal come to you?"

Rogue lets out a half-hearted laugh. "I owed him a favor. He decided this was how he wanted to use it. Or so I thought. My theory is I think he knew the Juman were out on the Tundra and got me involved to settle something of his own between them. Sure as hell had me fooled."

Isla cracks a small smile that fades as quick as it forms. She stares at him with more intensity. "This does sound true of how Prince Cal operates. Said rumor is true then. You possess immunity to the Hydra's Wake."

Archon's Wake

"That's how I survived the whole Camp Tor incident. Now it seems to work on other paranormal things, to an extent. I didn't vanish like the Juman soldiers in the crater. Or your people in Ghonda."

"There were penguins in Ghonda?" Isla sounds alarmed, but the rest of her face shows no change in her emotion, or any other sign of surprise.

"There had to be. I didn't see them. But what we found when my survivors and I got there? Everyone was gone, piles of clothes and tools on the floor where they stood as they vanished. Watched it happen myself at the crater, and it's the only way to explain what I saw in Ghonda."

Isla remains quiet. Her eyes are prying into his, searching him, and seeming to make decisions in her own mind, though what they are, she's keeping hidden. "What do you know of me?"

Rogue gives her an odd look. *That's an odd question.* "Uh, not that much. You're the Empress of the Blooming Sandseas, you throw amazing parties, and I had no idea you were out here. Cal did tell me that, and it's kinda throwing me for a loop right now. You'd think that'd be critical information if he knew."

"I must warn you against playing with generics. I require specifics," Isla says firmly.

What do I know of you? That question is as broad as it gets, woman. What is she digging into me for? Rogue becomes curious. "Regarding what? As in things I've read in the news about you? Things I know firsthand from your feats? I apologize, my head still hurts from back-to-back crash landings and Hondo's fist. A little help narrowing this down would be appreciated."

Isla turns her chair to sit across from him. "Mr. Whip, do not play coy with me. You will find that to be a fatal mistake. You bring up the immunity to Hydra's Wake and mention the Camp Tor event. What do you know about me? Truly."

"Why are you so interested in the Hydra's Wake? Is it the wake or Camp Tor?" Rogue asks. "You're not after my immunity, too, are you? If so, just give me a few days to recover from the blood loss the Juman already put me through. I'll cooperate, I promise."

"I have no interest regarding that. Actually, I reconsider, I do have a mild curiosity. Is this immunity natural? Something you were born with, perhaps?" Isla says.

"Camp Tor, then," Rogue mutters.

"I care not a damn for Camp Tor," Isla corrects him.

What the hell are you after? He hesitates then nods. "Understood. No. I was not born with some genetic mutation. I did, in fact, acquire it from a facility found in the mines at Camp Tor."

Isla stares into his eyes intensely, studying them, searching, deciding how to proceed.

Something's clearly under her skin. But what? What is she hiding? He opens his mouth to speak.

"Not a word!" She cuts him off with a fierce and forceful tone.

He maintains eye contact and nods slightly.

"I do not take pleasure in repeating myself." She stands up and heads to the doctor's desk, lifting a large syringe with a thick sloshing violet serum.

Rogue's eyes widen and he squirms in the chair.

"This elicits a reaction out of you. Progress," She says coldly, and looks over him like she's about to tear him to pieces.

"No shit! You're holding a syringe designed by Lord Albert Richtoff." He stops for a moment and looks at her with terror. "Wait a minute. You were one of his victims, supposedly. Why do you have his equipment?"

"These tools are my equipment. I am very much a victim of his, Mr. Whip. For six long, agonizing years, the likes of which you cannot imagine. But you don't survive such torment without taking away a few things," she says to him in a calm, controlled tone.

"Then you probably know that he was the one who shot me down and chased me to Camp Tor. I killed him in the events leading up to the explosion that killed the hydra."

"I know everything Acinvar redacted from the reports of the four survivors," Isla replies. "I gave you the option to tell me what you know of my involvement on your own free will. But now, in order to protect myself, I shall force it out of you."

"Your involvement?" Rogue asks. He chuffs then outright laughs. "Lady, are you ok? You? No. That's not possible. I searched all traces of everything surrounding that event. I followed the hexogen back to the manufacturers of its components. I followed the money; every cent related to it. And so did the Mining Conglomerate. We tore through dozens of companies, government officials, and even accidentally found a few corrupt dealings in the process. But nothing led back to you, or the Blooming Sandseas."

Isla glares at him. "I fail to believe you." Her well practiced emotionless face is giving way to an angry stare.

He forces himself to compose. "Sorry, whatever that goon drugged me with makes everything funny. But you're serious. You believe you had something to do with that whole thing?" Rogue wiggles his arm to flip it over under the rope. "Alright then, seems like I'm about to learn more about this than you will. Go ahead, the vein usually rolls to the right about an eighth of an inch if you want it to hit the artery; double the dose if you want."

She hesitates.

"Look, my body is in a lot of pain right now, that truth serum, well, mind wrack, really, will suppress the pain I'm in. And it'll be impossible for me to lie, so you'll have to accept my answers as the truth, and you'll probably tell me more about what I don't know just based on the questions you're going to ask. Sure, I'll need a lot of help from the Air Drop West neural docs when this ends, but it's a win all around for me."

"No one was supposed to survive that!" Isla shouts. "It is not supposed to be possible!"

"No shit!" Rogue replies. "I was there. I had to survive that whole damn thing."

"And I am sorry you did." She lowers her voice and puts the syringe down.

Rogue gawks at her. "Shit, I thought me being the one to slit his throat and stick a sword in his gut before kicking him off the side of a crashing airship put a target on my back. But this is nuts."

"No one can ever find out that I set it all up!" Isla stomps and pounds her fists on his legs. A tear rolls down her cheek; she wipes it away furiously.

"What?" He asks when his mind catches up and realizes what he's hearing.

"I had to stop him! I had to stop that monster! I had to end it! End his terror!" Isla tries to fight back the tears. "You cannot know what it is like to be the center of his attention. The motivational thing on his mind." She can't stop herself. She drops to her knees and buries her head in her arms on his knees sobbing.

Hondo overhears the shouting and looks at a guard who he had sneak up to the doorway. He shakes his head and forms an X with his arms. "What? No," Hondo whispers, then gestures for him to come over.

The guard crawls away until he can crouch walk to Hondo without his footsteps making too much sound. "Sir, uh, I can't believe what I just heard."

"We're intervening." Hondo takes a step, but the guard gets in his way.

"You do not want to do that. You will lose your life, and possibly more. No, you will definitely lose more than just your life. Don't risk her rage. She won't stop with killing you. Not if what I just heard is true," the guard says, in a shaky voice. "I think I'm dead. Sir, please, don't make anyone else try to look into this, for your sake and theirs."

Hondo pats his shoulder. The guard is scared shitless in a way he's never seen before. "Whatever it is, keep it to yourself. Go join the group at the lab entrance."

"Sir, can I just, take a minute in the transport?"

Hondo looks over at the building. He's never seen a man so shaken. Then again, he's never been threatened with orders to kill himself before either. "You're off duty until further notice. At ease. I'll take your advice under consideration."

The guard gulps and nods. "Thank you, sir. I really hope I wasn't seen."

Hondo walks up to another guard. "Let's give that space a bit of a wider berth."

"Wider? You want us further away?" the second guard asks.

"I'm starting to think there might not be a minimum safe distance." Hondo glances again at the building.

"I really had no idea," Rogue mutters.

Isla looks up at Rogue with bloodshot eyes. "I am so sorry I put you through that. You must understand, I had no choice."

"It's ok, your high-" Rogue starts to say.

"Isla, please; I do not deserve my title, not right now." She cuts him off and lowers her head back down.

Rogue keeps twisting his arm, trying to loosen the rope, but it's tightening the knot out of his reach. "Isla, I'm not a threat to you. I want you to know that. If anything, I'm happy about my experience. You gave me an opportunity to make Yeraputs a better place."

She gets up and turns her back to him. "Stop lying about what you know!"

"What?" Rogue splutters. "The Mining Conglomerate, the Acinvar Military Intelligence, and I searched everything. We followed the Hexogen back to the component manufacturers. We dug into finances going back years on any company, government official, or person related to any of it. We dug into Richtoff and Fire Team Dark. We tore his entire operation to shreds. The Lotus Islands even opened up about the spy Albert confused me for. It looked like a genuine accident; we found nothing to suggest otherwise. Albert Richtoff fucked up in a big way."

Isla faces him again and puts her finger in his face, she's not hiding her emotions anymore. "I will stop at nothing to ensure there is no risk that anyone can trace this plot back to me! Do you know how many people are looking into his disappearance? How many monsters on his level are still searching for the answers they deem acceptable? I had to go to extremes to hide from my part in the plot to murder Lord Albert Richtoff!" Isla stops shouting through her sobs when she's out of breath.

Rogue is speechless.

"I... I can't believe I just said that out loud." Isla starts hyperventilating and puts her hands on his knees to support herself.

"Hey, hey, easy. Breathe," Rogue exaggerates a few breaths. "In, out, in, out. That's it, squeeze my leg, hard as you can, focus. Breathe."

Isla controls her breathing and shakes her head, wiping tears on her sleeves. "I've never said it out loud before. I've had to keep it all in. For years. I've been scared to death, fearing any mistake no matter how minor. And then a nightmare happened two days after the attack. Three people survived and reached Acinvar. And then they found a fourth survivor. How many loose ends were there? I freaked out and had nowhere to run, nowhere to hide... nowhere safe, anyway." Isla sneezes and sobs some more. She looks at him and stares in silence for a few moments.

He keeps quiet and keeps a blank expression on his face.

"Oh goodness, you are still detained. I apologize." She reaches for her belt and pulls a knife out. Then cuts away at the rope. "I should've done that earlier, Mr. Whip."

"Rogue. Please. And it's ok. I understand you're nervous." He rubs his arms when they're free and wiggles them to get the blood flowing. "Here, um, let me help you." He offers her his hand and helps her back into the other chair. "Wow, that, uh... I'm stunned."

Isla gives a half smile at seeing his face. "It helps to finally say it. I never expected I'd feel this vulnerable, especially around you. You were my biggest nightmare. It kept me up at night. What if you found out? What if you wanted revenge? What if you told someone who would want revenge for Albert?"

Rogue looks off to the side at the wall. *Wait, a weapon that can make people vanish into thin air. That's the kind of weapon someone could use to fight the people who would scare her.*

Archon's Wake

Isla's smile fades when she sees the wheels turning in his head and she stands up quickly. "Oh gods. What have I done? I... I must not let you live. I am sorry. But you are a risk I cannot tolerate."

"Wait, please." Rogue sits her back down and kneels before her. "Can we talk, please? I beg you."

"No, you will certainly destroy me!" she shouts.

"I'm not... no, absolutely not. I offer you my service if it helps," Rogue says. "But please, don't throw my life away. I'm not going hurt you."

"You've no idea what I have endured!"

"I don't know what you've been through. But I can understand that it's not easy to live with. I see the nightmare around me every day. One of the other survivors, she... look, I'd have done the same thing you did."

"Would you?" Isla grips his bandaged hand and squeezes.

He winces at the pain. "Yes, and you don't have to tell me details, or anything. In fact, I don't need to know. But if I knew, I would've killed that bastard right from the start. I would've been a willing participant. I wouldn't change a damn thing about what happened back there." Rogue, panicked, speaks as fast as he can. "I just want to talk; don't throw my life away. Please, I beg you."

Isla's eyes water up. "You'd do it all again? Exactly as it happened? Even if you knew?"

"I'd have done it even without the immunity I received. I'd have made sure that bastard died, without a second thought. I promise that."

She buries her head in her hands and cries even harder.

There's no way this is real. Sure as shit feels real though. Is this another wake trick?

"Ok." Isla calms down after a few minutes. "We can talk. I hope no one else sees me like this. You better take this sight to your grave. No empress should ever be seen crying like this."

Rogue hands her a clean cloth from the nearby desk. "You have my word. What happens in this room, stays in this room."

"Sounds so childish." She forces a laugh.

"It does. Um." He breathes in and sighs. "I know what I represent to those few who know I killed Richtoff. Let's be clear about this. He died by my hand. It has to be that way. I know you were a victim of his, and his death is a huge weight off your shoulders. I'm going to convince myself that all of this stuff you're saying is just some after effect of his experiments. I know the evidence; I've seen it all myself. Every paper trail. Nothing leads to you. Can we agree on that?"

Isla stares at him with a blank expression for a long moment. She wraps her arms around him and hugs him tightly. "You would really do that?"

He hugs her back. "Yes, Isla. I absolutely would. For you, for Crystal, and for anyone else who survived him."

She cries on his shoulder, and grips tighter. "You killed him. You actually did it. He is never coming back!"

"That's right, he's gone for good." Rogue strokes her back.

She lets go of him and wipes her face again.

He sits back down in the chair he was tied to and scoots it close to her. "You're free from him."

She stares into space and breathes. "Ugh, you got the better of me. I've never broken down like that before. I am usually far more in control of myself."

"I don't want that to be a bad thing," Rogue replies. "Truth be told, I can't really talk to many people about it, either. Crystal, she's-, well her recovery hasn't been easy. She's got so much going on, and I don't want to make it worse. Walker, he... he has his own way of dealing with it. He buries it and carries on in the whole soldering style thing. Hunter, well, he vanished while in Acinvar custody. I've only really talked to one person about it before. Jessie, my best friend, and she's my company's CEO; but she's been the only person I've talked about it with, and she just sits there and listens. It helps keep me sane."

"I barely know you. Saying such things would be alarming," Isla says.

"It doesn't have to be me; it can be someone you trust."

"I can't, not to anyone." She nods along. "But maybe."

They sit in an awkward silence for a long moment.

"How did you do it?" Rogue asks.

She gives a slight smile. "You said you didn't want to know."

"I can see it eating away at you and honestly, it's low key bugging me. Kinda like who thought it was a good idea to let Dura Fastner get his hands on that dress at your feat two years ago."

Isla laughs in a fit and wipes her nose. "I swear to my Goddess of Yathil that thing was hideous! No one knows where it came from. Or how he got it. My word, that's back on my mind and is going to as you say 'low key.' I like these Acinvar idioms. Low key bugging. You missed the feat last year, there was this portly…" She stops mid-sentence and gives him a solemn look.

She clears her throat. "You can read me like a book. You're nothing like what I expected you to be. What little I know of the real you is from fleeting glances and split-second formal greetings once a year. As well as what I have studied from afar."

Wow, this woman can shift her emotions in a heartbeat. You wouldn't know she was breaking down a few minutes ago. Something doesn't feel right about her. Obvious abuse victim trauma aside. Unless her brain is seriously messed up from captivity.

"Without getting into the technical details, I used his own methods against him. Hypnotized his inner circle using his own techniques, fed him false information, studied every factor. Low and behold, a Lotus Island spy by the name of Raw-gue Wheap, earned his focus by shutting down a whopping sixteen percent of his income revenue. I happened to have been recently introduced to a Raw-gue Wheap who lived in Acinvar with a shipping company that crosses the Tradewinds. It was then I knew I could make you his target. It was just a matter of doing darker things from there."

How does someone feed him false information without him figuring it out? He's too damn smart for that, and Fire Team Dark has layers of people who would be able to realize it's coming from her if she was the one telling them.

"Hypnotizing friends and influencing shell companies indirectly to constantly test your routes to make sure the idea was foolproof. That hairpin turn you make at mount Hade over the Deep Forest Province was a standout maneuver with low traffic and less Tradewinds Compact security."

Oh. I need to stop thinking and just listen. She's full-on gloating.

"I sent a few murderers and other criminals from my land to test the wake. I told them if they could escape they were free, charges dropped. None of them made it. Then I had my people in Albert's information ring tell him his target was shipping large amounts of a high-grade explosives to an outpost in the Mining Conglomerate that didn't need it. Which got him watching records of these shipments. He tied them to his lotus island obsession. It happened much sooner than I expected. I was ready to send you dozens of those shipments. But he acted on the third one."

She's either deranged or she did do this. If it wasn't for that look on her face, I wouldn't believe her. But that look in her eye? She's dangerous. I need to be extremely careful.

Rogue's eye twitches. "That was a lot of information. Uh... um... so, Albert's hypnosis, that's a handy thing. I didn't even know he had a hypnosis method. Hunter and Walker never said anything about it. Did he use it on you?"

"The serum I threatened you with is his formula. I planned on hypnotizing you to tell me the truth. Then I'd know for a fact if you were sent to kill me, and I'd have the proof I need to have you killed in a way to warn everyone that I meant business."

"Send a warning to everyone? You mean use the Harbinger Weapon on me in front of a giant crowd," Rogue says.

Isla closes her mouth and eyes him. "That much is obvious to you?"

"You did bring hundreds of people across half a planet to a place where you have no diplomatic or trade relations. A place that is vastly unexplored because it's dangerous and difficult to reach."

A look of annoyance flashes across her face. "Do not you dare mock me, Rogue. It will do little to improve your chances of survival."

"I'm not mocking you, I swear. I... forgive me, I'm still trying to process your revelation. There is a lot I don't know, and I'm starting to think the less I know, the better. I shouldn't have asked. I... I-" He pauses to stop stammering. "I, uh... I should shut up."

"The functioning brain cell in your head seems to be frying," Isla replies.

"My point is, you're capable of defending yourself. I mean, using Albert on Albert without him seeing it coming. How'd you learn so much about his techniques?" Rogue can't hide how nervous he is, and is trying to keep her gloating.

"You wish to learn how I know his techniques? Has Crystal really taught you nothing of Albert's true terror?"

"He didn't exactly do a whole lot to her on account of her being mute. I guess he didn't like touching disabled people."

"Ah, yes, this is fact. Mutes in particular. A deaf person can still scream their head off and sing songs of pain. But a mute gives him silence. A missing sensation, one that is a critical necessity when crafting the art of excruciation. As he so eloquently put it."

Rogue gulps. "And what she told me was a nightmare. So, no. I don't need to hear it."

At first, she stops speaking, but the look on his face makes her feel powerful. "You got me going. I will speak and you will, what was her name to you? Jessie? Yes, you do for me as she did for you. You will sit and listen in silence while I unload on you. After all, you'll die, so I get the benefit of some much needed therapy, and the sense of security I'll get, knowing it'll stay between us."

She gets comfortable in her chair and takes a deep breath. "It started when I was six. Just so you know, I'm only telling you this to see if it helps me. I'm willing to try this talking therapy thing. I've never been given a true opportunity to unload my own trauma upon someone who matters to me in the way you do."

Rogue gulps, braces himself, and nods. "Of course."

She stares at him, tears form in her eyes and a dreadful expression forms. "I can't believe I'm doing this. It started with my grandfather. Emperor of the Blooming Sandseas. He angered Richtoff and was murdered. I was on his lap, a six-year-old girl playing with her puzzle box. My grandfather's face was cut off. His brain slipped out and fell next to me. That man was laughing at our side, wrapping his Urumi back around his waist. I could see my grandfather's blood still dripping from the flimsy metal. He took me away from my family. To remind them never to anger him again."

Isla stops for a moment, reliving her captivity. "I will never forget the cold of the metal tables in his labs. Being forced to cut myself open. Poke myself with needles, and put those tubes on my arteries and veins, dissecting myself. While he watched and drooled over me. Being hooked up to those machines that bathed my body in that disgusting slime that he invented to make people survive his experiments. He trained us on how to cut ourselves open. First on dummies, then on non-lethal parts, and eventually the day would come where we would go all the way. If we got it wrong, we'd die, and if we couldn't get it right fast enough, he'd hypnotize us, and he'd make sure we felt it all, remembered it all. You have no idea what it was like to hold my beating heart in my hand while he played cat's cradle with my intestines. Skin and flesh peeled back to my sides and my organs casually out in the open covered in his special jelly to keep me alive. I felt all of it. He thought it was hilarious. And worse, he took a moment to be his version of a father. He taught me how to play cat's cradle."

Isla pretends to play cat's cradle in front of him. "What girl learns to play cat's cradle from a madman using her own intestines while they're still attached to her body. Keep your thumbs out, put your fingers in the loops… but the fucking string is your actual intestines. Right out of your belly, and you're alive, awake, and actively playing it! What girl learns how to sew by stitching her body closed every day?" She screams at the top of her lungs and gets in Rogue's face. Tears flow down her face again in uncontrollable rivers.

Rogue forces himself to not throw up at the imagery he's coming up with in his head. "Isla, you don't need to…"

"Yes! I do! I've never been able to tell anyone about my torment. Not my parents, not my mentors, not my doctors, not any of my friends. You're my only chance to get all of this off my chest. You want me not to kill you? You want to avoid being the shining example of what happens when Isla's plans go wrong by the slightest inconvenience? I've been praying to every god my whole life that I'd find just one day of emotional rest. Just one; just an hour where I'm not tormented by my own mind. I am not living a worthy life, so you... no! You will hear me! You will sit! And you will listen to everything I have to say. How dare you! How dare you think you can control what I give you?"

Ok, I guess we're doing this. It's just words, right? That's all it is; her lived memories coming out in words. I can do this. If it saves my life, I can listen to her story. Maybe if I try being supportive and comforting? Rogue puts his hands up then puts them over hers to try to comfort her. "Forgive me; you're right. You have every right."

She slaps him across the face. Then again, and again, then grabs the cut Hondo made and squeezes blood out of it. It remined her of the feeling of control she felt when helping Albert torture others. It's a sick and dark feeling but in this moment, it's one she finds herself craving. To feel power over another person in a close, intimate setting. "How dare you touch me, you peasant! As for rights? I am an Empress! I have every right! As a victim, I have more than every right! That man! That monster! He took everything from me! How dare you try to exert control over me! I will control what I tell you! How exposed and vulnerable I am. And I don't care how uncomfortable you get."

She unbuttons her blouse and tosses it aside to reveal the scars on her body then takes her walking trousers off, throws her arms out to give him a view of as much as her as she can. "Look at the real me! I'll never get rid of them! Believe me, I've tried!"

He stares at them in shock. Not a single spot of her body from the neck down is unmarred from a surgical incision.

She looks at his hands. "Don't be shy. This is a hands-on experience." She grabs his hands and puts them on her stomach. "Seriously? I'm not delicate cargo in need of special handling. Put some muscle into it." She rips the bandage off his hand, intending to make him feel her with the skin of his hands. But the flap of skin on his palm tear off with the bandage and blood spurts all over her.

"Gyah!" Rogue does his best to not shout, but the pain in his hand is excruciating. "Isla, please!"

Why is every woman on this tundra batshit crazy and getting crazier by the day? Actually, they're crazier every time I survive a crash. I hope I don't survive a third crash. I don't wanna see level three crazy.

Her train of thought is gone, and she forgot what she was going to do to him next. She stares down at his hand, covered in blood, mesmerized by the warm liquid on her skin. She trembles and lifts his hand up to her face and rests her cheek on it, holding it tight like a treasure. "I miss the feeling of blood on my face." She kisses his hand, then licks it. "The taste of blood and flesh. A craving I haven't indulged since I left."

"No. That was him. That is him. Don't become him. Don't let him come back through you," Rogue pleads.

Her entire body shakes as he speaks. She holds his hand up in front of him and stares. "What am I doing?" Tears flow down her face, and she collapses on him, wrapping her arms around his neck and burying her head on his shoulder. "I'm sorry. I'm so sorry."

Thank fuck that's over. I'm not sure how much more of it I can handle.

"I've never done that to anyone since I was freed." She sobs louder. "I was twelve when he was teaching me and training me to be his assistant. That part just came back, and I don't know how to stop it. You must think I'm a monster like him."

"You're not a monster, Isla. You're an Empress, loved by her people."

"I'm hideous."

He grabs her shoulders and moves her back to look her in the eyes. "You're a kind leader. You make sure your people are taken care of. There's no hunger and no homelessness in the Shimmering City because of you. Your parents would be proud of the Empress you became."

She raises her hand to hit him again at the mention of her parents but stops. "Stop it! Albert, he murdered them, too! He took them away right as I was healing from six years of his torture!"

Rogue winces and feels bad. "I thought…"

"Don't you dare say it. Think about it. What happened to my parents? Don't you dare tell me anything else."

Rogue tries to think.

Archon's Wake

"You're in too much pain, and I bet you didn't even care about what was going on in my life at the time." She starts to get off him.

He sits her back down on his lap. "They were on a train that derailed, just outside the Shimmering City; no one survived. Locomotive's boiler melted and the steam pressure system blew up. I remember the newspaper that day."

"There was no evidence of anything, of course. But I'll always know in my heart it was him." She slides off his lap and quickly dresses herself.

Rogue gets up and looks at the medical supplies. There's not a lot of bandaging; most of it is different kinds of syringes filled with various colored serums. His head is throbbing, and he can barely register what he's seeing. "Uh, which one makes pain stop?"

Isla picks up a small one with a brownish syrupy looking liquid. "It's the least I can do. Give me your wrist. Just a quick pinch."

He does as she asks and stumbles after his body numbs over entirely. "That's some powerful stuff," he says and accidentally bites on his tongue.

"Don't speak; stay still and let it circulate for a minute. First few seconds that it's in your arteries it locks you down. Hits your brain stem hard, too. As it circulates and disperses, you'll get your motor skills back." She helps him back into the chair. "EVAN!!" She screams at the top of her lungs out the doorway.

Almost a minute later, Minatra is back in the room. "Yes, Isla?"

She notices her blouse is buttoned unevenly and turns her back to fix them. "Tend to his wounds, please."

Hondo's metal stomping is right behind him. "Your highness... they're ready when you are."

She stares at him blankly. "Ready?"

"To breach the laboratory," Hondo elaborates.

"Oh, yes, right. Do that immediately." She turns back to face them and smiles.

"Isla!" Hondo exclaims, when he sees the blood on her face. A large blade comes out of his arm, and he prepares to

145

Daniel Jones

kill Rogue.

Isla jumps in front of the blade. "I gave you no orders of any kind!"

"He hurt you! Your face is bleeding! That man is dangerous and must be punished!"

Isla grabs the hypnosis serum from the table and threatens Hondo with it. "I've had it with your impulses on this trip!"

"It's not my fault this place has me on edge all the time!" Hondo screams back. After a second, he realizes what he did and kneels. "I... I'm so sorry. I cannot be forgiven."

"It's the tundra," Rogue says. "It made me change a bit at the Penguin Crater. That would explain why we are having a hard time controlling ourselves."

Isla lowers the syringe. "That must be why there are so few people who survive this place."

"We should leave. Now," Minatra says.

An explosion goes off outside. "Not when we are so close to the finish line, Evan. But yes, we will be on our way home in a few short hours, I daresay," Isla says, while leaving the room. "And Hondo, if you lay so much as a finger on Rogue, I will kill you myself."

"The rotor will need repairs before we can go anywhere." Formalia throws a wrench at Hunter's head, who's tied up to one of the benches in the back.

"I couldn't tell if I was going to die or not. In Tor, a lot of people did die during those paranormal moments!" Hunter shouts back. "What the hell was I supposed to do?"

"Not shoot at our ride out of here!" Liliana screams. "Damnit, dumbass! You fucking fuck! You shot the air intake!"

"I need to clear my head. Your asinine moment has me too angry to concentrate." Formalia rushes out the side door and looks over at the barracks.

Kita is out of her bed and standing on the other side of the room.

"Has everyone lost their minds today? I told that girl to

stay in bed! Not move to a different one!" Formalia storms inside.

Kita lays down on the bed next to Cinder's bowls of food and water.

"What are you doing?" Formalia scolds her.

"I got up to relieve myself, then it occurred to me that Cinder hasn't been fed all day. I wanted to fix that," Kita answers. "I know it was not wise to get off the bed, but I had no idea how long you would be. I needed to take care of him."

Formalia calms down and slows her rush to a walk. Cinder is face down in his food, chomping away. "I see. You were able to walk some significant distance unaided, then. Are you in any pain?"

"No, my body is still numb. Truth be told, balancing was the hardest part," Kita replies.

"It seems that we are not so lucky. The vehicle we came on took some damage from Mr. Smith's hallucinatory episode." Formalia does little to hide her anger over the situation.

"I see. If Rogue is truly on his way to Black Sand City, he will get another airship to come back and retrieve us. He's not one to leave people behind, if he can help it. Surviving here for a few days shouldn't be a problem, right?"

"If Mr. Smith's episodes begin to spread to us, that will become an impossible challenge to overcome. I worry about the effects of this place. Our Mistress does not call off such endeavors this quickly, and she was rather hasty in doing so on this occasion. In fact, alarmingly so." Formalia checks on Kita's bandages to make sure they're still good and haven't shifted from her moving around.

"What do you mean if his episodes spread? Are you saying you or Liliana could be prone to those hallucinations?" Kita panics.

"Hunter was near the penguins when they activated their ability to make others disappear. Despite being some distance from the actual penguins, he's encountering paranormal situations. We were in the same proximity; thus, I cannot rule it out."

"He was also fully exposed to Hydra's Wake. But that

shouldn't matter, unless the phenomena are related."

"That is the running theory, as Liliana and I have yet to see any delusions or hallucinations. If there is a proximity impact simply by being near the penguins, I am wary of our own safety."

Kita gulps and looks over at the osprey. "Could that be what happened to Titania? The reason she attacked us?"

"No, she intended to do that, and was free to do so. Our orders changed. That is all. Titania enjoys the carnal horror of a painful and bloody show. I prefer to destroy the senses, put my victims in darkness and silence and let my victims' minds do the work. My sister Guariana is much the same way. We take away taste, smell, sight, and hearing before our victims know what's happened," Formalia corrects her.

Kita gulps. "You mean gouge eyes out and smash ear canals in."

"Rip off tongues and destroy nasal cavities. Sensory deprivation in full." She smiles. "Liliana is not so creative. If you want any of us to come after you, she is the one of us who values her time and makes it quick. That may be from her background in stealth combat."

Kita shudders.

"We are no different from Titania. We follow orders. We slaughter who we are tasked to. We protect those who we are tasked to. If Titania were tasked with your protection, you would her find as pleasant and attentive to you as I have been. We are soldiers, regardless of the rumors. Understood?"

Kita nods. "Yes ma'am."

Formalia takes her chest armor off and sets it on a nearby bed, which compresses and the wooden frame creaks when she does. The inside is lined with leather pouches and pockets, and ammunition for her gunblade.

"That's a lot of equipment," Kita mutters.

One of the bed's legs gives out and it slides into the floor, putting a dent in the concrete.

"And too heavy for these cheap beds." Formalia picks it back up and tries another bed.

"What are you searching for?" Kita asks.

"I am going to give you a vitality booster. Small doses

only, to ensure it doesn't interfere with your body's healing. But I can see that your pain wipe is wearing off. This should keep you comfortable." Formalia opens a small metal tin, picks up a small white pill, and hands it to her.

Kita takes the pill without question. "Thank you."

Inside the osprey, the restraints on Hunter fall through his body. "Oh, that's interesting."

Liliana side eyes him getting up. "Hey, sit your ass back down, or I swear-"

"I have a leg cramp, and that shit was uncomfortable. I'm unarmed; I'm not going to do any more damage. You can easily take me down with both hands tied behind your back and we both know it, so calm your tiny murder tits!" Hunter says.

"I'm not going to take this crap from you!" Liliana draws her gunblade and comes at Hunter, who smiles at her, as her blade passes through him.

After enjoying her frustration for a moment, he walks through the side of the osprey and jumps down to the ground.

Liliana runs out the side door. "Where the hell do you think you're going?"

"To have a look around, genius. I don't control when this happens to me. But as long as I'm ghosting through shit, might as well see if I can find interesting secrets left by the desert folk or Shiv. Better than being babysat by you." Hunter waves her off.

"If you get hurt, I'm going to come find you and I'm going to make Titania look tame!" Liliana shouts.

"Hah! Your creativity is as tiny as you are!" Hunter gives her two middle fingers.

Kita and Formalia watch him through the window.

"Maybe that's for the best." Kita shudders at seeing him.

"Liliana, let him be!" Formalia shouts.

"We need to kill him the first chance we get!" Liliana shouts back. "Tiny murder-, I AM GOING TO KILL YOU!"

"In time, Liliana, all in due time," Formalia replies.

Liliana shoots at Hunter until her gunblade is out of ammo. Each shot goes through his head. He raises his middle finger at her, with the last shot going through it.

"That man's mutilation is long overdue. He is lucky he makes himself of value to our Mistress," Formalia whispers to herself.

6: Lines That Should Not Be Crossed

Titania kneels over James' body and smiles at Bifo. "You've done well, soldier."

"Thank you, ma'am." Bifo slams his forearms together.

Titania holds up a telegram transcript. "The location of Ihuit, and the knowledge that the Pyrite Nest will have to refuel at Ghonda before everyone leaves, is useful information."

"Once Amenaza has her prize, they will use the transports to begin rounding up the expedition teams and return everyone to the airship. They'll also take their equipment with them to leave no trace that they were ever here. That is why all stations received those orders to break down in full," Bifo replies.

"So, I could simply camp here and await them?" Titania approaches him and puts her hand on his face, pinching his cheek.

"Ma'am, yes ma'am. But the tear down at Ghonda will likely take the longest; days, even."

"If they don't react in fear to the fact their colleagues there are missing, certainly." Titania pinches hard enough to draw blood with her nails. "Do you have more words for me?"

Daniel Jones

"This place was once a cargo airfield. We've had trouble accessing its underground, but we have found evidence of a Rim Cart system. It stands to reason a Rim Cart network under the tundra would be how the Shiv moved their supplies around. It may lead you to other locations, ones even Amenaza doesn't know about," Bifo adds.

Titania lets go of him and laughs in his face. "You are full of surprises, aren't you? Tell me, are you after my heart?" She puts her hand over her heart and winks at him. She knows full well this man isn't a hypnotized soldier, but his attempt to hide himself as one is amusing to her.

"I am loyal to the Mistress and the sovereignty of Juman. I will relay information of importance to my superiors," Bifo replies, without hesitation.

Titania rolls her eyes. "Ugh, hypnosis. I hate how it slaps you across the face, just when you're having fun."

"May I escort you to the blocked entrance to the underground?" Bifo asks.

"I'll find it myself, thank you. You're not fun enough for me." Titania shoves him to the ground and kicks him in the gut. "Bore me further and I'll dispose of you."

Bifo lays still on the ground and watches her walk away. When she leaves the hangar, he lays on his back and exhales. "Gods be damned she's scary."

Titania hears the remark and glances back at the hangar's entrance, smirking. "Good boy; I like a little game while I wait," she whispers, then looks at the other buildings on the airfield. Most of them are reduced to rubble. A group of archons overhead fly silently toward the setting sun. "Night will soon be upon us. Can't travel at night. The air freezes just about any machine."

Bifo gets up and walks to his desk. He starts thumbing through a pile of maps until he finds a specific one. "Bingo."

"Ah, that is useful." Titania snatches it out of his hand.

He turns around to see her towering over him with a gleeful smile. "Take your clothes off."

"What?" Bifo asks.

Titania grabs his neck. "A Juman strips when ordered, my little desert mouse."

Archon's Wake

Bifo gulps and starts unbuttoning his shirt.

She rips it open and stares at his stomach with glee. "Oh dear. You seem to have forgotten to get your obligatory Juman crest emblazoned upon your chest. I'll applaud you on your performance until the end here. Almost had me convinced."

"Gotta put on a show for the ladies, right?" Bifo says nervously, while trying to keep cheerful.

"Oh, I do love a bloody good show." Titania leans in close to him, moving her lips close to his and then blows on him. "I should warn you, the level of amusement required to stave off my insatiable bloodthirst is beyond reason. You're so squishy and round. Jiggly flesh and all. How much blood can I spill out of you, I wonder?"

"Good thing I know how to work a Shiv Rim Cart." Bifo's shaky voice gets worse, and he trembles under her grip.

Titania glances at the map in her other hand. "That's only useful if the underground access is open. Night is coming quick; that will force the Pyrite Nest to land and halt progress, regardless of their location. Finish stripping, then go outside, and open the path for me. If you succeed, you'll get to warm up in the underground facility. Fail, and you freeze to death. Then I get to desecrate, dismember, and disembowel your corpse, however I decide to do so, in the morning. Either way, I win, because I get to watch you suffer for my sole amusement."

Bifo starts to unbuckle his pants.

"Oh, and if it turns out you can simply open a door, I'm going to find that rather anticlimactic. The absolute worst-case scenario for you."

The telegraph starts tapping away.

Bifo stops and gulps loudly. "I'll have the door opened for you swiftly ma'am." Bifo buckles his pants and rushes to the hangar exit.

Titania reaches him before he gets a foot out onto the tarmac and grabs his shoulder, digging her fingers into it, making him yelp and drop to his knees. "Do not call me ma'am, unless you intend to serve me the rest of your miserable life. And how dare you disobey my orders. You were clearly told to strip, not keep your soiled pants on."

"Yes, ma'am; understood ma'am," Bifo replies.

She stomps on his foot and twists his ankle under her boot then presses her armor's weight down on it, making sure to crush every bone. He screams in pain, but to her surprise doesn't grab at her or his foot or plead for her to stop. She smirks and lifts her boot enough for him to slide his foot out. "Hurry up, I don't like waiting. My patience makes me think, and I always think about how to hurt my new toys."

Bifo hops down the tarmac, trying to get as far away from her as he can. He looks over his shoulder and finds she's not at the hangar entrance anymore. The pain in his foot is insane and he does his best to not scream, but falls over. He crawls to a nearby pile of rubble.

"Tsk, tsk, the map of this place says it's not here, silly." Titania waves it around over him.

Bifo's eyes widen. How'd she get to him so fast?

She stabs his arm with her gunblade, then stomps on the wound. "Oh look, stubby fingers to cut off." She shoves the tip of her blade through his middle finger, cutting it off. Then cuts his thumb off and grabs it. "I'd give you a thumbs up, but you're failing to open my door for me; such a rude, heartless, belligerent man." She slices off the rest of his fingers on both hands one by one.

Bifo's screaming seems to only make the excitement on her face grow. He finally puts his arms up toward her like he wants her to stop.

She swings her sword, cutting both his arms clean off at the elbows. "Hehe, ah, haha, HA!" She straddles him and puts her hands on his head, running her fingers through his hair.

Bifo cries and stop squirming around. "No! I want to see my family again."

"Your family will see you again, if you believe in that sort of afterlife thing." She leans in close. "Your wife might not like how you kissed another woman before you died, though. Such a bad, unfaithful husband you are."

Bifo shakes his head no, but she presses her lips to his, forces his mouth open with her tongue, and feels the air leave his lungs while she cuts through his neck with her sword.

Titania stands up and wipes her lips. "Raw broccoli breath

with tobacco smoke, ick. I swear the health risks I take doing this silly ritual sometimes." She looks at the map and heads across the tarmac to a pile of rubble that appears to be excavated. There is a stairway going down with rubble still blocking the way at the bottom. "I prefer doing everything myself, anyway."

Guariana surveys the canyon near a massive concrete wall that spans miles in both directions and at least a hundred feet above the tundra surface. The wall is covered in massive ice buildup, almost disguised as a natural formation. There are dozens of armed soldiers in Blooming Sandseas uniforms walking around. The sides of the canyon are lined with crumbling ruins of old buildings. Dozens of rail lines lead out from the base of the wall, where a big gaping hole has been made.

Three large, two-story armored transports are parked near the most intact buildings, which look like they've been turned into a makeshift camp. She spots Rogue walking out of one of the buildings with a bowl of food. "He's alright? Thank goodness," she says; speaking aloud makes her flinch at the pain in her side. She didn't escape the wreck uninjured, and the wound is bleeding, despite her efforts to close it.

Gunshots ring out from inside the facility. Everyone on the canyon floor appears caught off guard, and many start running toward the entrance. The popping sounds of gunfire are joined by the booms of grenades. One of the transports roars to life and rolls toward the entrance.

She keeps her eyes on Rogue, who watches the commotion from where he's standing. He's quick to shovel the food into his mouth then runs up to a soldier, who stops to say something to him and points to a second transport.

The first transport going to the facility crashes into the wall. When she looks, she finds the soldiers near it are missing, and penguins are waddling out of the facility with glowing green eyes. "Rogue!" She looks down the canyon wall. It's further than she can jump, and there isn't an obvious way to slide down. "Damnit."

Pale blue mist forms around her, and it feels as though a wall is pushing her. She turns around to see nothing behind her. It's the same as at the penguin crater and crash site. But this one is moving, and it's soon going to force her off the cliff. "No, damnit. Not this again!"

Rogue jogs up to one of the transports where several soldiers are grabbing their weapons.

"Get inside, Mr. Whip!" One of the soldiers grabs his shoulder and pushes him.

He looks up and sees someone dangling in midair above the canyon wall. "Hey someone's falling!" He points. But on second look, the person is held up by something. The longer Rogue looks, the more he can make out the shape of a shadowy figure behind them. It's got its hand wrapped around their body, moving them further away from the ledge.

"What? Did we have anyone up there?" another soldier asks.

"I don't think so," a third says.

The person is dropped by the shadow figure to fall to their death. Rogue realizes who it is. "Guariana!"

"Juman Venator!" someone shouts. Several of the soldiers aim their weapons at her when she lands on a solid stone ledge about two thirds the way down. Other soldiers back away and talk to each other, they seem unsettled.

Oh no, she's not moving after that landing. That thing... that thing looked right at me when it did that.

"Did she just commit suicide?" one of the soldiers asks.

"Movement!" another shouts, as she moves her arms to push herself up.

"Cease fire! Hold Fire! Don't shoot!" Rogue shouts. "I know that one! She can help clear the penguins!"

"She can slaughter Isla easily while she's at it. She's a threat," the soldier behind Rogue says, and puts a gun at his

Archon's Wake

back.

He raises his hands. "I can promise you on my life, she won't harm the Empress."

The soldier keeps watching her and mutters just loud enough for Rogue to hear. "She will harm some of these men though."

Rogue glances over his shoulder. "I don't fear her, nor should you."

The soldier steps closer and speaks in a quieter voice. "Me, no. Isla and her soldiers? Maybe."

"What the hell does that mean?" Rogue keeps his voice down. "Who are you?"

"It seems our cover is about to be blown. You know the Venator? How?" The soldier steps back and holds his weapon with a steadier grip.

"She has orders to watch over me," Rogue replies.

"I see. Lucky for you then," the soldier replies.

"Isla said to respect him as we do her. She must know something of this," Dr. Minatra says, as he comes out of the transport. "Lads, give him the benefit of the doubt until she steps out of line. Help her get down."

The soldiers all shake their heads, but most of them lower their weapons, to Rogue's relief.

One of the soldiers brushes past Minatra. "You can do it yourself. We're going to fight for our empress."

The soldier with the gun at Rogue's back stays, while the rest run down the canyon.

"You gonna help me or go run at the penguins to die?" Rogue asks.

The soldier watches as several of the soldiers closest to the lab start vanishing. Their weapons and clothes drop to the ground, causing the ones running at them to run for cover in the nearby buildings.

"Whatever it is you're doing, and whoever's people you are, you need to stop being a fool." Rogue turns around and tries to grab his gun to lower it, but his hand passes through it.

"What just happened to you?" The soldier takes several steps back.

"That was peculiar to see firsthand," Minatra comments.

"I'll remain in the transport."

"Minatra, get inside where it's safe!" Rogue shouts.

Minatra shrugs and closes the door.

Rogue looks up at Guariana and waves his arms in the air.

She waves back and watches him gesture to go away from the facility.

Rogue runs to the base of the canyon wall. "Go that way, it's not as far a drop!"

Guariana looks where he's pointing. She'll have to climb down several steep, but small drops, to get there. The problem is, she's in too much pain to crawl along it. Her attempt to twist around causes her to lose balance and she slides off the ledge and falls to the ground with a hard landing.

Rogue gets to her quickly; she's awake, but in intense pain. "Hey, I'm here, I got you." His hands go through her when he tries to touch her. "Damnit, I can't touch you. There's a doctor nearby who can help. Ok, just hang on."

"Rogue, stop, I'm not-" Guariana looks at the soldier coming up behind Rogue. She recognizes him and her eyes widen.

"You're not expected here, ma'am." the soldier says.

Guariana's face gets serious. "You're not desert folk. Rogue, get out of here. Now," she says, through gritted teeth.

"You're not authorized to inform anyone of our presence here," the soldier replies.

Rogue looks at the soldier. "Your cover is blown? Juman? Somehow, I shouldn't be surprised."

"Call two. Cease Operation." Guariana reaches for her gunblade.

"You're not my handler, ma'am. Risk point assessment dictates Call Nine!" the soldier shouts, and tries to shoot at Rogue, but his bullets pass through him. Several more soldiers echo, saying, "Call Nine!" and start shooting at Amenaza's real soldiers.

"Cease command!" Guariana shouts, but the shooting continues for several seconds as the ambush happens.

"Damnit!" She shoots the soldier behind Rogue. "They're Juman spies."

"Point down! Call Three!" a spy shouts, and shoots at

Guariana, who deflects the bullets with her blade,

"What's Call Three?" Rogue tries to grab her again, and this time he is able to grab her. Her armor makes it impossible to lift her, so he tries to drag her to cover. Each shot fired from the hypnotized soldiers is alarmingly accurate in aiming for her exposed head. She manages to deflect each shot they take. When they start shooting at her armor, the bullets just bounce off, until one finds its way into the crack at her hip.

She screams and grabs at her hip. "They're going to try to kill me for jeopardizing their operation, whatever it was, which is foolish of them." She screams again when Rogue deadlifts her chest to keep dragging her behind the ruins of a half standing building. "Stop! Please."

"I can't do nothing!" Rouge sees blood is leaking through her armor.

Dr. Minatra runs out of the transport as it's being shot by the Juman spies. "Ahh! Help me!"

Guariana peeks around the corner of the rubble they're hiding behind and lays down cover fire for him. "This way!"

"This has to stop." Rogue looks around the rubble. A shot whizzes through his head. "I'm starting to like 'ghost' me."

"I wish I could do that; I'd make them regret it," Guariana groans.

Rogue walks through the rubble. "That gives me an idea. Keep that man alive whatever you do! He's Isla's cousin! When this dust settles, he can reason with her to keep us alive!"

Guariana waves Minatra over and puts him behind her.

"Thank you. Thank you so much," Minatra says, before getting a good look at her. "Oh, my goodness, you're severely wounded."

"No kidding," Guariana mutters. "What is he doing? I need to tell him something."

Rogue walks to the center of the canyon. He has the attention of the spies, and he takes stock of them as they shoot. Bullets whizz through his head in all directions. The penguins are getting closer. He goes to the two spies hiding in the building where penguins are already wandering around. Their eyes glow at him and they react like the ones in the crater, making the same panicked braying noise. Rogue walks through the wall to where the closer spy is and grabs them. They pull a knife out to stab Rogue, but their hand passes right through like he's not there. The second opens fire on him while backpedaling toward the doorway. A penguin waddles in and makes him vanish.

Rogue smirks and throws the spy in his grip through the window. The soldier lands in front of the penguins and vanishes.

"Ok. That, is brilliant," Guariana chuckles, then flinches in pain and grabs at her hip.

"This armor needs to come off." Minatra tries tugging at her back plate. "What is with this armor? It's not budging."

Just lift up, it comes right off," Guariana replies.

"What? No, I can't even budge it; did it get bent somewhere?" Minatra tries harder and barely gets it up an inch. "Do you seriously wear armor that heavy all the time?"

"Every day, all day." A spy comes up behind them and Guariana shoots him before he can shoot them.

Minatra glances behind him and gawks as the body drops. "How'd you know he was there?"

"I'm a Venator. Not an amateur," Guariana replies. "Even on my deathbed, I'm as dangerous as they come."

"I'm thankful for that," Minatra says.

Guariana shoots a penguin getting too close for comfort.

Rogue walks across the canyon, to another building where two spies are shooting at him. The spies stop to reload, and he picks up a penguin and throws it through the doorway. One of them vanishes and the other tries to shoot it, but his gun jams, and he vanishes.

His body starts feeling tight and heavy. "Damnit. Not

now," he mumbles. Blood starts raining from clouds that appear in an instant.

"What's happening to him?" Minatra watches Rogue look to the ground and slip.

"It's like at the Penguin Crater," Guariana replies. "Have your people encountered any illusions or hallucinations?"

"Plenty of paranormal activity reported, yes," Minatra replies. "Every time we got closer to here."

Rogue crawls toward a pile of rubble where one of the soldiers is hiding. "I gotta stop them."

Something in the rubble makes a gurgling, "gug, gug, gug" noise. A man walks out of the rubble; he's skinless and his flesh, muscle, fat, and sinew is exposed. A black oily substance bubbles out of his mouth, and his eyes are glowing green. He stumbles ahead of Rogue and starts vomiting the oil all over the back of Rogue's head.

Rogue rolls away, but the man grabs his arm, pins him down on his back, and continues vomiting the oil all over his face.

Guariana watches in horror as Rogue's veins turn jet black and his body writhes all over the ground like he's having a seizure. Bony spines burst from his chest and arms. His body levitates off the ground, rolling around in midair and bending in unnatural ways. "What is happening to him? Rogue! No!"

Rogue's pain filled screams echo around the canyon. The shape of a shadowy figure looms over Rogue, though it's not very visible. Thin, black smoke is seeping into Rogue's body.

Minatra can't believe his eyes. "What in the name of the gods?"

The spines they can see start dripping with Rogue's blood,

his skin dries up and cracks apart until it flakes off, letting strings of flesh dangle off his body.

Guariana turns away, unable to bear watching anymore.

The skinless man grabs Rogue's head and forces his mouth open. A long, rope-like tongue drops out of his mouth and slithers around Rogue's neck. A blood funnel shoots out of Rogue's mouth. The man's tongue grows teeth at its tip and starts eating its way into Rogue's chest over his heart. Rogue tries to grab it, but when he does, it feels like grabbing a burning piece of coal. Everything feels real, and the pain is beyond anything he's felt. His eyes look over at the half of building standing near the transport where Guariana is hiding.

The man grows a third arm out of his skull with two hands on it, and he uses it to push Rogue's head back until his neck breaks. Then his thumbs gouge into Rogue's eyes.

"Give up," a voice echoes in his head. "I see you here. I see you clear. But you will see no more. No one leaves my domain. You're mine, all mine. Give up. Give in. There's nothing tying you to this world. It's not real. It's all a ploy. You're being played by all, but too blind to see. Give up. Give in. To me."

Rogue tries to force his body to roll, but every effort to squirm or struggle is in vain.

"Come to us, come to me. You're in my grasp and cannot flee," the voice continues. "No hope, no will. One's touch is but a lie. Best you die. One's touch is a but a ploy. Depriving you of joy."

Rogue manages to close his mouth, but blood still forces its way out of his lips. He opens it again when the tongue eating into his chest bites into his heart, and the rest of it slithering on his neck keeps coiling around tighter until he feels his neck tearing.

The man stops when all that's connecting Rogue's head to his body is his esophagus. He lowers his head to the open tube and vomits more black oil into the hole. After a few more heaves, the man drops to the ground, lifeless. Rogue's nearly decapitated body lands next to him, writhing in an unnatural seizure.

"Now you are mine," the voice finishes. "You'll set me

Archon's Wake

free."

Minatra watches Rogue drop to the ground.

Guariana hears the thud and gulps.

"He's not moving," Minatra mutters.

Rogue lies still and the spines retract back into his body. But the black veins remain. His body grows a black shadowy shroud, and his body withers down to his skeleton.

"Oh my goodness." Minatra ducks back behind the rubble.

Guariana finally brings herself to take a peek, and watches the ghostly skeleton get up. "What happened to him?"

Rogue looks down at his body and screams. His scream reverberates through the canyon and shakes boulders and ice loose. Sections of the canyon buckle and cause small landslides.

Guariana covers her ears until the building they're hiding behind crumbles further, and she pushes Minatra out of the way of the wall coming down.

Rogue looks ahead of him; some Juman spies are peeking out of their hiding place and Rogue screams again.

The spies vanish in an instant; all of them at once. He then looks back at the lab and the penguins around him and screams at them. The penguins in his view vanish. His screaming is cut short when he blacks out.

"No. This cannot be. You did not die. You did not Perish. Nothing more than a memory is what you should be. Why can I not leave? You. What in this dark world are you? Master I cannot flee! He is not the bridge you seek!" The voice echoes around Rogue's mind.

Rogue can feel his brain throbbing. It's pulsing and pounding like his heartbeat; every bone and muscle feels like it's being ripped from his body but isn't tearing. The pain and pressure are unbearable.

"What are you? Skin of heart? You are not human. You are a prison of unknown design!" the voice screams.

Rogue can see himself in the hydra containment facility under Camp Tor. The memory of him drinking the clear liquid is replayed in his mind dozens of times.

"I understand now," the voice says, and Rogue's body stops feeling pain. "You are not the bridge I sought, servant of mine. Free you from him, I cannot. Do so yourself, you must. Return to me."

Guariana and Minatra look up when it's over to find no sign of the soldiers or penguins, and Rogue is laying in the middle of the ground, unconscious; his veins darken until they're pitch black.

"His body is back, sort of." Guariana takes several deep breaths.

"I... yeah... that was... I can't wrap my head around that." Minatra hides behind the rubble.

Guariana crawls toward him.

"Hey, stop! What are you doing?" Minatra reaches his arm out toward her but won't dare come out from behind the rubble.

"I have to know. I have to see if he's ok. If it's the last thing I do. I have to check on him," she mutters, and keeps crawling until she's at his side. She lifts his head and shakes him gently. "Rogue, talk to me, wake up."

Rogue opens his eyes; his pupils now glow green like the penguins'.

Guariana scoots away from him in terror. "Your eyes! They're glowing!"

"It's ok, Guariana." Rogue looks in her direction causing her to flinch until she realizes she's not vanishing.

She tries to calm down. "You don't look ok! Do you even know what happened to you a second ago?"

Rogue gets to his feet. "Yes. I do. And I know what I did."

Minatra comes up clapping. "Alright Rogue! You wiped away all the bad guys and those pesky penguins!"

Rogue looks his way.

"Oh, my goodness me, your eyes." Minatra puts his hands over his face. "How far did your uh, special ability go? Did anyone in the lab survive that?"

"I spared the humans still alive in the facility. None of them are hypnotized Jumans," Rogue replies. "I'm going to drag them out of there."

"This is Dr. Lourcer's lab, right?" Minatra asks. "She won't leave it empty handed."

"Yes, it's called pain. My body is experiencing much of it.

Archon's Wake

From injuries," Rogue says.

"You are injured, and so is she. You two need to let me try to help you," Minatra says.

"Why are your eyes glowing?" Guariana asks.

"Yes, her injuries are severe. And yes, I'm upset about it," Rogue says, while turning his head to the side.

"Rogue… don't-" Guariana starts to say.

"Obviously I don't want her to die!" Rogue shouts.

"I don't think he's talking to us," Minatra says.

Guariana watches Rogue appear to argue with himself.

"Heal her if you can. Call it a gesture of goodwill." Rogue returns his attention to them, staring down at Guariana with tears running down his face. "Please, she's important to me. I need her by my side."

Guariana tears up at seeing him say that to her. "That's all I want before I go," she whispers to herself.

"Rogue, she's been shot, and fell off a cliff, and I'm assuming she came from the same crash you did, so who knows how badly she's injured? We don't have that kind of medical equipment out here," Minatra says. "I'm sorry."

"I'm not talking to you," Rogue tells Minatra.

"Who the hell are you talking to?" Minatra asks.

Rogue coughs and starts heaving, he throws up some black oil then gets back up, wipes his mouth clean on his sleeve. The bruises on his body heal, and the black veins and glowing eyes disappear. "An introduction is mandated. I'm borrowing Rogue Whip to fulfil a small task to rectify an unforeseen circumstance." Rogue gives them a quick showman's bow. "Doctor Shoujin Lourcer, at your service." His body flashes into the ghastly skeleton it was a moment ago before returning to normal.

Guariana pounds on the ground. "Get out of him!"

"I would, truly, but I find myself stuck. I intended to kill him and move on, but well, as I said, I find myself in a situation I could not foresee. I imagine we will require something that can warp reality to fix this, and I am afraid that device is not here. It lies beneath Ghonda, in a hidden facility in the magma pit caves, that you people failed to search properly. This facility here is nothing more than a testing site.

Your empress will find nothing here," Dr. Lourcer replies.

"What exactly do you want?" Guariana asks. As he finishes, she can feel herself slipping into darkness.

"Hasty woman, are you not? Patience, please." He puts Rogue's hand on her injured hip, making sure to get under her armor and bodysuit to touch her flesh directly.

"Don't touch me." Guariana shoves his hand off, but in the split second his hand does touch her, the pain stops and she feels normal, even rejuvenated.

"You are most welcome. I have removed the bullet from your body and these small bits of debris that tore your insides." Rogue's hand drops a handful of metal bits, and a Juman's assault rifle bullet is among them. "Nasty airship wreck you were in. You'll find that not so much as a scar remains. Full revitalization. A gesture of goodwill as I agreed with this… Rogue Whip. He asks you to calm down and trust him." Dr. Lourcer gestures to her side.

She stands up and puts her hand on her side and then opens her armor to see her wounds are healed. "I will cut that hand off if it touches me again while under your control."

"And I shall regrow it back." Dr. Lourcer smiles. "I can do that, you know. I can do, oh, a great many things." The bruises and cuts on Rogue's body fade away and he looks as good as new. "Mr. Whip, you may have control of this body back. I've restored this body to perfect health to do as we need. Speak your peace to assure your woman, so we may begin. We require her to not interfere." He coughs the same way as before and Rogue's eyes glow again and his veins turn black.

He looks at the two of them. "That was probably the easiest way to explain it."

Guariana gawks at him. "Ok, I am a hundred and ten percent past my freak out point."

"I'm declaring myself to be dead! There's no way this is real anymore. Can I roll with that?" Minatra asks. "I died! A soldier shot me, a penguin zapped my body into nothingness, and now my soul is floating in nightmare land. That's my story and no one can convince me otherwise."

Rogue side eyes him. "Yeah, sure, go with that; whatever makes you feel sane. If Isla and Hondo come out before I do,

Archon's Wake

make sure they don't kill Guariana, and if possible, try to leave me something to ride to Ghonda. Please. I'm counting on you Minatra, you just saw the new side of me perform a miracle; don't test its power to destroy."

Minatra looks exasperated. "We already saw that! Why not take her with you? I can stall and prepare them to not give her a harsh welcome?"

"Because to do what I need to do here, is gonna require some ghosting stuff. I can't exactly take her all the way, and if they find her in there, Hondo won't hold back. I need to reach them first but it's possible I might not, they've had plenty of time to get far," Rogue replies.

"I need a word with Rogue, in private," Guariana says.

Minatra walks away. "I'll be in the last transport making some coffee. Yes, coffee, that's a good start. Let's wake up from this nightmare. I wonder what coffee tastes like when I'm dead?"

Rogue embraces her tightly. "I knew you somehow survived that wreck."

"This is you, right?" she asks, before lifting her arms.

"Yeah, it's me. I'm me. It's complicated. But-"

She wraps her arms around him and hugs him tight. "I didn't think you survived."

"I did. I'm alive. And I'm happy to see you're ok. Seeing you back on your feet is more than I could've asked ten minutes ago."

She kisses him, and he kisses back and holds her tighter.

You will want to see this memory from her mind. Dr. Lourcer's voice says in Rogue's head.

Rogue sees a memory flash before his eyes. Guariana is with the Mistress on the observation deck looking down at his crash site. He can feel how Guariana feels repulsed, upset, even used. Her orders aren't to supervise over Rogue, but rather to manipulate him for when the Mistress needs access to him after they collect the penguin specimens. Guariana's mind pictures Rogue as an uncultured, unmannered, uncaring, musclebound Acinvar man. And it makes her stomach churn. She doesn't want to get close to him, let alone befriend him.

She was ordered to more or less seduce you for long term plans of this

Daniel Jones

Mistress of hers. I gave you glimpses to skip the full conversation; it is unpleasant even for me.

Rogue looks at his hands as they're holding onto Guariana's hips, and he lets go then looks up at her smiling face. "Why'd you follow me after the crash?"

Grab her skin again. I was not finished.

Her smile shrinks when his fades away, and she looks hurt. The accusation in his tone takes her aback. "I needed to know you were still alive. You're important to me, too. More than I thought you'd be."

"I've seen what I need to see," Rogue mutters under his breath.

Not from what I witnessed. There's more truth to see.

Guariana's smile fades entirely. "What is that supposed to mean?"

"Not you; the guy in my head," Rogue replies. "I, uh, yeah; let's see if we can get out of this place and then we can get back to our lives."

"Rogue, are you really ok?" She puts her hand on his cheek.

Hah, yes, let's dig some more into her mind.

Rogue sees her holding his hand while he's unconscious in the hospital bed. She's worried about him and refuses to leave his side, not because of her orders, but because she wants to be there. The Mistress arrives with a serious vibe, she looks emotionless, but Guariana can tell what her mood is. The Mistress speaks to her about leaving the airship to deal with Hurlua, regarding what she did to Prince Cal. After that they speak at length, while Rogue can't make any of it out, he can feel a strong sensation of surprise and joy. The idea of freedom is on her mind. Along with images of Rogue and her doing normal people type things. As well as fleeting thoughts to reflect on her Venator sisters.

At first glance I wanted to inform you that you had me waste my power on your own assassin. And while that may still be the case, it is a kindness of sorts and a delightful demon in the same, that she finds herself so attached to you. A simple conundrum for you both. How I wish I could have studied such dilemmas in my life. How do you handle this, knowing these truths from her mind? Knowing she cannot tell you at the same time.

Archon's Wake

For reasons that should be obvious.

Rogue looks away. "Lourcer, stop it and let me think."

But you can't think. Just as I cannot speak. Whoever controls the body does just that. While the other does the thinking. I've already figured this nonsense out. You possess enough residual cognizance through your mind to maintain focus and access your memory to make decisions. Forces whoever is in control of this body to be impulsive, but at least every act we make won't be random.

"You're right," Rogue says, after he tries to think, but all he can do is bring memories to mind, not generate thoughts of his own. But he can comprehend his surroundings, control his body, and make physical decisions. "That's annoying. I'm not gonna get used to this."

"I should give you some space." Guariana backs up a bit.

He grabs her wrist at the armor. "Wait."

Make this quick. I don't enjoy wasting time.

"Yes?" she asks.

"Why'd the Mistress choose you to supervise me? Was there any particular reason?" Rogue asks.

She hesitates then nods. "Yes, there was. We Venators are a unique bunch. Each of us is highly trained in various forms of combat and we don't get to express ourselves much. When we do show our personalities, we find ourselves doing so in an all-out manner. I would like to think the Mistress took my personality into consideration when pairing me with you. It is common knowledge that when a genuine desire to cooperate is present, it makes the team stronger. It's my assumption that she chose me as the best candidate she had to team up with you."

"Sounds like you want to say more." Rogue folds his arms and gives her an inquisitive glare.

She sighs and gives a slight nod. "Yes, but it's not important right now. It will be something we can talk about later. After you have just one person in your body." She forces her smile to return.

He wraps her arm around her back and lowers her to his level, giving her the best kiss he can. "I like it better when your smiles are real."

Her forced smile turns genuine. "Go, do whatever it is you

need to do; I'll be right here waiting for you."

"Nightfall is almost here. Please, stay safe; don't fight Isla's soldiers. If they won't listen to Minatra, then I want you to run, and I'll find you," Rogue says, before coughing again.

Guariana looks away at the sound of Rogue throwing up. "Oh, gods, eww, that's gonna make me do the same." She walks away and covers her ears.

"Your moment has been had, and time is moving along." Lourcer jogs to the facility. "Honestly, I did not anticipate that to drag. Next time, a peck please, not whatever mouth action that was."

We've had one hell of a day Lourcer, and your little memory trick didn't help. Wait a minute, I was in control of the body when you did that, did you just conjure that up?

"Considering I cannot block out what the body experiences and does, I despise romance at face value. And no, what you saw was her true lived experience. I can tap into anyone's memory when I have physical contact," Dr. Lourcer mutters under his breath, as he jogs faster to the facility. "Besides, you have known her for all of a few hours. You must be a fool to-"

It's called love at first sight, dumbass. While this is the first time I've seen it like this, I have seen the emotions before. How about you dig around my mind and learn what real love looks like.

"I do not accuse her feelings as a farce. I accuse the pretenses that formed the foundations of such, and that often leads to crushed dreams and destroyed lives. Though you are right, she demonstrates a display of emotions reminiscent of your second romantic partner, not that I care."

Terry has a name, asshole.

"An outside observation on you and Terry, if you'll permit me. Had you paid attention to the hooligans you passed on the way to the lunar festival that year, you might have had second thoughts of taking her to the circus. She would definitely be alive right now." Dr Lourcer sounds like he's enjoying the conversation. "Ah, yes, the smell of her flesh burning under the beam. Both of you covered in the fiery scene of a flaming circus tent, on an otherwise lovely beach. The screams of injured and dying people around you. And your feeble attempts to free her from a thick log and twisted mess of broken bleachers that today you could likely lift with ease. Even in her dying breath, she did nothing but watch your face with love and passion. You on the other hand passed the moment by and failed to return her love to her. Not once, did you look down to return her gaze or tell her you love her in her finality. I despise romance, but even I know the right thing to do when it counts. And I could see her doing such through your own memories. You saw it, but paid no heed."

I was trying to save her life.

"In a situation you could do little about. I have humored this conversation long enough. Ihuit awaits." Dr. Lourcer steps into the facility. Inside, it looks like a regular cargo bay, and the equipment is still in place. Loading cranes, wooden crates and containers, smaller tracks leading away with hand carts still on them. Even the turntable at the end of the main rails looks untouched by the weathering that's happened in the canyon.

He steps through and finds the whole place is a massive building. The canyon walls have been dug out and there are dozens of floors, levels leading to the ceiling. Light fills the building from reflective surfaces on the ceiling. Shiv Empire signage and propaganda is all over the place.

Whoa.

"Yes, marvel at the grandeur of the Ihuit research facility. Crown Jewel of all science in Yeraputs. At least in my time." Dr. Lourcer reaches the end of the tracks, passes the turntable, and heads to where the building opens into a tridecagon shaped room. It's so large the first thing that comes to mind is the hydra container in Tor. Another surprise is that the level he's on is halfway from the top or bottom.

Hundreds of suspended rails cross the room from one side to the other with dangling passenger vehicles. *This place is so massive it needs its own Rim Cart network. That's crazy.*

"Yes, the transit system was required. It demanded a labor force of forty thousand men and women, and took three years to construct this place in what was once a cavern under the ice," Dr. Lourcer replies.

Ninety-two floors in thirteen wings and over thirty million square feet per floor. This place is a small city.

Dr. Lourcer chuckles. "It would take that idiot Empress and her goons years to explore it all."

Something nearby catches his attention: an armored vehicle parked near elevator shafts. The front has significant ramming damage, and the sides are covered in scrape marks.

That's not Shiv; someone has been here before. Well, a few decades ago, anyway.

"Indeed, an unexpected sight. Let's have a look, shall we?"

He approaches the back of the vehicle, where a loading ramp is lowered, and freezes in shock. An insignia is on the inside of the transport. A thick navy-blue ring around a black and grey camouflage pattern with the letters L. A. R. on the top and F. T. D. on the bottom.

Fire Team Dark was here? Albert really did find this place.

He walks into the transport, discovering Yensi's Military hardware. All mechanical with magnetic gears. "At least we have a ride out if we can get this thing unlocked. You have knowledge to do so, and I know where such tools are. We no longer require the assistance of the Empress and her transportation."

Well, that's making a lot of assumptions. Look for an ignition plate slot.

"Like that one?" Dr. Lourcer points to it. "Ah, I see the problem you allude to."

Unless we find a really big portable source of electricity in here, which there isn't, this thing ain't moving.

"Are you trying to aggravate me on purpose? Your immunity to paranormal effects is quite literally trapping my soul in your body. The only thing that might help us both is my weapon. Otherwise, we're going to be stuck like this forever."

I'm giving your theory a lot of faith. Take that at the value you need to.

"You do take the word of strangers at face value far too much for my liking."

You make it sound like I have a second choice that lets me survive such encounters.

"I admit, you handled those events better than most. Between your ability to 'roll with it,' as you say, and my natural critical thinking capabilities, we could do quite a lot. But I sense that we lack the kind of compatibility to make such a union a success."

Don't get comfortable.

"I don't plan to. You're too restrained, peaceful, and unscientific for my taste." Lourcer snaps his fingers and falls through several floors, stopping at the third one up from the ground. He follows the massive walkway that forms a ring connecting the wings around the central gap. For miles they walk until they arrive at the entrance of the seventh wing. "Awfully quiet on the way over; are you alright in there?"

Just taking a stroll through your demented mind. You're an evil son of a bitch. All those people you 'tested' your science on. It's probably a good thing you got warped into your own little dimensional prison.

"I may have found a way to amuse myself in my work, but what genius doesn't? And besides, you overlook my loyalty to the Shiv Empire. Those subjects were criminals. Many of them for crimes you would also consider crimes in Acinvar: murder, rape, and the like."

Not all of them. Some were little kids screaming for their parents. And that newborn baby, right at the moment of birth? You made that woman deliver her child in front of you only to have her watch her child zapped into nothingness.

"I had forgotten about that one-off test. I needed to be sure that there was no stage of life that the effects did not cover. One test of such circumstances sufficed for the paperwork. Besides, she joined her child mere seconds after; a kindness of its own under the necessity of data. You again failed to disclose that she was a serial killer. The security team needed some amusement of their own. It provided me with the rare opportunity to generate a test during the seconds' old stage of life. A nine-month wait was not too much to ask for."

Alleged serial killer, not proven. You even suspected the evidence of that case was shaky.

"This was hundreds of years ago. Her trial was not rigged. Who cares in today's world? It's all meaningless in the grandest scopes of the here and now." Dr. Lourcer walks past several security checkpoints and makes his way down a series of hallways.

Daniel Jones

I can overlook the acts themselves, as disturbing as they were; it's the fact that you enjoyed it that I take issue with.

Dr. Lourcer stops when a certain memory comes to mind. "Get that particular memory you've found out of our head. I healed your romantic curiosity as a kindness, to show a willingness to cooperate with you. And I further provided context for her feelings, revealing their dark origin and bright truth. I can just as easily destroy the spark she has for you."

You've already dug through my head; I'm simply returning the favor. Don't worry, that was so disturbing, I don't think I'll revisit it.

"I think it's time you drive. Your selection of memories on Memory Lane is lousy." Lourcer hunches over and throws up some oil.

"Ugh, yuck. Wow, is there a better way to do that?"

No.

"This place looks creepier in the front seat," Rogue says.

Move it. You know where we're going.

"I swear I'm going to need a few lobotomies when this is over. And seriously, you don't need to threaten me like that; it's petty for someone as smart as you."

I have little else to do for amusement in my current state. Petty yes, but it's not nothing.

Rogue follows the hallways, until he reaches a set of double doors, locked with a puzzle mechanism. It's covered in handles, levers, and knobs. He pulls down on a lever on the top and twists it clockwise twice. Then grabs a handle in the middle of the door and moves it halfway up the moving slat, then turns it two hundred and seventy degrees clockwise. The door makes several clicking sounds and new handles pop out along the sides. He grabs the seventh one down and tugs hard. The door swings open.

And here I thought you'd need my direction. Why didn't you just walk through it, leave it locked?

"I like puzzles."

Just get to the containment room, you idiot oaf.

"Go watch a memory. You know what, have a truly fascinating one: the Camp Tor incident. Should amuse you for a bit." Rogue walks into a large room covered in panes of frosted and lenticular glass on all sides. He walks to the back of the room and through the wall into another glass room; this one is pitch black. He follows Lourcer's memory and walks through several walls. Then he stops and snaps his fingers, rising through the ceiling into a massive room. The floor is littered with metal ankle cuffs on short chains secured to the concrete floor. Half of them are empty, and the other half have skeletons locked in them. "Are you fucking for real?"

I had no control over this. The facility must've been evacuated when the incident in Ghonda occurred.

"Obviously, not everyone was evacuated!" Rogue shouts.

Clearly not. And I will remind you, it's not my place to apologize.

"The hell it isn't. The people in this room were your cache of expendable humans to experiment on. It's even on the wall still!" Rogue points to a massive banner with a cartoon drawing that reads:

HOORAY!
YOU WILL BE PART OF A GREAT
SCIENCE PROJECT THAT WILL
FURTHER HUMANITY. YOUR DEATH
SENTENCE WILL BE TURNED INTO
KNOWLEDGE AND POWER FOR THE
GOOD OF THE EMPIRE!

I never liked that sign. Made the test subjects rather combative and waste plenty of my time. It's accompanied illustration is rather abhorrent as well.

"Of everything in this room, that's the thing you don't like?"

Not a fan of that artistic style. I'm less fond of caricature and more-

"Shut it. I'm not interested." Rogue walks to the back of the room; some of the skeletons look like people were trying to cut off their legs to escape before they starved to death.

My experiments granted a quick fate. I'm not above recognizing suffering.

"Say that to the illusions you've been making us endure all day." Rogue walks through a wall into another glass room with a smaller glass room inside. He walks into the glass and bounces backward.

You can't walk through that one? Interesting. Oh well, just use the

Daniel Jones

door.

Rogue walks around the smaller room and steps inside. It feels strange; he can't explain it, but the sensation is making his skin crawl. His flesh and blood feel like they're burning. The sensation subsides after a few seconds.

Wait, no this isn't right. This is backwards, this is supposed to be in Ghonda.

Rogue stares at a large metal obelisk laying on its side. A cavity has been carved out in the top and a large metal plate is hovering above it. "Yeah, I was expecting a giant ball full of wires and cables."

I suppose we get to test my theory early. Though I must admit, I don't know what will happen when you fire the Harbinger Weapon at yourself.

"Hold up, I thought you built the Harbinger Weapon, and that bomb device was-"

No, it's the other way around, you fool!

"Alright, sheesh." He walks up to the obelisk and finds the cavity empty.

What? That's impossible!

"Someone already found it. Richtoff. Where the hell would he have taken it?"

This room was sealed by that lock, there's no way anyone who didn't know its design could get past it. Proven by a lack of damage to the room.

"Maybe it is in Ghonda," Rogue mutters.

How do you mean?

Rogue closes his eyes. He sees himself as Dr. Lourcer. The device he's holding, it's a strange metal that feels smooth and gives off a static sensation to the touch. "Norgut Metal. Where did you find that thing?"

I lobotomized myself because of that information. I fail to recall where, but it's my understanding that I did not find it in the tundra. Leave; there is nothing more to do here. I will attempt to conjure up a backup plan.

Rogue follows the hallways back to the central gap. As he exits the wing, a metal coated arm grabs him and slams him into the ground. "Hondo, what the hell?"

"Rogue?" Hondo immediately helps him up. "Wait a minute, you came out of there? How'd you get by us?"

"I came to tell you guys something important. The

penguins, when they attacked the surface-"

"They appeared out of nowhere, all over the facility, and disappeared just as instantly as they appeared," Isla cuts him off, as she comes from behind Hondo. "We were headed straight here; how did you get by us so quickly?"

"You've been in here for hours?"

Yes, but they had to zig zag to reach the proper stairways to come down this far. We simply ghosted our way down in a matter of seconds. If she was heading directly here as if she knew the way, then she's been taking the best path, which begs the question, how did she know where she was going?

"Scratch that, I came in, looked for you guys, and ended up ghosting through the floors," Rogue clarifies.

"Ghosting?" Hondo asks.

Rogue sticks his arm through Hondo's chest like he's not even there.

Hondo yelps and backs away. "Don't do that to me! You couldn't do the wall or something? Point made."

Isla laughs. "I must admit, that was rather fun to watch. And you can do this at will? It seems as though you've encountered something up there. And I see your body has miraculously healed."

"During the penguin attack, I picked up some new abilities."

Isla pokes his arm out of curiosity. "You don't feel any different to the touch. Explain these new abilities."

"Well, truth be told, they're not mine. They belong to Dr. Shoujin Lourcer. He is a trans-dimensional being now, confined to the Tundra by the constraints of his existence. He got there by using the Harbinger Weapon. And while he has some difficult-to-explain gifts, his existence is a curse. Isla, I went in there to get you out before you made the worst mistake of your life. Because if you touched that Weapon, you would end up like him. Trapped here, cursed to suffer for all eternity. Never to see your people again, and you would never live the life you are looking for."

Ooh, nice deception narrative. I can spin a memory of that to put into her head and make her believe it. You must make physical contact with her. Skin to skin.

Rogue puts his hand on her cheek and looks her in the eyes. She seems to freeze in time. "As long as she gives up her hunt for he Harbinger Weapon," Rogue whispers under his breath.

I am implanting the vision into her mind now. But at the same time, I'm travelling her entire life's memory, and I've gotta say, this woman has endured torture that is far worse than anything I have; scratch that, everything I have ever done combined that could possibly be considered evil. She's in great fear for her life. Paranoia on a scale that's difficult to control. This is not a simple ask to simply make her lose interest. This will require me to manipulate her real memories and make her forget quite a few things. This damage will be permanent. It will cause her to become mentally unstable for some time, while her brain adjusts.

"Can you do it?" Rogue asks.

Of course I can do it. Here's a neat little secret: the behavioral changes everyone has experienced out here. That's my doing. My master cannot reach your reality, so I do so in the form of what you might call a haunting influence. To those who are not already exposed to other dimensions, it's not powerful, but it's enough to cause people to become forgetful, ignorant, aggressive, and create situations where mistakes happen in the unforgiving natural environment of the Harbinger Tundra. Which, as you know all too well, is deadly. Before the Shiv Empire, this tundra was relatively simple to leave. All one had to do was take underground pathways. Shame that Shiv collapsed them all. Flying over that storm is a fool's errand.

Isla's eyes roll to the back of her head.

"How long is this going to take?" Rogue whispers under his breath.

Rogue, my boy, you are experiencing time far faster than usual while I do what I am doing. Now, where was I? You know what, who cares? What's important is that you get me out of your body, and I will put in a good word with my master to simplify your escape. Well, make the case to allow your escape, to be precise. We either need to locate the device everyone insists on calling 'The Harbinger Weapon,' or we need to detonate my invention, the dimensional bomb. Which is what I consider the Harbinger Weapon. But in order for that to work, you would need to detonate it from my side of the dimensional rift your existence is wedged in.

"How in the hell do I cross into your dimension to do that?" Rogue asks.

My master would need to enter your body. Though I am unsure how that would work with the obstacle in your DNA. No matter, we will figure it out, I'm sure. Or, if your hunch is correct, the Harbinger Weapon that I used to create my dimensional bomb will be near the Ghonda facility. We'll use that and split me from you and, well, what's left will ultimately be up to you, I guess. And I'll keep doing what I do. Existing at the pleasure of my master. I'm done. Isla will be very interested in going home and will want nothing to do with trying to threaten dangerous people, such as the Maroon Mistress.

Isla's eyes come back, and she gasps at Rogue's gentle touch.

She will pass out soon; be ready to catch her.

"I want you to live the life you deserve. Please," Rogue tells her gently.

"Oi! Remove your hand from her this instant!" Hondo shouts.

"Enough Hondo!" Isla says, while cupping her hand over Rogue's. "He means me no harm." She passes out and falls into his arms.

Rogue picks her up in his arms while Hondo is raging red in the face. "You don't have to trust me for anything, but you need to understand she can't go down that hallway. It's better if I stop her like this. She needs you to defend her. She can hate me all she wants when she wakes up. At least she will be safe, and on her way back to her people, where she belongs. Tell me any of that is wrong."

Hondo calms down and puts his anger in check. "All of that sounds good to me. But hand her to me; I don't want your demonic hands all over her."

Rogue hands Isla to Hondo and leads the way out.

"They've been gone for several hours now." Minatra says, after taking a sip of hot chocolate.

Guariana takes a sip of hers and looks at the chessboard between them. "They'll be fine."

Minatra claps his hands and offers his to shake. "Good

game. No matter what I do, you will win in two turns. You're amazing at this."

Guariana smiles and shakes his hand. "You flatter me." Then she sees lights in the canyon. "They're back."

"What the hell happened? Two of our transports got destroyed?" Hondo looks at the transport that got shot up earlier.

Minatra jumps out of the last transport. "Hondo! Hey! Oh heavens, is Isla alright?" He panics when he sees Hondo carrying the empress's body.

"Doc, she's unconscious, breathing, looks stable; happened in the lab." Hondo hands him Isla's body.

"Oh dear, this is unexpected. And speaking of unexpected, Rogue's Juman friend showed up. She's friendly, so whatever you do, please, do not engage her."

Hondo side eyes Rogue to find him giving him the same concerned look that Minatra has. "An actual Juman, huh? A woman then. I don't hit women. Why are you both looking at me like I'm a problem?

"I'm delighted to hear you refrain from assaulting females." Guariana walks out of the transport.

Hondo's eye twitches. "Minatra, that's-"

"A lovely Juman Venator named Guariana. Yes, and she is Rogue's bodyguard no less. She saved my life when the penguins attacked. Twice. Isla would be waking up to one less family member if it wasn't for this woman. So please. Please."

Hondo brushes past him, making sure to smack Minatra's shoulder hard and walks up to Guariana. His exosuit extends in the arms and legs, making him taller than her. "We thought we were dealing with Huntresses out on the tundra, but no, Venators, I've waited my whole life to test my might against one of you."

Rogue, switch with me, now. I'll cut this distraction short.

"I will not engage in combat with you." Guariana looks over at Rogue, who's coughing up oil. "Do not force this upon me, Hondo. Grand General of Empress Isla Amenaza's personal security detail. I beseech you peacefully."

Hondo laughs. "Hold up; a Juman, A Venator, a fabled slaughterhouse assassin, asking nicely to avoid a fight!? I finally meet a Venator and she's a coward? Beseech me? Oh, what in the gods is going on here? Have you no shame or pride? Have the Venators gone soft? Is it possibly just a rouse, all that hearsay surrounding you?"

"If you want a fight, there is a Venator in the tundra who will gladly oblige. Her name is Titania. She will make a worthy opponent for you." Guariana is quick to say. "And I daresay you may have your chance if Ghonda is our destination. I, however, have standing orders from Rogue not to engage you in combat. So, I will not."

"I don't care who any of you are. I have seen your crimes on my land more times than I'd like to. I'll take my country's revenge out in blood from any of you." Hondo pokes her in the chest as hard as he can, she lets herself be pushed a few steps back. Hondo spits on her face.

"Guariana, don't engage." Dr. Lourcer walks up behind Hondo.

"We might agree on a few things, Mr. Whip, but I'm not giving the Maroon Mistress's hand maidens an inch." Hondo swings at Rogue.

Dr. Lourcer catches his metal fist, stopping its force with ease. "Show restraint. This skirmish is fruitless."

"The hell it is. Order her to attack me. I demand my chance for valor and honor! She defends you, right? Maybe I'll attack you and it'll happen then." Hondo yanks his fist out of Lourcer's grip.

"Hondo! At attention, stand down and present yourself accordingly!" Isla screams at the top of her lungs.

Hondo snaps to attention. "Your highness! It's good to-"

"I said at attention, soldier!" Isla shouts even louder. "Do not make me repeat myself a third time." She stops to catch her breath, and she's red in the face.

Hondo snaps to perfect attention.

"I saw the truth Rogue spoke of in the vision I had after Rogue touched me. He just saved my life. The least I can do to repay him is oblige his request to bring her along!" She screams, "Am! I! Clear!?"

"Perfectly." Hondo's exo-suit retracts back down to normal.

7: Demons In Plain Sight

"Whoa." Hondo stops the transport outside the hangar as dawn rises the next day. "Isla, we have a problem."

Isla looks out the window, to see James lying face down on the ground in a massive pool of blood, and Bifo, dismembered, near one of the building ruins by the tarmac.

"Titania," Guariana says, when she takes a look. "She's still acting on her orders to find the Harbinger Weapon. Well, specifically, her orders to find you, your highness, and her side-quest for the Harbinger Weapon."

"Is there a chance she's still here?" Rogue asks.

"If so, Hondo gets first shot at her," Guariana says.

"Damn straight." Hondo kicks the door open and walks out. "Detail, search the premises. Venator, keep the royals and guest safe for me."

"Sure thing, boss." Guariana gives him a sarcastic salute.

Isla looks to Rogue. "I should have stopped when I knew they were here. What have I done?" She lowers her head into her hands and sobs.

"Don't blame yourself," Minatra says. "That's Juman's doing, not yours. We can make this right in the long run, but not here."

"She's been devolving emotionally," Guariana whispers in

Rogue's ear.

"Lourcer said that she'd be encountering wild mood swings until her brain stabilizes," Rogue whispers back.

"Can't you fix her brain with whatever that ability was? Make this a whole thing a lot less annoying on us all," she whispers.

What am I? A miracle worker?

"I tried to, when she broke down over the sweetness of sugar in her coffee," Rogue replies in a low voice.

Hey, it's sugar, the kiss of life that keeps people going. I sympathize. Not like that dark bland mug of crap you drank earlier.

"It's ok, Isla; you've got us around to help you through this." Minatra grabs Rogue's shoulder. "Right, Rogue?"

"Why would I want his help? He did this to me!" she shouts.

"For the last time, Lourcer did that to you. The moment he's out of my body, you can kick his ass all you want," Rogue replies. "And you don't have to see me ever again."

Oh, I hadn't considered if I'd get my own body back when we separate. It's unlikely, but a pleasant thought.

"I don't want that anymore." Isla looks right into his eyes. "In fact, I want you to visit on a regular basis. Once you're free of that manipulative trash."

"Uh, come again?" Rogue asks.

It's a phase, ignore it. Oh wait, you're the manipulative trash. She's talking to you. Hah.

"I am going to offer a trade landing port to Acinvar. They don't have much on the northern half of Inner Shell, and it would place them uncomfortably close to Juman."

"Acinvar won't say yes to something like that," Minatra replies.

"No, but we have an airship pilot, with a new rescue division that could use a new skyport, located on the northern side of Inner Shell where half of his rescue missions have happened so far. Places him in an advantageous location to make hours and minutes count. He'd make a strong case for Acinvar to sign off on it."

Rogue's jaw drops. "Uh, I mean, we fly out to you guys for trade, as it is. What did you have in mind?"

Daniel Jones

"There is open land on the south side of the Glistening City that's been set aside for political reasons and never developed. It's about fourteen thousand acres and is well out of the way of the current trade port. All you have to do is say yes and I'll build whatever you want on it. Perhaps a pair of skyports, the main trade port, and locomotive ready exchange. As well as a new headquarters for your rescue division." She gives him a look.

That didn't sound like a suggestion. Great offer with what I know of your business.

"Uh, wow. You thought of that while sleeping last night?" Rogue asks.

Guariana gives her a quick sideways glance. "Makes it easy to keep him close to you at all times. Would certainly send Juman a message."

Oof, that look, that tone. I apologize, I was out of place yesterday. You. Are. In. Trouble. A lot of it. And it happened without my pushing. You need all your manipulative powers when that hits the fan.

"We'll have that conversation once I get Jessie involved. She'd have to sign off on it," Rogue replies.

Lackluster save.

Rogue turns away. "Lourcer stop it; it's too early for this."

"You still own the company, though. Why get your second in command involved?" Isla comments.

"Own, yes; run and make the big decisions? Not anymore. Jessie is the real CEO these days. I gave her the top spot so I could pursue a personal agenda. Heart has some… problematic… universal travel space laws. But yeah, that kind of thing would have to go through her, per the procedures and such," Rogue replies.

"Ah. I forget when it comes to business, you are a man of protocol and procedure," Isla remarks.

Not to mention the Tradewinds Compact regulations you'd need to get familiar with. It's giving me a headache, and I dealt with scientific regulations.

Minatra heads toward the back of the transport. "Coffee, anyone?"

"Yeah, I need a second cup." Rogue follows him.

Hey, you need to put some sugar in that coffee! How can you drink it black?

"I didn't know you had a say about what goes in my body, Lourcer," Rogue whispers.

I'm living experiences for the first time in hundreds of years through you. Do you realize that I haven't slept in the whole time I've been in a different dimension? And I experienced sleep last night. You have no idea what an enjoyable experience that was! Please, oh please, let me taste some sugar. Just a little. I beg you. At least some cream or milk.

Minatra pours a cup at the small kitchenette in the back of the transport. "Black?"

Rogue shakes his head. "Uh, you know, add some cream and sugar to this one."

Yes! Wait, you're doing this to make me be nicer, aren't you? Ok, fine.

Minatra raises a suspicious eyebrow. "I thought you said-"

"It's for the guest in my body," Rogue replies.

Minatra chuckles "He's a guest now?"

"Pest," Rogue corrects himself.

Paranormal existential parasite, actually.

Rogue turns his head. "You attacked me. You got yourself into this, dumbass."

How the hell was I supposed to know I'd get myself into this nightmare?

"He's chatty?" Minatra pours himself a cup.

"It's like a thing that won't shut up and stops you from having your own thoughts. It is not a fun experience."

I concur!

Isla watches the group head underground. "Looks like they found something." She gets up and Guariana puts her arm in her way. "Tight spaces are Titania's favorite place. Not even I can hold my own against her in such environments."

Isla sits back down. "Can you beat her at all? If you had to, I mean?"

"I can defeat her in wide open spaces where I can overwhelm her with wide sweeps and high energy physical contact. She is a master at bouncing off walls, though, and she's deadliest in places like narrow hallways and tight alleys," Guariana replies.

Isla looks out the window. "They're walking into a trap?"

Guariana shakes her head. "She's not the patient type."

Several hours later, while they're traveling, Rogue is sitting on his bunk at the back of the upper level of the transport, reading a book, while drinking his coffee. "I wonder if the penguin crater would be a good place to revisit. Their ability uses dimensional rifts."

I doubt it. Right now, your physical state is trying to balance between two dimensions. The penguins' ability is a one-way trip. It's been tearing you out of your reality and placing it where I could access you.

"I like how I can follow your thoughts as you think them. There's something that you're not saying."

You're not oblivious. My master, what you call a shadow figure, has lost its grip on me in your body, but I still possess the abilities it granted me, abilities you are subsequently using yourself.

"For those abilities to work in my reality, won't they have to have an already established point here to work? My body isn't the only point tying it to my reality, it's gotta have something to anchor it here, right?"

You're making an assumption that it is like the hydra. No, this is a free roaming being that was-

"Cut the crap. If it was new to this world, because of your experiment gone wrong, then the harbinger penguins wouldn't have existed before you, yet they did. I've seen that shadow figure and it's not all that different from the one I saw in Tor. Come to think of it, the one here couldn't touch me at all, but you could. You're trapped in its realm by unusual means. Either you're still taking orders or you're running."

Escape was never possible! Now it is! Ok. Yes, I am considering that it is finally possible for me to leave that infernal prison! But for four hundred and eighteen years, I watched day and night in a realm alone, taking occasional orders to torment people who showed up that it couldn't reach. Almost all those people had never had a connection to another dimension. You and that Hunter Smith are like glowing beacons to us.

Rogue stands up. "Shut up Lourcer." He looks out the back window where the shadow figure is lurking in plain view.

It heard all of that, didn't it?

The shadow figure fades away.

Look, I know I've been rude, but I can't exist in that space anymore. If you can leave, just take us out of here. I'll build a new machine well outside its grasp and you can be free of me somewhere that isn't so dangerous. I'll be the best brain guest you ever had until then.

Rogue chuckles. "That was painful to hear. That will take too long for me. Sorry doc, you're coming out of my head here."

I'm not going to go quietly.

Titania walks to the center of the Ihuit research facility. "You've gotta be fucking kidding me." She marvels at how massive it is, then shirks at the idea of searching. "How'd they even build this place with those pesky archons all over the sky?"

She heads to the left and soon spots the Fire Team Dark armored transport. "You are a sexy beast of a tank, aren't you? Dumped in an icy grave left to be forgotten. So sad." She walks up the ramp and heads to the cockpit. There's a small leatherbound journal wedged in the cushions of the driver's seat. She almost didn't notice it. "What have we here?"

She opens it, finding nothing but blank pages. She thumbs through it and eventually comes across a note written in Lord Richtoff's handwriting.

> To whomever beyond my time finds this. I congratulate you. This is the Ihuit research facility of the Shiv Empire. This is the laboratory associated with Dr. Shoujin Lourcer. His weapon was found in an obelisk made of natural magnetic repelling metal. Quite a sight to see such a device levitating in what can be at best described as a tomb, located deep located in level six of the electromagnetic radiation research wing.

Daniel Jones

>Access can only be made to that area through the third level. But you will not find the weapon there.
>
>In my short experience, I discovered the device is more a tool than a weapon. I learned that it does not simply make people vanish. Rather it displaces them into an alternate reality, or dimension. Those unfortunate enough to be displaced are not dead. And there is one particular specter who has made this venture take some rather unnatural and deadly turns. The more use I made of the device, the more serious the encounters.
>
>At one point we found ourselves in what can only be described as a fractured reality. Invisible barriers blocking paths and appearing and disappearing at random. It is clear this device creates rifts between realities that cannot be allowed to converge. I have tried to destroy it in the magma pits beneath Ghonda, to no avail. The material used to make it is indestructible, and it remains active. Thus, I had to leave it where it lay. It is my demand that you leave this place immediately.
>
>Lord Albert Richtoff.

Titania throws the notebook through the windshield and screams. "Curse you! You old dead bastard!" She grabs her gunblade and slashes everything in the transport.

When she finishes her tantrum, she walks out and huffs. Nearby, she spots bullet casings. "I missed a real fun party too!? COME ON! I've been traveling in the freezing cold looking for a good time and all I get is an empty tank with a note full of bad news and spent bullet casing confetti!?"

She walks up to kick the casings. "Hold on, these are not Yensi casings. These are cheap military crap. Desert people."

Archon's Wake

She looks around the central gap and shrugs. "It is a big place, and they did seem to crash their transport like fools. Piles of clothes by that hole says the penguins were here. But where are the penguins, and why am I compelled to talk to myself today?"

She stares at one of the Rim Cart rails that's thicker than the others and painted bright blue. "I wonder where the pretty color standout goes?"

Hunter rolls up next to the osprey on a small cycle type vehicle. "Liliana, Formalia, help!"

Kita and Formalia turn their attention to the window.

Formalia grabs her gunblade. "What is he doing back here?"

Hunter runs up to a broken window. "I just went to Rogue's crashed airship, keeping my distance away from you two until things cooled off. But while walking through walls, I found more survivors in a part of the wreck that's caved in. Six crew are still alive, and they're trapped. They need your Venator strength to get them out."

Liliana jumps out of the osprey with her gunblade in hand; she heard every word. "I'll do it. Prepare to receive them." She grabs Hunter by the back of his neck and drags him away from the window. "You're coming with me for your last ride; we'll save them, then you and I have a date, where you make up for all the crap you put me through."

Hunter lets her drag him to the back of the osprey.

"This is for causing me trouble." She kicks him in the crotch then slams his head into the floor. "Stay down, if you know what's good for you."

Hunter groans and rolls onto his back. Soon the osprey's engines roar to life and he can feel the aircraft lifting up. "There's something else." He crawls to get closer to her.

"You don't take direction well." Liliana rolls to the side to throw him around.

"Stop it! The paranormal activity stopped at some point

before sunset last night!" Hunter shouts.

Liliana levels out and looks back at him. "That's not saying much."

"I couldn't walk through walls anymore, and whatever had been messing up my mind stopped at the same time. I don't know what caused it, but I got trapped in the wreck and had to break my way out. Then I had to dig that cycle out of the cargo hold. That's why it took me so long to get back."

I don't know what its connection to the corporeal world is. But you might be right about its existence. I've simply never paid the detail any heed.

"I've already figured it out," Rogue mutters. "Don't stress yourself over it."

You know what it is?

"You told me when you said it can see me like a damn beacon," Rogue replies. "And I've seen it. The shadow figure has the skeleton of a man, but the skull of a lion."

Great, what is it? I'll help you kill it. What about, if I help you kill its connection to your world, would you be a little more open to giving me control over how I separate myself from you?

"Kill it? No, if I'm right, nothing in this world can take it down," Rogue replies.

The Gigas Archon that approached you after you crashed. The same one that took out the Juman airship.

"The same one tailing the transport." Rogue gives the back window a quick glance.

Give me time to think of a plan.

"You can do what you want; I know what I'm doing when we get to Ghonda." Rogue turns his attention to the front of the transport where Minatra and Hondo sound excited. The Pyrite Nest is coming into view. "Looks like we're just a few hours from there."

Guariana walks back to him. "Isla's going to order the crew to stop at Ghonda, collect the information from the operations center and refuel, and then she's leaving. Seems the crew on board already rounded up everyone from the tundra after Titania's first attack. If we're not ready in the time it takes them to do their thing, she wants to leave us behind, in order to take care of her people."

"That's fine. You said Formalia and Liliana have an osprey, right? The one they took when the Mistress abandoned the Luscious?"

"They'll be chasing after Titania."

"I can sense Hunter in Ghonda. They're there. We'll catch them," Rogue interrupts her.

She blinks for a moment. "You... can sense him?"

"Yeah... somehow. He's not far from Ghonda. He's moving, but not fast enough to be in an aircraft," Rogue replies. "Regardless, I agree that we shouldn't put her people in danger. You and I can figure this out."

Hondo overhears Rogue. "Your highness, the Juman have murdered many of our people; we can't let them walk away consequence free," he whispers in Isla's ear.

"The one they call Titania," Isla says loudly to Guariana. "Will she return to Ghonda, do you think?"

"Depends on what we find at Ghonda," Guariana replies. "But I can assume that is likely."

Isla looks at the airship ahead of them. "We'll discuss this when we know more."

Hondo is frustrated but nods. "As you wish."

A quick point of observation. You look like a demon. Care to switch? Going incognito and all might be of some assistance here.

Rogue rolls his eyes then glances at his arms. "You got a point there. Do anything out of line, and I will make you regret it."

Guariana's calm demeanor changes when Rogue's body returns to normal, and his face carries the grimace that Dr. Lourcer uses. "About time you came out."

"I'm not answering questions about intention. I'm simply blending in for our benefit," Lourcer says.

Isla watches him change back to clear skin and normal eyes. "Are you certain you aren't Rogue when you look human?"

"As has been said before, Empress, I did not choose

which aesthetic this body develops. Unless you'd like to explain to everyone on board why Rogue looks like a monster. This is for the sake of simplicity. Nothing more," Lourcer replies.

Isla hugs as many people on board as she can, while making her way through the crowded walkway to the bridge. "I'm so thrilled to see everyone! We're going home!" she shouts.

Lourcer claps along with the cheering researchers.

"I had no idea there were this many people out here." Guariana stops counting after a hundred people.

Hondo grabs her arm and grips it as tight as he can. "There are two hundred and seven people on board. "There should be nearly twice that. Show some respect." He shoves her against the wall.

Lourcer slides between them. "Rest assured, they will get their justice, Hondo. When this Titania person gets to Ghonda, we can-"

Hondo pokes Lourcer's chest as hard as he can and presses him to the wall. "And you, I didn't like you to start with. Well, Rogue, the person who was born in that body. Actually, scratch that. Both of you are piles of shit. I think you're far more dangerous than Isla is willing to see. While she's with her people, she has no need to have you around."

"We'll go to a cabin and stay there until summoned," Lourcer says quickly.

"Not good enough." Hondo backs up a few steps and a pair of soldiers come up with shackles in their hands. "You'll take the secure cabin. It's called the brig. I'll be kind and let you share a space together. Just the three of you, all to your lonesome."

Lourcer offers his hands in front of him and gestures for Guariana to do the same.

She reluctantly follows his lead.

Hondo yanks her gunblade off her back and puts the tip at Rogue's neck.

Archon's Wake

Guariana restrains her anger but does little to hide her thoughts.

"That makes you angry, doesn't it, bitch? You seem like you might actually care for this pathetic Acinvar man. What's the matter? No muscly pilot men in Juman catch your fancy?" Hondo digs the tip into Rogue's neck, drawing blood, as a large machine gun opens out of his back and aims over his shoulder at Guariana. "And you, no ghosting or touching me, else I'll do her in."

"You don't need to threaten us to get what you want. We'll do it peacefully," Lourcer replies.

Hondo digs deeper and twists the blade while keeping his focus on Guariana. The two soldiers with him exchange concerned glances. "It's not about that. It's about pain and suffering. It's about hurting Juman as much as possible. If I could make her cry from watching Mr. Whip die, by the gods of all, I will do it. Lucky for you, Isla wants him for other reasons. Take them away, and don't stop by the medical bay, he can make that wound heal itself, as we've seen already." Hondo slashes the side of Rogue's neck and watches it heal over. "Hmph."

The soldiers take them to the rear of the airship, with Hondo following behind them. He stops the one escorting Guariana before they enter. "I've got more to say to this filth."

Guariana doesn't react.

Hondo spits on her face, then uses his thumb to smear it around on her cheek. "There, that speck of dirt was annoying me. We're done." He gestures to the soldier to put her in.

Rogue and Guariana are pushed into a cell made of steel on all sides; thick bars lower from the ceiling halfway. The soldiers hold Rogue's and Guariana's shackles so they're wrapped around one of the bars when they lower into the ground.

"He's wearing my nerves thin. I can tolerate buffoons and suffer some humiliation for show, but I might need to return the favor later," Guariana mutters.

"It certainly isn't helping my image of them right now. Rogue says he will make it up to you when this is over," Lourcer replies. "I beg your pardon, but I'm not saying that in your place, have some decorum," he whispers.

"When this is over. If things were going to plan, I'd be taking Rogue on a train over the southern coast of Juman right now. We call it the Flaming Coast. Sunset on the water is an enchanting sight; beautiful as can be. I'd have liked to show it to him." Guariana looks over at him with a pained expression.

"I know the coast you speak of. It is worth one's life to see a clear autumn sunset. High tide once every three years, when two of the moons are full and rise in the sky after the sun fully sets. You see this magnificent fire on the sea and are treated to a moon glow that reflects off the water, and the shimmering shells on the seafloor below."

Are you trying to piss me off? I mean, really *trying to piss me off? You're bringing up the Eve of Twins with her now? You know I lost someone I loved on that night. Remember?*

Guariana closes her eyes. "It's my favorite night. The Eve of Twins. We don't do festivals like what Heart does. It's not really celebrated on Shell, but it's, well, that's something I'll tell him directly. No offense, Lourcer."

"None taken. It's a shame your culture doesn't celebrate it. We used to go all out. I'd go to that coast every third year just for the view. My daughters loved it dearly," Lourcer replies.

It used to be my favorite night. Every year my mom would take me to the Acinvar Lunar Festival. And even after she passed, I went and always had a great time. Until nine years ago.

"Something wrong?" Guariana asks, when she sees Lourcer frown.

"Rogue's memory of that night is dark. He lost someone important in a heinous act of violence."

Wait a minute, hey, drop it Lourcer! I can't help it if bringing the topic brings the memories to mind, but don't share them, please!

Guariana looks at him in surprise. "That's horrible. Family?"

Don't. Not now! I like her, I want her, but I don't know if I need her in my life all the way yet. That's not something I would share at this stage. I haven't even had a proper date with her, so don't.

"That's for him to say when he's ready. He's screaming at me, currently."

Damn straight I'm screaming at you. You did it to me all night the

Archon's Wake

first day you were stuck in my head. I was nice, but this is my body, and those are my memories. It's my life you're visiting in the sickest, most invasive way possible.

"Stop it, Rogue. Yes, I know I was annoying at first, but I know better than to tell her your wife died nine years ago," Lourcer whispers, as quietly as possible.

SHUT UP!

Guariana audibly gasps and looks away. She wants to tell Rogue how sorry she is, but decides not to.

I swear, I'm going to put you back in your body just to kick your scrawny old ass with my own hands. You better hope our separation either wipes me away or puts you back in your damn prison.

"Control isn't easy when emotions are running high. I can't think; remember, you're in the thinking chair. I'm in the doing chair. It came out," Lourcer says.

"What was her name?" Guariana can't help but ask.

Switch us, NOW!

Hondo walks into the brig with a set of new soldiers; his face is red with anger.

"Something the matter?" Lourcer asks.

Why the hell couldn't he have barged in here ten seconds ago?!?

"Her highness wants you both on the observation deck," Hondo says, through gritted teeth.

"She has no idea you've arrested us, I take it?" Guariana asks.

"Why are you all the way back here?" Isla walks into the brig.

"We asked for a cabin to ourselves. Hondo was generous enough to bunk us here," Lourcer replies.

Isla takes a deep breath to control her anger and embarrassment. "Hondo, if they're not out of there by the time I finish this sentence, I swear upon my life I will have you thrown in front of a penguin!"

Hondo fumbles through a key ring to open the cell and take their shackles off, but she finishes speaking before he finishes with Guariana's. "I will sort this out properly."

"No. You will not," Isla replies in a cold, dead tone. She turned to Lourcer and Guariana. "Come, let me introduce you to the captain, who will see to it you are treated properly as my guests. Because you are guests. Hondo, what does the word guest mean?"

Guariana walks up to Hondo and takes her gunblade off the strap around his back and looks closely at the blade tip. "Thank you for cleaning it for me. Looks better than a spit shine," she whispers to him.

They follow Isla along the length of the airship to the flight deck.

"Terry," Lourcer whispers to Guariana. "She was a brilliant scholar of the botanical sciences."

You can't drop it, can you?

"What is there to keep hidden, Rogue? It's part of who you are, and a larger part than you admit to yourself. If you're truly ready to move on, you'll open this door. Coming from someone who's experienced similar pain and succeeded in making himself whole again. I understand your pain, which is why it surprised me so when I came across the memory in your mind. It pained me in that moment which is why I said what I did. For that I am truly sorry. If there is any lesson you'll take from having an old man in your head, it should be that your darkest moments are a strong foundation to build light from. I lost my first wife Hoyamata to an act of war. And it took seven years before my heart would flourish again. This new woman by your side should be given the chance to know where your rock bottom is, so she can bring you up. As my dear Meiko did for me. You already are aware of her rock bottom. A child sold by her family, for a mere week's worth of food. Your rock bottom is that your wife of three years died in an arson attack at the Acinvar Lunar Festival on the Eve of Twins. Arson also claimed your mother when you were fourteen. You both have overcome these events as individuals. I intend to leave you both to overcome them as partners," Lourcer says, at regular volume.

Guariana keeps a blank expression on her face while Lourcer speaks. "I'd prefer that you stop inserting yourself into our lives, Lourcer."

"I've said my peace," Lourcer replies.

Isla does her best to mind her own business, but hearing their conversation makes her look at Rogue with a new mindset. "I can arrange for separate rooms if you need," she says directly to Guariana.

"I'll be fine. I'm taking what's said with a grain of salt, given it's coming from a body snatching specter who supposedly died four hundred years ago. Besides, I think I heard Rogue give me permission to damage his body for Lourcer's remarks."

Uh, actually, yeah, I'm good with that.

Lourcer shrugs. "If you must. The message was more for him, anyway."

I'm angrier on principal than I am at the context.

"Once we land, of course. I don't want to spill blood all over your fine airship, your highness. Your cleaning crew doesn't deserve that mess." Guariana walks faster to join the empress.

Once we land, we switch and stay switched. I don't care that I look like a demon. She at least hasn't shied away from me. And that's saying something, because I can't even with these eyes in the mirror. Also, you're wrong. HAVING AN OLD MANIACAL MASS MURDERER SHARE MY BRAIN AND BODY IS THE ROCK BOTTOM MOMENT OF MY DAMN LIFE! Seriously, you are nothing but a trauma generator!

Lourcer remains quiet for the rest of the walk to the bridge, giving the women ahead of him some extra space as they chat.

"Is everything alright, your highness?" The captain asks, when he sees her unsettled expression.

"Nothing that concerns you, my good and reliable friend. Captain Norte, meet Rogue Whip, pilot extraordinaire and famed hydra slayer. And his guardian, Guariana," Isla says.

The pilots and crew in the room look up from their work at him.

"It's an honor to have you both aboard." Norte shakes their hands. "I thought you'd be on the observation deck, your highness."

"There seems to have been a mix-up with accommodations. I need you to have this sorted at once, if you please," Isla replies. "I need to have a quick meeting with my security team, then I'll return to the observation deck."

"Of course, your highness; it is my honor," Norte replies, with a slight bow.

"There are some researchers who would like to meet you, Mr. Whip. You'd be doing me a great service in appeasing them once you're settled in. In fact, I insist on it," Isla says, before she storms down the hallway as Hondo is coming toward them.

"Your high-"

Isla slaps Hondo as hard as she can. "What in the absent mind do you think you attempted just now?"

"The Juman-"

"Guariana. You will not call her 'the Juman,' or 'a Juman;' you will address her by her name. And furthermore, do not dare degrade her again!" she shouts, and slaps him again. "How dare you! She offered to assist in detaining the one who murdered my people. She offered this to me in private, before we boarded. That is why I asked you to look after them. I specifically tasked you with this. You failed me, and worse, you possibly jeopardized the one chance we have to give justice to those whom Titania killed. You are no match for a Venator, despite what you think you can do in that noisy, rusty, piece of crap you're wearing." Isla stops, out of breath.

Hondo gulps and stands at attention. "I understand, your highness."

"I'm not convinced of that. Return to the brig until I summon you. Before I order you to jump overboard at elevation without that silly thing." Isla storms past him. "Soldiers, see to it he is located where he is ordered. He so much as lets his breath leave the brig, I need to know immediately."

The soldiers following Hondo give him a surprised look. "Uh, sir, right this way, please. Her highness's orders."

Hondo sighs. "I hate this tundra. It's making everyone crazy."

"They've been gone a while," Kita mutters.

"Too long for my taste. Seven hours, really?" Formalia is quick to say. "I'm going to walk the perimeter."

"I'll be here. Making sure lunch is cooking." Kita smiles and stirs a small pot of boiling water and looks over at Cinder. "Let's make some Black bean chili. Not quite for kitties, but we won't tell her if I sneak you some."

Formalia gets halfway down the street when she spots the Pyrite Nest airship approaching the town.

Twenty minutes go by and Kita strokes Cinder's fur. "She's never taken more than a few minutes to sweep the perimeter. It's going to be alright. It has to be alright. You made it as long as you did on your own, right?" She hugs the cat tight.

"Kita? Kita Reinhart?" A voice calls out.

She turns her head to see a group of people walking in with a medical stretcher coming her way. "What? Who are you guys?"

"It's ok, Kita." Formalia walks in after them. "They're the researchers from the Blooming Sandseas. They're here to take you home."

Kita grips Cinder tighter and tears up instantly. "It's over? This nightmare is over?"

The men move her to the stretcher.

"Is she the only one?" one of them asks Formalia.

"Yes, she's the only survivor here," Formalia replies.

"What about the survivors Hunter talked about? You can't leave them!" Kita pleads.

"From Tradewinds Goliath? They're already on board. We picked them up before we landed here," another man tells her.

"Was there a man named Edward with them?" she asks.

"Ed made it," Lourcer says, as he walks in. "So did Duncan, Shelly, Rico, Wayne, Carla, and unfortunately, Nick."

Kita gawks when she sees Rogue walking toward her. "I thought you were gone. The Jumans, they took you, Rogue! What happened?"

"Turns out the archons really like destroying red colored airships, but don't care for beige." Lourcer walks up and gives her a hug the way Rogue would. "I'm sorry you got hurt."

"I think this will be the last time I come along on one of

your rescues," she says to him.

Lourcer nods. "Tell Empress Amenaza I'm going to finish up my business here."

"You're not coming with me?" Kita asks.

He shakes his head. "I've got a paranormal problem that I need to sort out before I can leave. It's a serious one."

"No! Nothing could be so serious to keep you here!" Kita cries.

Lourcer, it's time to switch.

"Please don't freak out. I promise I'm alright," Lourcer says, then coughs until he vomits black oil. Rogue's veins turn jet black, and his eyes glow green.

Kita stares in horror, and the medics look away, but they act like they've seen this before. 'Uh. I. Whoa. That looks serious. I'm freaking out," she rambles.

Rogue places his hand on her. "It's alright."

Kita feels her body go numb and her flesh moves in her side where her rib was yanked out, her toes grow back, popping her foot bandage off, and her leg doesn't feel pain anymore. She takes her bandages off and stares at her healed skin. "You picked up some magic. Uh, exactly how'd this happen and is it permanent?"

"I hope not. It's a long story; I'll fill you in later," Rogue is quick to say. "But I owe it to you to make sure you get home in one piece. Guys, she's all yours; get her onboard with everyone else."

"Yes sir, Mr. Whip." They push the stretcher out of the building.

Formalia stares at him in shock. "Uh, that… wow, what a party trick; does Guariana know about this?"

"Oh yeah, she knows. We're both going to need a lifetime of therapy to get over this experience. Well, I will. Anyway, Liliana said that tracking down Titania was your task, right? You need to go help her talk down Isla Amenaza and her head of security. They want to arrest her for her murdering spree on the tundra. Specifically, they want her dead," Rogue replies. "Guariana has already agreed to help them arrest her. But the goalpost is moving."

Formalia nods. "Thanks for the heads up. Good luck with,

Archon's Wake

uh, figuring out whatever that is. Your eyes glow like the penguins, you realize that, right?"

"I'm well aware. It's been good for spooking people." Rogue follows her out but stops to hang back for a few seconds. "Thank you for doing right by my crew. But that doesn't make up for the gaffe with Guariana this morning."

I'm well aware the chances of my surviving what comes next are nonexistent. Chalk my behavior up to last acts of will in the hopes it does something productive. I was ripped from my time four hundred years ago. I've lost my family, my world, and my body. Apparently, my soul is next.

The shadow figure rises from the floor behind Rogue.

I'm not prepared to return. I'd rather any other outcome.

"You earned your prison," Rogue mutters. "Tough shit if you're not prepared."

"I see many. I see plenty," The Shadow Figure says.

"You see one, you see me," Rogue retorts. "We see the same, we see the need."

"Cost is high, price not paid," The Figure says.

"Fee is fair, offer is made," Rogue retorts.

"Terms in stone. Reflect and choose." The Figure vanishes.

I'm lost. What is happening?

"In exchange for letting Isla fly her researchers and my crew away safely, I guarantee it gets you back," Rogue says aloud.

You can't guarantee that. I can't even guess what happens when we reach my bomb and reverse detonate it.

"I'll figure it out from here. Stay back and wallow in your fate. It's my body, my life, and my future that's at stake." Rogue hurries to catch up with Formalia.

"It'll take us three hours to refuel and then we'll be headed to the Shimmering City. We'll arrange for the transport of your people back to Acinvar from there," Norte says to Rogue on the flight deck.

Rogue nods. "That's all I ask. They're aware I'm not

coming along."

"If you can sort yourself out in time, we'll gladly take you," Isla replies. "This bout with Titania is not your business."

He glances over to Guariana. "I uh, need to ride back with the Venators. Take a breath from all of this and see a few sights. I admit I need time to think about what I am going to tell my CEO about this trip, because she is going to tear me more than a few new ones." His joke garners a few chuckles from the others in the room.

Guariana has a small smile on her face and makes eye contact with him.

"That's settled then." Hondo bangs his chest. "The security detail and I will wait here with Formalia and her warriors to apprehend Titania."

"The terms of her arrest must be sorted out now," Formalia demands.

Hondo nods. "Agreed. Being on the same page will make this simpler. We arrest her, we take her to the Blooming Sandseas, we try her, and we execute her."

"You may arrest her, but you will not take her to the Blooming Sandseas. You will take her to Black Sand City, since the arrest is made on Hurluan soil, and it will be up to King Soto of Hurlua to make the determination of custody. You will be permitted to make your case to the king. We will assist in apprehending her on your behalf. Her only defense from us will be presenting the king with her military orders," Formalia says back, fiercely.

"Tradewinds Compact does not apply here!" Hondo slams his fist on a nearby table.

"No, Hurluan law does. If you leave with her in your custody without their direction and permission, Hurluan authorities will come to retrieve her, and that will force an unnecessary confrontation. One Juman will gladly provide military assistance for," Formalia says. "I am not saying it is impossible for you to receive your desired execution, but I am demanding you follow proper procedure."

Isla shakes her head. "King Soto's son invited us as his guests. You invaded."

"True. Which one would assume would lend itself your

Archon's Wake

way in the king's court," Liliana adds.

"Hold your tongue, sister. This is not your conversation," Formalia snaps.

Hondo's eyes narrow in anger at the Venators. "It's an unnecessary delay. More opportunities for Titania to escape, no doubt."

"We're not ruling that out. In fact, we're not ruling out that she can escape your custody before you leave the tundra," Formalia says. "Right now, we agree to apprehend her for you. Not keep her detained. But that can be arranged. You are speaking of holding a Venator in your grasp. One who has no regard for you, and Titania is as capable as any Venator. Your highness, my point is this. You will do this our way to attain your desired justice. Because the alternative is that you will lose more lives to something your people are not capable of handling."

Minatra clears his throat. "Hurlua's laws are clear on the matter. While that should be the end of it, I agree with the circumstances around Formalia's request. We can't win against a foe like Hurlua, much less Juman, who is capable of going toe-to-toe with Acinvar's might, in case Hondo needs a reminder."

"There's also the matter of Juman's spies among my ranks. Including my own security detail," Isla replies. "What say you to that?"

"Those actions are the result of orders from the Inner Council of Security in Juman. Black Sand City is but a train ride away for them, putting a Venator in their custody will force the council to send a representative to do one of two things. Either they will show their hand and make it clear you have an enemy in Juman, or they will discuss the matter with you in a manner that seeks a resolution. In either case, you will find the justice you desire for your people can be had with greater simplicity," Formalia says.

"We've done nothing to Juman!" Hondo shouts.

Formalia keeps her tone calm and controlled. "I know not what that answer is behind Juman's actions. It's above my pay grade, as they say. But at this moment, I must insist on procedure and order. I offer my condolences for the people you've lost. I also offer my agreement that Titania's acts can be considered a heinous crime as the basis for this cooperation."

"I've had enough of this crap!" Hondo raises his voice even louder.

"You are well reasoned and generous, Formalia." Isla raises her hand to cut Hondo off. "I accept your suggestions and requests in full. Hondo, I order you to bring Titania to King Soto. I will ensure Minatra is there to establish our grievances, accusations, and evidence. Meanwhile, I will prepare for the inevitable conversation with who I assume will be the Maroon Mistress."

"If necessary, I'll make myself available as witness to the desecrated corpses and trail of blood we followed from Ihuit to Ghonda," Rogue cuts in.

"Watch it, delivery boy," Hondo says, through gritted teeth.

"Can you not control yourself today?" Isla asks him. "They've admitted Titania's acts have gone too far. They're willing to sign a Cooperate de Tare. I want justice for my people. I want peace in my land. You seem insistent on blood alone, and I cannot tolerate it. Not from you. These Venators desire peace more than you do."

"What is the method of transport you have in mind? Your rotor wing vehicle will not fit my men," Hondo says, in a forced calm tone.

"I will send transport once I arrive in Black Sand City," Minatra replies. "Captain, it seems we will need to drop me off at Black Sand City to arrange this in a timely manner."

"It's a twenty-hour flight one way, if we're to avoid the gigas archons. So, you're looking at nearly two days," Norte says.

Formalia nods. "So be it. Are we in agreement then?" She offers her hand to Isla.

"Thank you for giving your concern to my people. It gives me respect for you." Isla shakes her hand. "We'll leave behind any supplies you want."

"May I ask one thing?" Formalia keeps grip of her hand.

"Of course," Isla replies.

"Why did you come out here, chasing the Harbinger

Archon's Wake

Weapon myth?" she asks.

"I honestly can't remember. In the Ihuit laboratory, Lourcer, through Rogue's body, erased long periods of my memory. I have nothing more than glimpses of great pain. Sensations of horror and fear; my body trembled, though I don't remember why. Hondo tells me I was obsessed over my own protection. That I was a victim of a famous torturer. One who must've put such fear into my heart to make me treat irrational actions as reasonable. But I have nothing to fear anymore; it's been told that said torturer was murdered. By none other than Rogue Whip." She stops after saying his name and stares at him. Her lip trembles. "Have I started a war with Juman? By coming here? Was Juman who I feared?"

"Formalia, I can attest to that. Lourcer did wipe her memory clean. I even witnessed Rogue further heal her body clear of Albert's scars," Guariana says, before Formalia can reply. "We know Rogue is currently experiencing some unusual phenomena that grant him extraordinary abilities. You've seen this firsthand by now, yes?"

Formalia puts her free hand gently over Isla's. "That makes this simple then. I will advise my Mistress that your intention out here was what you stated to Prince Cal. A scientific endeavor to better understand the nature of the tundra on his behalf. Done in a manner regarding dealings that are between you and the prince alone. We will be sure to include this in the agreement that is submitted to King Soto for consideration of Titania's fate. Our invasion of his land against a non-military operation that has no dealing with us will certainly carry weight in the direction of a desirable decision for you."

Isla looks over at Hondo. "It will be in writing. Can you please not be the one who messes this up?"

Hondo unfolds his arms and kneels. "Forgive me, your highness. I will take you at your word, Venator Formalia. You know Titania best; I will follow your direction and advisement on her capture and detainment."

Oof; can I just say, that was painful to watch him say?

Rogue stifles a laugh at Lourcer's remark. "You're not wrong," he whispers under his breath.

Several hours later, Hunter walks up to Liliana in the osprey; she's working on something in the cockpit. "Formalia said you wanted to see me."

Liliana shakes her head. "No. Why the hell would I want your ugly mug around?"

"Sorry to bother you then." Hunter turns around.

"Sit," she demands.

Hunter sighs. "I'm sorry, again."

"I said sit." Liliana pushes him into the copilot's chair.

Hunter makes himself comfortable. "I'm on my ass, what's next?"

"Could do with less attitude, set your snark to zero." Liliana forms a fist with her hand then lowers it. "You did good today. Wanted to say I'm glad you found those people."

"It's not every day you get to save lives, not destroy them," Hunter says over her.

"It's a good feeling. Shit, I can't do small talk with you. It angers me. What do you know of Hondo?" Liliana turns her body to face him.

"You mean from my days under Richtoff? Of course that's what this is about." Hunter chuckles. "You're right not to trust him. I don't know much. But I know when Isla's parents were murdered by Richtoff, he mysteriously wasn't in country to defend them. And he ordered his security thin that day. He's unreliable, when it counts."

"That much is obvious," she replies coldly.

"Hey look, I was under contract with the Suran government at the time, putting down rebellion leaders. I don't know much," Hunter reiterates. "The whispers I heard were that he's all bravado. Frankly, what I've seen of him in the past few hours doesn't discount that theory."

"I'm not comfortable with letting my sister get executed for following orders," Liliana replies.

"I agree with you and Formalia. Hell, Guariana had some ideas that made me shudder. Hondo must've royally pissed her

Archon's Wake

off. When are you gonna spring on him and his men?"

She shrugs. "Formalia wants to leave his men out of it. I could care less. His exo suit... it's Yensi tech, right?"

"Magnetic gears and electric powered, with a hydraulic mainframe. He can easily lift a ton and move as fast as a champion boxer. But he's still no match for any of you in a serious situation," Hunter replies.

"If he somehow does force that to happen, and we don't defend her, you'll make up my anger by breaking her out when we get to Black Sand City..."

"...and get her to the safehouse where the Mistress is staying. Formalia said the same thing after Isla took off. I got you; your sister will be by your side when this is done. I promise," he cuts her off and finishes.

Liliana smiles a little. "I think that will help me start to forgive you." She pats his shoulder. "What did they leave for food? Any idea?"

"I heard the soldiers saying something about cactus stew in that makeshift mess hall of theirs."

Liliana's face scrunches at the idea. "Ugh, nope. Cactus Stew? Really? Desert people are weird."

"I'll grab us some meat if I can find it." Hunter laughs.

"Yes, thank you. Real food, please." Liliana's stomach growls.

Rogue walks down a dark cavern with a spark light in his hand lighting the way. "We've been down this cavern a few times now. Your memory is shit."

Watch it again, then.

"I know you changed it. You're making sure I don't find the lab."

Boo-hoo. I don't want to go back to that thing.

"You are pissing me off."

Don't care anymore.

Rogue looks behind him to the paved pathway that leads from the Rim Cart station to Ghonda's Underground area. "I know what's right. It's an offshoot of this cavern."

It's not right, right, or left, not left, but right, not right. Idiot.

"These are really your last words?"

Left, left, left right left.

"The most intelligent man of his time and he is only now figuring out which side of his body is what." Rogue studies the crevices hard and slowly walks deeper into the cavern. Taking it step by step and flashing the spark-light in all directions.

The Shadow Figure rises up ahead of him and points.

That's cheating! A clear breach of your agreement!

Roge follows the shadow figure, until they reach an offshoot of the cavern, and walks to the end of it.

There's really nothing I can do to make you reconsider this. Fine, we'll die then.

Rogue's hands wither down to the bone, and his skin and flesh turn to dust. He focuses on regenerating his body. "Oh no, you don't."

I'm sorry, but I'm not going back; I'd rather die.

"Well, well, well. What do we have here?" Titania comes up behind Rogue and watches his hands wither and regenerate. "That's spooky. You don't look like you're up to finish our stroll from earlier."

"I need your help. Please," Rogue says. "The Harbinger Weapon Lourcer made is here."

Titania laughs, puts her hand on his shoulder and swings around into his view while holding a strange object made of Norgut Metal, with glowing blue features. "I have it in my hands, darling. Isn't it lovely?"

"That's the device he used to reverse engineer his mechanical weapon," Rogue replies.

It can't be. She actually has it. How does she have that!?

Titania gives him a curious look. "Alright, I'll bite." She lowers herself to his eye level and bites his cheek seductively. "How do I make this weapon appear? Tell me now, while I'm in a good mood."

"Stalagmite with mushroom top. Push down. Twist right," Rogue grunts.

How can you match my proficiency of using my abilities? Lourcer tries to force Rogue's brain to wither away inside his head.

Archon's Wake

Rogue drops to his knees and fights to stop it.

Titania feels around the rock formations until she finds one that presses down and makes a clicking noise. She twists it to the right and there are several more mechanical clicks inside the cave wall. A handle-like object pops out. She turns it and pulls. The cave wall opens up to reveal a room similar to the one in the Ihuit lab with the reverse magnetized pillar. The walls are made of frosted and lenticular glass and lined with thick metal plates. Electric lights flood the cavern, making it as bright as day. In the center of the room is a massive metal sphere on a pillar, with several mechanical consoles surrounding it and thousands of wires jutting out of the sphere and going up into the ceiling and down into the floor.

"Oh-ho! Oh my goodness, Rogue, baby, damn you delivered. I knew I liked you from the moment we met!"

If she activates it, everyone on the surface will die the way I did! Not lying!

"That's why we're reversing it!" Rogue replies.

"What are we reversing?" Titania turns around with a puzzled look on her face.

Rogue realizes a problem. "I'd have to fire it from the other dimension. To get this thing out of me."

Titania looks around her, searching for an answer to his awkward babbling. "Ok, I assume some super fucked up shit is going on with you. I mean, your veins are popping out of whatever is left of you and you're oozing black oil like a machine, and those green penguin eyes are a bit of a trip. Ruins the whole vibe for me." She grabs his neck with her bare hand. He puts the memory of Lourcer forcing himself into his body into her head.

"Help. Me," he pleads.

Titania's smirk fades and she gets serious. "You're serious. Ok, yeah, uh, how, exactly do we get you into this other dimension to use this?"

"Get me inside there," Rogue says as best he can, while screaming in pain.

Titania picks him up over her shoulder with her free hand and heads to the doorway, but something is stopping her, pushing back as she tries to force her way in. She sets Rogue down and is able to walk inside without a problem. "That's not going to be easy."

You'll be dead before she figures it out.

Titania looks around the room then at the weapon in her hand. She fiddles around with it until it shoots a bright flash of light at the wall. She then points it at Rogue. "Let's try this!"

No! Damn that woman! If this is my fate, at least you're forced to always remember me.

Rogue closes his eyes and braces himself. He feels a pulse ripple through his body. His body stops withering from the inside and he feels it regenerating. Then his whole body goes numb, and he loses consciousness for a few seconds.

"Hey, wake up." Titania's voice echoes in his mind. "Yeraputs to Rogue, did you die on me?"

Rogue opens his eyes and rolls over to cough.

"Had me worried there for a few seconds; you dropped like a brick." Titania holds him on his side. "Easy, don't choke."

He spits out normal blood. "It's blood. It's blood! Not oil!" He laughs. "It's not oil!"

Wait, if I'm here, and she's here, that didn't work. Damnit, how the hell am I going to get this bastard out of my head? Lourcer I swear to… wait a minute, I'm thinking.

"To think, I'm excited over blood coming out of a body." Titania lays him flat on his back. "You alright, now?"

He looks up at her. "I can think to myself. I can think to myself!" He wraps his arms around her and hugs her tight. "That got him out of my body! You did it!"

Titania pulls his arms off her. "Hey, easy; you put a lot of your memories into my head."

"I only gave you the memory of Lourcer getting inside me," Rogue says. "What'd you see?"

"You gave me far more than that." She helps him to his feet, but keeps hold of his hand. "Can you still give or take memories? Just as a test, I mean."

Rogue tries to focus on a memory and the sensation he felt of sending it to her. "Anything?"

"No."

"Ok, guess not," Rogue replies.

"Good, because otherwise I'd be slaughtering you right now. I don't need any man being in my head more than that. You owe me big. So, save my life." Titania throws his hand out of hers and pushes him back. "So, the matter at hand, this is his weapon. Not very portable. How am I going to get this to my Mistress?"

"It's a dimensional bomb. Cables lead to geothermal power generators all over the magma pit caverns," Rogue says. "Hang on, how'd you get here? Ghonda is covered in soldiers."

"Rim Cart Station isn't. Took it from Ihuit to here. It was a six-hundred-mile trip. Then I had to scour these caverns for where Albert Richtoff dumped this thing. Took me a whole day I think; got lost in here. Then I saw you wandering around. Caught up to you in time to save your lucky ass," Titania answers.

"I'm grateful for that," Rogue replies.

"Are you?" Titania grabs him by the neck and lifts him up to her eyes level. "How grateful are you?"

"What. Are. You. Doing?" Rogue tries to speak while gasping for air.

"I saved your life, which means I missed out on a dying breath." She puts her lips close to his. "What does Rogue's dying breath taste like? I need to know."

Rogue grabs at the dimensional weapon when her lips touch his. His grip and her pulling it away activates the device, causing a blinding flash of light. His body feels heavy and tight; the same sensation from when the penguins first glared at him, and he's instantly exhausted.

Titania's body feels drained of energy and weak. She can't stand under the weight of her armor and collapses.

Rogue lands on his back and her body falls on him. "Ouch. Damn, your armor weighs a lot!" He struggles to move her off him. He gasps for air when he finally succeeds and discovers she's unconscious. "Ugh. Not good." He can't keep his eyes open and passes out with her.

8: Light Another Fuse, Run Like Hell

Dawn rises the next day and Guariana wakes up before anyone else in the osprey. Liliana and Formalia are sleeping in the cockpit chairs, and Hunter is tied up to a soldier's bench in the back, snoring like a chainsaw. "Rogue?" She doesn't see any sign of him. "Something's wrong. I need to find him." She stretches and quietly leaves the aircraft.

She rushes down the street as a few of the soldiers are getting some exercise in. "Morning fellas! Has anyone seen Rogue has come back up yet?"

"Haven't seen him, miss," one of the soldiers replies.

"Try Hondo; I know you two don't get along well, but if Rogue returned, he'd be the first to know," the other says.

The idea of speaking to Hondo makes her sick to her stomach. "Right. Just how I want to start my day."

She walks by the makeshift mess hall that's in front of the barracks.

The man sitting by several oven pots covered in hot coals waves to her. "Morning, Guariana!"

The smell of coffee and something sweet make her come closer. "Morning, Ferdinand. What's for breakfast?"

"Doing something a little different this morning. Found a few bags of flour, and used that with the molasses, ginger root, and a pinch of sugar, to make some ginger bread. First batch will be ready soon," he replies, and opens one of the oven pots to let her smell.

"That smells so good. So was the Cactus Stew last night. You're an amazing field chef." Guariana looks over at a steaming pitcher full of fresh coffee. "May I?"

"Of course." He reaches into a crate and hands her a clean mug. "No sign of your guy, though. Hope he's ok. I know Hondo and a few guys were doing something with the underground entrances. No idea what, though. Seemed real hush-hush about it. He's holed up in the ops center right now."

His remark gives her a bad feeling and she sprints to the operations center, dropping her mug in the street. A few soldiers sidestep out of her way while she runs inside. "Has anyone seen Rogue?" She asks the pair of soldiers by the door.

"No, ma'am. But we have to ask you to leave the building," one of them says.

"He should have been back by now!" Guariana barges past them and heads for the entrance at the back of the warehouse. She growls in frustration when she sees it's been sealed off with discarded junk.

Hondo steps up to her while laughing. "Took you a while to come see my project. Good morning. I have to advise you that I will not let him come back up here. His unnatural abilities are a threat to us, and potentially to you. He's definitely a threat to himself. This is a matter of safety and taking precautions. When we have Titania and the transport, then I'll let you search for him."

Guariana shakes her head in disbelief. "How could you?"

Hondo grins. "It was easy. We just broke up a bunch of tables, grabbed things from the dismantled vehicles in the next building over and piled them up in the stairways. All eight entrances. Not to worry though, he'll be safe when the shooting starts. Least he won't die to friendly fire. Right?"

She looks at the pile of debris. "Did you kill him?"

"No, and that's a baseless accusation." Hondo points his

finger at her. "Watch yourself, bitch."

"What about food or water? Did you at least ensure he has that if he comes this way?" She is trying to keep control of herself with every fiber of her being.

Hondo shrugs. "Did anyone think of that? Did we make sure we left him anything before we started?"

The soldiers around him remain silent.

"Guess not. To be fair, we were more concerned about our safety, not necessarily his. But hey, he is a famed survivor of extreme situations, right? He'll be fine, I guess. Maybe. Who cares? Now get the hell out of my ops center." Hondo gets in her face.

"I should've gone with him. I should've known you'd do something like this," Guariana mutters to herself.

Hondo laughs heartily. "Well, you could beseech me to let you join him. I have no qualms about burying you both together. Go ahead, politely beseech me to order my men to open it up and let you search for him. Go on, beg! Haha, Everything I've ever heard of Venators and there seems to be only one of you out here doing that reputation any service. Sure isn't you. You're pathetic."

Guariana calms down visibly; her face and body become devoid of all emotion.

"Whoa. Look at that, boys; made her calm down right quick. Guess we're about to see a mighty warrior get down on all fours and beg!" Hondo laughs.

She gives him a thousand-yard stare that sends chills down his spine. "Your men will clear that entrance, organize a search party, and bring him to me, alive and well,. If they know what's good for them. And when they're done? You will grovel at my feet and beg for mercy."

Hondo's toothy smile beams from ear to ear. "That finally sounds like a threat. And when I beat your ass to a pulp? I'll do whatever I want to you. Then I'll go find that fool Rogue and make him watch me cut you open and butcher you into pieces, before I put a bullet in his head. And I'll came back up and beat your sisters into a broken mess to set an example for that Titania bitch. I'm gonna do some dark shit to that unfortunate woman."

Archon's Wake

Nearly all of the soldiers in the room back away from them. "Clear the underground passage! Quick!" someone shouts.

"Hondo can take her! Hondo can do anything!" another soldier shouts and pumps his fist in the air.

Guariana grabs her gunblade and fires at the soldier's fist. It pops into a bloody pulp. She lunges at Hondo, jamming her blade into the machine gun coming out of Hondo's arm and cuts through the mount at the same instant she's parallel to his side. She thrusts her free hand into his gut.

Hondo barely saw it happen. One instant she was standing before him, now she's next to him, a soldier is screaming somewhere to the side, after a loud gunshot. He hunches forward in pain and his mouth opens to scream.

She jams her fingers into his mouth, grabs his bottom jaw, and presses her knuckles against his upper lip. His bottom jaw dislocates as she pulls forward. Then she pulls her fingers out of his mouth, and slams his jaw shut with her palm. Most of his teeth crack and break apart from the force she's using.

In one smooth motion she wraps her fingers around his face and pushes his head backward then down to the floor. She digs her fingers into his nose, breaks it, then rips the flesh upwards, tearing it off. Next, she rolls her hand along until her knuckles are on his forehead, presses down until she hears his skull crack, but stops before she does enough to kill him.

Hondo can't make sense of what's up or down; the attack is too fast for him to keep up with. His whole face is screaming in pain, and he can't breathe through his mouth or nose. When his mind catches up, he's on the ground and sees her standing over him, turning her attention to his men who've begun shooting at her.

Guariana shoots her attackers in quick succession. Most of the soldiers drop their weapons and raise their hands, while a small handful decide to engage. Their bullets strike her body and bounce off her armor. After a full sweep she puts her weapon away. "Those of you who chose not to engage me have heard what I want. Get to it!"

Hondo tries to sit up, but Guariana puts her foot on his chest and kneels on him. The weight of her armor crushes his chest.

"What's the matter? Jaw ripped off your skull? All your pearly teeth broken up? Your nose is missing; should get a bandage on that." She grabs his shoulder, digs her fingers in, and dislocates his shoulder with ease. She puts her other knee on his good arm, letting her armor's weight press down into his exo suit and do the damage.

He can't breathe; he can barely tell what's going on. "No," he manages to stammer out in a gurgled plea.

She puts her hands on the sides of his head and strokes his eyes with her thumbs. "You don't have permission to lay your eyes upon me." She presses her thumbs into his eye sockets and gouges them out, then takes hold of his eyeballs after they pop out and rips them all the way off his head. She returns her hands to the sides of his head and digs her index fingers into the ear canal, destroying his sense of hearing.

"Ma'am please. Just put him out of his misery," a soldier says, in a shaky voice.

Guariana looks up at him and gets off Hondo, who makes an audible gasp for air.

The soldier takes several steps back and raises his hands. "Please, he was wrong to do what he did, yes, but he don't deserve to be tortured."

She shakes her head. "I should be doing this far slower."

Hondo rolls over and starts crawling away. Something resembling a whimper is coming from him.

"Toma, don't get involved, help us clear the entrance," another soldier says, while rushing past him.

Toma lowers his arms and turns to help.

"I'm not done with you Toma." Guariana's words make him freeze in fear.

"Ma'am." He trembles and looks down at Hondo feeling around him, leaving a large smear of blood on the ground.

"Find whoever is next in command and bring them to me. Inform them of Hondo's mistake. Can you do this for me?" She leans in close to him. He whimpers and cowers in front of her.

"That would be him. Coyaru." Toma points to a man who's still gawking at the scene with his mouth open in disbelief. Toma puts his hands in front of his face and bends his knees to lower himself.

Coyaru barely registers her assault, it happens in seconds. And now she's got him in her sights. Her face is heart attack inducing.

Guariana steps on the back of Hondo's neck and twists her foot, breaking it to put him down for good, as she walks over to Coyaru. "I'm told these are your men now. Is that correct?"

Coyaru hears her, but is too terrified to understand.

She grabs him by the neck and lifts him up to eye level. "I asked you a question."

Several more armed soldiers rush into the warehouse after hearing the gunfire.

"Hold your fire!" Coyaru screams.

Guariana uses her free hand to wipe Coyaru's spit off her neck. "What is it with you desert people and spitting your words?" she mumbles. "Go, explain to them what's happened. And let them know I'm very happy to take on dissenters."

Coyaru looks at his men in terror. "Don't engage! I repeat! Do not engage!"

Rogue's mind is filled with thoughts and memories of someone else. A young woman crying on a metal table, in a room made of porcelain tile with a single oil lamp burning in the corner. "Why am I being punished? I didn't do anything wrong." Rogue hears the words but can't make out who's saying them.

A man comes into view. "Hello darling, you are a special one." Rogue recognizes him: Lord Albert Richtoff.

"Please, let me go; I'll be good. I promise!" a little girl's voice cries out. "Not the punishment table!" He can feel her struggling against the metal cuffs chaining her down.

"You misunderstand, dear Tabatha. You are not here to be punished. You are going to become a better version of yourself. Your Mistress asked me to help you join the

Venators. A great honor. Can I tell you a secret? Just between us?" Albert takes a seat by the table and scoots closer.

"I'm going to become a Venator?" Tabatha asks, and Rogue can feel the girl's sudden excitement. Ideas of an all grown up woman, in Venator armor standing like a hero, pop into the girl's head.

Albert smiles and nods. "Yes, you will. But here is the secret. I do not always hurt people. Your Mistress gives me girls like you every year to turn into strong, powerful people. And you are one of them. But do not tell anyone that I made you a better person, alright? I need to pretend that I do nothing but make people scream." Albert tickles Tabatha's side while he speaks with a kind voice. "Can you keep this secret?"

Tabatha gasps. "Well, yeah; no one would believe me if I said you were secretly nice."

"I suspect you are correct." He stands up and leaves Tabatha's view.

Tabatha lays her head down and daydreams of all the strength she'll have. "A Venator. Wow."

Several years flash by in an instant. Glimpses of people screaming and begging for mercy flicker in his mind. All of them are being murdered. And the more murders he witnesses, the more he feels the murderer wishing for freedom.

Rogue opens his eyes to a sleeping Venator curled up with him, using his arm as a pillow. "Guariana?" He says with a yawn, then realizes the woman has long red hair, not short brunette.

Titania rolls over and wraps her arm and leg around him, cuddling him while tightening her grip.

He tries to wiggle his way out of her grip. Her hand flattens out on his chest and presses him down, stopping him from moving.

"Excuse me?" She opens her eyes and looks at him with a hurt look.

"Titania. Wait, we-"

"Shut up." She presses down on his chest harder.

"How long were we out?" Rogue asks, while trying to breathe.

"I said shut up!" She sighs and looks away. "It's probably

been a while; feels like a day but I don't care. I woke up a few minutes ago. Your arm was comfortable, so I got cozy. Too cozy." She presses down on his chest and leans in close to his face, her eyes staring deeply into his. "Calling her name out in that soft, gentle, pleasant tone. Completely ruined my moment."

"I am sorry." Rogue gently grabs her hand. "Please."

She slaps him across the face, grabs his neck and leans in closer. "When a woman cozies up to you, at least get her name right."

"Ok, Tabatha, I'm sorry." Rogue says, before thinking. He relaxes and stares at her in awe.

Titania is stunned, her feigned hurt expression is now real. She moves her hand and leg to sit up and stare at the floor. "Did Guariana seriously tell you my name?"

"No, woke up knowing that. I could see your memories in my dreams. Paranormal abilities must still be lingering," Rogue says, when he sees the Harbinger Weapon above his head.

"Don't ever say that name ever again." She turns fully away from him while screaming and fighting back tears. "That girl died. Long ago. You have no right to say her name!"

Rogue gets to his feet and picks up the Harbinger Weapon. *And I thought Isla was a mental case.*

"When I found that thing, I was overjoyed. If it does make people vanish, I could use it on the Mistress. I could be the hero I always wanted to be. Not the brainwashed murderer. I don't like hurting people. But this tundra, this place, I loved it. I was the monster I feared. And I was getting so damn excited about it." Titania throws her gunblade out into the caverns.

Rogue places his hand on her shoulder. "You asked me to save you back, right?"

"That's an impossible ask; I was fucking with you. You were nothing more than my next thrill. Till you grabbed that." She gestures to the Harbinger Weapon. "I woke up feeling like myself. The calm, closeted girl I am. After two days of being something I'm not."

Rogue nods. "This place has been changing everyone's personalities. I've been a lot more aggressive and passionate here than usual. I wonder if what Guariana and I have is even

Daniel Jones

real."

Titania wipes her nose. "About that. How are you still here? You should be on a train to Black Sand City by now."

"The Luscious crashed."

Titania jumps to her feet. Her face lights up with excitement and she grabs his shoulders. "What!?" She stares at him in disbelief until she realizes he's being serious. "Please, tell me the Mistress is dead."

"She left in her Alticopter. Sent Hunter and two Venators, I think their names were Liliana and Formalia, to look for you. Guariana was with me when an archon attacked."

Titania looks away and holds herself tight, obviously terrified. "You're saying my Mistress survived."

"Yeah. Yeah, she did." Rogue looks out to the caverns. "Look, uh Titania, I could use your help."

"With what?"

"I can't let your Mistress have this bomb." Rogue gestures to the giant orb thing in the middle of the room. "It's not something we can destroy, but I can bury it. And I'd like your help."

She stares at the Harbinger Weapon in his hands. "What about that?"

Rogue shrugs. "Seems portable to me. Might come in handy later, I guess."

Titania straightens up and stands at attention. "Venator Tita-, No. Tabatha Farsides, at your service, Mr. Whip."

Rogue backs up and gestures the caverns. "I'll take Tabatha or the Titan, either way, ladies first, grab your weapon. I have a feeling we'll need it. The plan is to go to Ghonda's third sub level, D wing. We're activating the town's self-destruct."

Titania gasps in shock and grabs his shoulder tight. She wants to stop him. He can't do that. "You're out of your mind. Do you know what that mechanism does?" She gives him a concerned look and sees the determination on his face, it genuinely scares her. "Of course you do. Rogue, we can't outrun it!"

"There's an osprey with your sisters and Hunter up there. That can outrun what I'll be setting into motion," He retorts.

Archon's Wake

She keeps a firm grip on his arm and pulls him back. "Stop, for a second. This town's self-destruct makes the whole area implode into the magma pits. This location wasn't selected by accident; it's a choke point that will cause a volcanic eruption." Titania looks up. "We've been out a while. It could've been hours or days; let's at least check the surface before you do this."

"It's not just to bury this place. Besides, we have to set it in motion first, otherwise it'll be impossible to escape that thing." Rogue points to the Shadow Figure, which has reappeared in the caverns.

Coyaru walks up to Formalia. "Everyone's on edge after Guariana's actions."

"We tried to give you all the support we could. Hondo thought it would be a good idea to trap Rogue underground," Formalia replies, as calmly as she can. "Everyone was aware of her orders to protect Rogue. The men who died this morning, including Hondo, were killed in accordance with that directive. You can't wiggle your way out of it."

"We're not trying to," Coyaru is quick to say. "At the time, Hondo's argument seemed well reasoned. Rogue does have paranormal things going on and could become a literal monster. Even you must acknowledge there's no guarantee he won't be a threat."

"We're done. You can arrest Titania on your own. Be warned, she'll slaughter you all, unless you beg for mercy and find ways to amuse her. Liliana, you and Hunter need to protect the osprey, I'm helping Guariana get Rogue, we're out of here!" She puts her hand on Coyaru's shoulder and brings him down to his knees. "If your men put so much as a scratch on my bird, or my sisters, you'll find out what a Venator leader does for fun long before Titania gets here."

Coyaru is about to respond when the bellowing roar of a gigas archon in the distance cuts him off. "Fine, we'll stay out of your way. Good luck getting past that thing."

Daniel Jones

Liliana and Formalia look up to see a massive archon pass in front of the sun, its shadow darkens the entire town for a few seconds.

Gunfire erupts across the town and guards are screaming one word in terror. "Penguins!"

Titania walks beside Rogue with her arms folded, keeping her focus on the side of the hallway. A quake causes the floor to rumble. She can barely stay on her feet.

Rogue stumbles and bumps into her. "Whoa!"

She catches him and grabs the wall. "Maybe you don't need to pull a lever after all."

The sound of an archon's roar is followed by several smaller tremors that shake the sublevels.

"There are still people up there," Rogue replies.

"Damnit." She pounds the wall, putting a huge fist size hole in it.

Rogue gets off her. "You ok?"

"No, I'm not. This means we have to leave your way," she says, after a quick moment of silence. "Hang on to that device. Don't let it get buried. I can't go back to my Mistress empty handed."

"I think she'll understand the circumstances." Rogue hurries down the hallway.

"That won't stop her from punishing me for my failure,." Titania mutters. "I can't endure that again."

"We're not far! Come on!"

Titania sits down and stares at the ceiling. She's not about to hand herself to her Mistress, only to die on sight. That will likely be the cost of her failure. "Go on without me."

Rogue looks up when another tremor is joined by the sound of a building getting crushed. "You want this, or not?" He holds up the Harbinger Weapon.

"You're not that stupid." She huffs and gives him a quick glance. To her surprise, he's coming back for her.

Another tremor knocks him down. He slides the weapon

Archon's Wake

at her. "It's yours if it gets you moving."

She rolls her eyes and picks it up. "You don't get it, do you?" She looks down at the weapon.

"What is there to get?" Rogue is back on his feet. He offers her a hand, but she bats it away.

"The punishment for failing a second task in one's life as a Venator is death. I've already done so once before." She puts the weapon back in his arms.

"She ran, Titania. The Maroon Mistress ran like a coward. She's not so invincible after all." He puts the weapon back in her hands. "Anyone else would look at your actions over the past two days and give up on you. And as sick and twisted as it is, I choose to see past that. Damnit, you have allies. Me, your sisters on the surface. My heart might belong to Guariana, but damn if I don't see a woman before me, who could become a hero one day" Rogue says, to try to get Titania moving.

She looks away. "Are you done? Then fuck off."

"Fine." Rogue nods. "Don't come with me. Stay here and die. Anyone you could save in the future loses." He leaves her side and runs to an intersection up ahead.

The ceiling comes crashing down and Titania yanks him away from it in the nick of time.

Rogue looks at her. "Thank you."

"You did that on purpose." She lets go of him and slaps him across the face. "Eventually I'm going to stop saving you."

Rogue looks to their left. "There. Those double doors. We pass that and we're in the security center."

"That looks jammed. Hold my prize for me." She hands him the Harbinger Weapon and cracks her knuckles.

Rogue watches her rip the doors off their hinges and throw them his way. "Showoff."

Titania grabs her gunblade and shoots at something out of his view. "Penguins! Stay back!"

Rogue runs past her. "I got this!"

She watches him run past several penguins with glowing eyes. "Hey! I can't do that!"

"I see you here. I see you clear." The Shadow Figure emerges in front of Titania. "Soul of wrath, bringer of rage."

She backs away from it. "Rogue! Help!"

Rogue turns around and watches the Shadow Figure grab her. He aims the weapon and fires. The bolt of light strikes the figure and makes it vanish. Then he starts using it on the penguins. Each of them vanishes; warped away into another dimension, until the whole hallway is clear.

Titania rubs her neck and walks up to him. "Nice save." She shoots over his shoulder at a penguin without looking at it. "Guess I have to stick with you; that shadowy thing has a taste for me, it seems."

Rogue aims the Harbinger Weapon behind her and fires, the bolt of light misses the penguin, but Titania's bullet doesn't.

"New rule; I kill small waddling birds. You zap big bad, easy-to-hit ghosties." She walks past him.

"I'm more of a swordfighter than a gunslinger." Rogue leads her past the security checkpoints until they reach a heavy puzzle vaulted door.

"There's no way I'm ripping this off its hinges." Titania fiddles with some of the knobs and studies the design.

Rogue puts his free hand on the door and closes his eyes. The device in his other hand glows brighter and he walks through it.

Titania stares at where Rogue was just standing. "Just when I thought he couldn't get any more interesting. Hey, you better let me in! What if that thing shows up again?"

Rogue enters a room full of desks, with consoles of all kinds lining the walls. Pipes and intricate gear mechanisms hang from the ceiling. "This isn't the security room! This is the heat management room," he mutters. "Whatever; this looks like the right place from Lourcer's memory."

"I see you here. I see you clear." The Shadow Figure appears again, next to Titania.

She shoots at it with her gunblade, but it turns into cloudy vapor, before her shot can hit its target. The vapor engulfs her body and seeps into her nose and mouth. She swats the air around her and tries to cover her nose and mouth, but she can feel her lungs fill with what feels like smoke.

Rogue finishes turning a dial on a console, and a large slot in the wall next to him opens. It reveals a large, red-handled lever, labeled MELTDOWN PROTOCOL, behind several layers of glass. Rogue punches through them and yanks the lever down.

Electric rotating lights in the room turn on and an airhorn siren sounds.

Formalia jumps out of a building before the archon stomps on it. "Shit!"

The archon roars at the next building, shaking it with its infrasound and shattering every window in range.

The roar is debilitating this close, even for her. Some guards come out of a nearby pile of rubble and shoot at it, getting its attention.

The archon inhales to prepare a dedicated roar, when airhorn sirens start going off around the town. Instead of roaring, it growls and visibly tenses.

Liliana jumps out of the rubble behind her and grabs Formalia's arm. "That's not good!"

"What's not good?" Formalia asks.

"If my Shiv language skills are right, that's the meltdown siren. The desert folks had a description of this in their ops center research," Liliana answers.

"This place can blow up?" Formalia grabs her by the shoulders. "Are you certain?"

"It's worse; it doesn't blow up. Magnetic plates reverse magnetize and shake underground at various geologic weak spots. It implodes the caverns and magma pits beneath Ghonda, to clog a high-pressure magma river deep underground. It's going to build up pressure very quickly, and that's what blows up," Liliana says.

"Shiv's meltdown protocol is cracking open a volcano?" Formalia gawks, as Liliana nods her head.

Titania coughs and drops to her hands and knees.

Rogue ghosts back through the door. "It's done."

She slams Rogue into the door then shoves him into the ground. "I was the one who made Lourcer disappear. Such was your charge. Now, I am its instrument, and I will exact the cost."

Rogue aims the device at her, and she punches him in the face, then kicks him into the wall. His head spins and he slumps over.

She stomps on his leg. "I have men to murder, sisters to slaughter, and a master to please. But you may watch it all. You have set this place's demise in motion. That will end mankind's desire to trespass into my domain. I cannot cross the final barrier between us, but I will still choose who dies and in what order. I've chosen you to die last."

The archon's paws slam through the ceiling ahead of them, and lift back up, causing large piles of rubble to fill the hole it made. Titania heads to the surface behind it.

"I'm getting out here, and there's nothing you can do about it," Rogue groans.

Titania looks behind her and grins. "I love that you believe that." She walks back to Rogue. "This woman, she tends to provide acts of tenderness before one passes, yes?"

Rogue punches her in the face. "I'm done getting kissed by her."

Titania touches her cheek where Rogue hit her; she's bleeding. "You die first." She throws a punch back at him, but her fist goes through him.

He punches her again and grabs her chest armor, yanking the plate off and kicks her in the stomach. "You have her body, but you can't hit as hard."

"Rogue!" Guariana shouts, from farther down the hallway. "I've been searching everywhere for you!"

"Guariana! Run! Get out of here!" Rogue screams.

Titania laughs and watches her climb over the collapsed rubble to get to him. "Sister, welcome; how are you?"

"She's a Shadow Figure! Not Lourcer, but worse! Evil possessed! Evil possessed!" Rogue points at her.

Archon's Wake

"Spoiler alert!" Titania smacks him; this time her hand hits him and she knocks him into the wall again. "Oh, well."

Guariana grabs her gunblade. "Get out of my sister's body. And don't you dare touch him again."

"Make me." Titania lunges at her, passing through her gunblade and grabbing her neck.

Guariana struggles in her grasp, but can't grab her.

Rogue aims the device at Titania and fires it.

Guariana breaks free of her hold.

Titania jumps at the wall, using Guariana's shoulder to balance herself and get above her head. She drops down, wraps her leg around Guariana's head and pulls it sideways, forcing her off balance and positions her knee on the back of her neck.

Guariana rolls into her as they land, causing Titania's knee to slam into the ground. She grabs Titania's side and throws her off.

Rogue grabs Titania's gunblade and slashes at her from the side.

Titania grimaces as she looks at her sword, sticking in her gut at Rogue's hand. "All this does is waste time. Time you don't have." She rips her sword through her and screams at Rogue with an archon's roar. The Harbinger Weapon glows in Rogue's hands. She slashes her blade at him, but he runs through her body and runs to Guariana.

"We gotta run like hell!" He helps Guariana up and leads her up the pile of rubble to the surface.

Titania removes the sword from her side and follows them.

Rogue and Guariana reach the surface; most of the town is completely leveled.

"This place got flattened," Rogue remarks.

Guariana can't believe her eyes. "It didn't look this way this morning."

"How are Hondo and his men handling things?" Rogue runs a down the street but can't recognize where in the town he is or where they're going.

"I killed that son of a bitch, cleaner than he deserved," Guariana says coldly. "He pushed me too far."

"Really? That's awesome! I wish I could've been there to

see it." The sound of sirens and gunfire are all over the town with the archon smashing buildings and roaring at soldiers wherever it finds them.

Gunfire goes off behind them. They turn around, expecting to see Titania.

"Where have you two been hiding? Let's go!" Formalia shoots some penguins coming out of a large pile of rubble near them.

Another gunblade shot goes off and Formalia stumbles forward and falls over, lifeless. Titania is holding her gunblade outstretched with a big grin on her face.

Liliana comes out from behind Formalia. "Friendly fire!"

Guariana shoots at Titania's head, but she deflects the shot with her gunblade. "She's compromised!"

"Nothing you do can save you!" Titania looks at her gunblade; Guariana's shot destroyed the revolver mechanism.

"Rogue, get the osprey going, pick us up here. We'll deal with our sister." Liliana reaches into her chest armor and holds out an ignition plate to him. "Hunter can lead you to it."

Rogue grabs the plate and sprints to Hunter, who's waving them down.

Guariana and Liliana stand side by side.

"Defensive only. Drag this out. Keep it here. We're buying time," Guariana whispers.

The archon roars in their direction.

"While also not getting eaten or stomped on, being surrounded by penguins who make people poof into nothing? Yeah, sure, why not?" Liliana replies.

"The hell is going on over there?" Hunter asks.

Rogue fires the device at a penguin that pops out in front of them. "A shadow figure has Titania. Yes, I said shadow figure, and yes, it's exactly what you're thinking."

Hunter's eyes widen and he sprints down the corridor. "A what has who!? She doesn't need any more power!"

The archon leaps to the sound of gunblade fire behind

Archon's Wake

them. Its landing causes tremors that knock them off their feet.

"And take a wild guess what this shadow figure is linked to." Rogue helps Hunter back to his feet.

"Why are you so calm about this?" Hunter looks up at the gigas archon and drops his shotgun.

"Because I have a plan." Rogue gets back up and shoots another penguin ahead of them. The Harbinger Weapon's blue glow dims, so Rogue panics and the glow brightens. "Think this thing is running out of energy. How far to the helo?"

Huh, that's odd. Why'd it do that?

Hunter sprints past him. "It's in front of the warehouses. Archon bypassed the whole street by sheer luck."

A soldier runs out in front of them and shoots at them with an assault rifle. "This is all your fault!"

Rogue aims the Harbinger Weapon at him and fires. The soldier vanishes into nothing, leaving only his clothes and weapon behind.

Hunter takes cover behind some rubble during the shooting. "Damn! I'm hit!"

Rogue runs at the rubble the guards are hiding behind. Their bullets whiz right through him. He grabs one and throws it at a penguin in the street below. The startled penguin's eyes glow and the guard vanishes. He fires the device at the other soldier. "Can you make it?"

"Maybe." Hunter looks at his leg, the shot is through and through, but he's bleeding like crazy. "I need help!"

Rogue comes back down and runs to him.

"Still got that healing trick from earlier?" Hunter asks.

"Maybe." Rogue focuses on replicating the sensation from when Lourcer was in his body, but nothing happens. "Nope. Come on, let's get you out of here."

Liliana ducks under Titania's swing and Guariana counters a strike with her gunblade. The two of them back up from Titania.

"How long can you two keep this up? Because if Rogue

activated the meltdown, we should start to see the effects, right about..." She throws her weapon to the ground and looks southward. "Now."

A huge quake shakes the ground, causing piles of rubble to spread out. Enormous chunks of ice and rock shoot into the sky in the distance south of the town.

The archon looks at it, roars, then leaps into the sky.

Titania uses the distraction to close the gap and tackles Liliana while swiping at Guariana's gunblade. In one swift, smooth motion, she slashes through Liliana's throat. "Made you look, little Lili."

Guariana pulls Titania off, but not before it's too late.

Titania laughs. "As I told Rogue, I choose who dies, and in what order. But don't worry, I'm still debating who dies first."

Guariana sprints to the middle of the street and tries to follow Rogue's tracks.

A small band of guards shoot at her and Titania.

Titania's body turns into a skeleton cloaked in a hazy shroud of dark gas and wails in their direction, making them vanish in an instant.

Guariana feels her head shake from the figure's wailing infrasound. Rubble collapses and scatters, blocking her path to follow Rogue.

"There we go! Let's finish this dance in peace." Titania's body reforms.

Guariana punches the ground and runs toward Titania. She dives when Titania tries to swing her sword and slides across the ground. When the blade passes over her head, she twists her body to sweep her leg into Titania's, knocking her to the ground. Then she puts her hands on the ground, swings her body up to pivot around and scrunch her body down.

Titania looks up in time to see Guariana's knees come down toward her head.

Guariana's attack goes through her.

Titania rolls away and gets back up. "Wow, that attack could've killed me, sis. Had no idea you had it in you"

Guariana kicks her leg back up and rushes at Titania with a continuous handstand flip. She picks up an object from one of the dead guard's bodies along the way and high jumps at

Titania when she's close enough.

Titania raises her fists and staggers her stance. "Foolish!"

Guariana dodges Titania's punch on the way down and slides the object under Titania's back armor and tucks into a rolling landing then dives behind a few big pieces of rubble.

Titania explodes from the grenade Guariana stuck in her armor.

When Guariana looks up, Titania is standing where she was, in nothing but her black cotton body suit and armor below her knees; the rest of her armor is scattered across the street. "Fuck! Thought I had you."

Titania chuckles. "Whew, that was flashy, and good too! Had I not realized what that was, I'd be gone. Got any last ditch attempts? You got time for maybe one more."

Rogue and Hunter get inside the osprey, where Rogue drops Hunter on a bench and runs to the cockpit. Outside the windscreen, he sees the archon is already far in the distance, flying away as fast as it can. "Yeah, that quake was just the first phase."

"How many phases are there?" Hunter takes an ammo belt and tries to make a tourniquet on his leg.

"Two; ten minutes apart," Rogue replies.

Hunter straps himself in tight. "That's cutting it close."

Rogue gets the engines turned on and the rotors start turning. "Open the loading bay!"

Hunter growls in frustration and unstraps himself, then scoots along to the back and pulls on a lever to open the loading ramp.

Rogue slides the Harbinger Weapon back to him. "Here! Use this to hit Titania; won't kill her with that thing inside her, but it will slow her down enough to give Guariana a chance. And whatever you do, don't shoot the wrong one."

"It's gonna be rough." Hunter picks up the weapon. "Hey, this is made of the same stuff as the facility in Camp Tor!"

"Yes, it is!" Rogue pulls on the controls and takes off.

"How does this thing work?" Hunter looks over the weapon and grips a spot towards the back; a bolt of light shoots out. "Never mind, I got it!"

Guariana's face slams into the ground, Titania's body rolls over her and she lands flat on her back.

Titania kneels on her chest armor and gently taps her cheek. "Oh my, I feel him coming this way, finally. You need to keep breathing. I want him to watch."

The osprey gets louder as it flies over them.

Rogue looks down at the street to see Titania waving to them while kneeling on Guariana. Liliana is lifeless on the ground, further down the street. "Shit."

Hunter fires at Titania when he has a good line of sight. The bolts of light cause Titania to stumble and fall off Guariana, who's not moving. "You're going to have to land!"

"I know!" Rogue shouts. "Keep Titania down!" He swings around and looks out the back while he brings it down in the middle of the street as close as he can to them. He grabs the Harbinger Weapon from Hunter and jumps out the back. Firing it a few more times at Titania to keep her on her hands and knees.

"Haha. That's annoying but it's not removing me. But that's fine." Titania forces herself to get back up. "It's fine. I have no more use for this vessel. You can have her back."

The ground shakes and shifts beneath them. Plumes of dust are rising in the distance and shooting into sky around them.

Rogue grabs Guariana and tries to lift her up. "Damnit." He searches for how to unhook her armor. "Guariana, you gotta get this off, so I can carry you!"

Guariana's vision is blurry, and she barely registers Rogue's voice. Titania gave her a serious thrashing.

"Yes, struggle in futility," the Figure's voice says from Titania's body, as it turns back into the shadow figure, rising above them with its arms outstretched, emitting massive plumes of black, hazy smoke from its body. Titania's body falls out of it, and she coughs the same way Rogue did when Lourcer was ripped out of his body. "I see you here. I see you clear. The end is here."

The device glows blindingly bright in Rogue's hand. He aims it at the shadow figure and a beam of light fires instead of a bolt. The Shadow Figure blocks the beam with its hands. "Affects me not; I am already home."

Rogue can feel the weapon reacting to his anger. "You want the barrier broken? Come on over then!" He shouts at the top of his lungs. The weapon's blue glow and the beam of light turn lightless black. The Shadow Figure's hazy form retracts into a towering man's skeleton with a lion's skull on it.

The figure hesitates. "You brought-"

Rogue fires the weapon again, the weapon's glow switches back to a blinding blue light, and he fires the beam. "One last place you must go!"

The Shadow Figure's form gets hazy and it stares at Rogue with green hateful eyes as it vanishes. Huge plumes of thick smoke fill the area and retract back into the shadow figure where the beam is hitting it. The Harbinger Weapon pulses and sends a massive bolt of white light. The Shadow Figure vanishes without a trace.

Titania puts her hands up when Rogue aims the weapon at her. "I'm me! I swear! I owe you everything!" The ground gives out beneath several buildings nearby. "Get to the cockpit! Now!"

Rogue glances behind him as the osprey tilts forward.

Hunter pulls on the controls and pokes his head around the pilot's chair. "Already on it! What are you waiting for?!"

Rogue grabs Guariana and tries to lift her up but can't.

Titania grabs her and picks her up. "I got her! You get in!"

They sprint for the osprey, but the ground beneath them gives out. Rogue jumps and grabs the loading ramp.

Titania lands inside the bay and sets Guariana down. "Hunter! Punch it!"

Rogue pulls himself up and swings his leg around. "Close the door!"

Titania pushes the lever on the controls.

Daniel Jones

The osprey shakes as dirt and rubble shoot up around it.

Rogue gets to the cockpit to help Hunter get them off the ground.

"What was that beam thing?" Hunter asks.

"I don't know! Dimensional light or some bullshit!" Rogue flies the osprey forward.

Titania kneels at Guariana's side and takes her armor off. Guariana is bleeding from several serious wounds. "Hang on, sis; I'm here, and I'm not losing another sister today."

Hunter looks behind them. "I'll help back there, you got this?"

Rogue's jaw drops as huge geysers of lava burst out of the ice ahead of them. "Hang onto something!" He rolls the osprey to avoid the lava spray.

Hunter grabs his heart. "Holy shit! Oh God, oh god, oh god."

"Shut up, shut up, shut up," Rogue replies.

"We're gonna die!" Hunter screams.

"Hunter! I swear to all the gods, shut the hell up and let the man fly!" Titania hangs onto the side with one hand and is keeping Guariana steady in the other. "Hey! No more acrobatics! She'll die if I can't stabilize her!"

"Make it work, Titania!" Rogue raises his voice, but keeps calm, as he veers around bursting lava geysers and billowing plumes of super-heated smoke. "No promises."

Titania watches Rogue's calm demeanor for a second, then returns her focus to Guariana. "How are you holding up?"

Guariana reaches up to Titania and smiles for a second before her eyes close and her arm goes limp.

"Damn it. No" Titania grabs the chest plate and digs through several pouches. "Come on. Where do you keep it?"

Rogue tries to keep the osprey steady while climbing in altitude and moving forward. Several warning lights are coming on all over the flight console.

"Turbines are losing air!" Hunter calls out.

Rogue looks around the console. "I can't see how to fix that. Intake is at thirty percent; gonna have to make that work for now."

"Turn on the turbo reservoir! Punch it in full, see if that

clears the debris!" Titania finds a foil wrapped pill bag and tears it open, then shoves the pills into Guariana's mouth.

"That would run all that crap through the engines. I'd like to avoid blowing them up! This is ash and rock, not sand!" Rogue replies.

"I may have shot it earlier while hallucinating," Hunter says. "Liliana's repairs might not be holding."

"Of course you did," Rogue mumbles.

The ground cracks apart and huge parts of land sink into the ground, while hundreds more jets of lava shoot into the sky.

"This shit is getting scarier by the second!" Hunter says.

"We're almost free! Altitude passing two thousand feet!" Rogue calls out. "Titania, how's it look back there?"

"I could really use that hand now, Hunter! Search her armor's pockets for biofoam canisters and a pump!" She shouts. "I really did a number on her while that thing was in me."

"Rogue, four o'clock!" Hunter points before getting out of the chair.

"Yeah, I see it." Rogue spots the gigas archon hurtling toward them and points the nose down. "Gonna dare that fucker to follow us through the lava geysers."

"You're going to what?!?" Hunter and Titania say together. Hunter re-straps himself into the pilot's chair and covers his eyes.

"To think, people say I'm insane." Titania straps Guariana into a seat as best as she can.

The archon stops its attack when a lava geyser shoots up in front of it.

"I don't like this plan!" Hunter screams.

Rogue maneuvers around geysers of lava and pillars of scorching hot smoke.

The archon's roar shakes the osprey and makes the geysers of lava ripple. The vehicle shakes and rattles. The flight console's alarm lights flicker. Titania finds two biofoam canisters and the pump. She jams it into Guariana's deepest wounds and fills them up.

Guariana grabs Titania's hand. "Ouch, damnit that stings!"

Titania is relieved to see her awake. "I thought I lost you, sis!"

Guariana smiles when she realizes Titania is her normal self. "I won't die that easily."

"That thing is really pissed off!" Hunter says.

"Seriously, shut the hell up!" Rogue retorts.

"Why is it so hot in here?" Guariana gasps when Titania plugs another deep wound.

"Because we're flying through hell!" Hunter screams. "Literal flying fire hell!" Hunter grips the bottom of his seat and pulls as hard as he can on it. "Whose bright ass idea was it to turn this place into an erupting volcano? We're going to die!"

Titania comes up to Hunter. "Hey, look at me; you're not going to die. Rogue can do this; you'll make it."

Hunter stares at her, then nods. "And just in case?"

Titania kisses him gently on the cheek. "Calm down."

"Rolling right!" Rogue calls out, before banking hard.

Titania braces herself and puts one foot on the wall to stay upright as Rogue rolls, getting her first good look out the windscreen; she can't believe what she's seeing. "You might actually be out of your fucking mind!"

"I told you! We're going to die!" Hunter screams.

The archon swoops down in a gap ahead of them and gets ready to roar again. Its eyes are locked onto the osprey, and it looks confident that it's finally cornered its prey.

"Uh, shit," Rogue mumbles, when he realizes there's no room to maneuver.

A new geyser bursts into the archon's wing, burning it clean off. The archon falls into the pooling lava below.

"Take that!" Hunter screams, at the top of his lungs.

Rogue levels out the osprey as they watch the archon writhe around and roar in pain at it's showered in falling lava and ash. Another geyser shoots up; this one is too close for Rogue's comfort, so he veers away. "I'd say time to go, but every time I do, it gets harder to leave." He forces the osprey to its limits while veering around lava geysers, until he can get above them and the pillars of ash shooting into the sky.

It takes a few minutes for him to navigate his way through

the field to find a path above the smoke that doesn't involve flying through it. When they get up above the smoke, everyone cheers at seeing the clear sky and bright sun above them.

"Alright, let's get the hell out of here." Rogue looks back at Guariana, who's smiling at him.

Along the way, huge portions of the tundra have become volcanically active. Flocks of smaller archons are pushed toward the Ring storm. Many are killed by flying through the super-heated smoke and plumes of ash falling from the darkening sky. At the Ring storm, the archons can't fly high enough to go over it, and seem to pass out when the atmosphere is too thin to breathe. The ones that do try to fly through it are shredded by the storm's powerful and icy winds. The volcanic ash cloud forming across the tundra keeps getting thicker and darker.

As they're almost over the Ring Storm, Titania walks to the cockpit. "Hunter's leg is patched and he's resting. Guariana is stable, but she'll need the infirmary."

Rogue keeps his eyes on the flight console and the controls. "How about you? You alright?"

"I just had a, whatever that thing was, completely take over my mind and body. I lost, um, was forced to kill, two of my sisters."

"I'm talking that bump on your head. You're bleeding." Rogue reaches over and moves her hair aside to take a better look.

Titania runs her hand over the wound and looks at the blood. "It doesn't hurt; I'll be fine. I, uh... I'm sorry... for what I did back there. Before I got possessed. Never felt myself lose control like that before."

Rogue nods. "I am sorry for your sisters; they didn't deserve that."

"Your bearing is south, southeast? Not going to Black Sand City?"

"I am. But it will mean something to Guariana if she takes

me to watch a sunset on the Flaming Coast. Something about it being one of the best sights I might ever see. Can't pass that up. So, we'll land this thing in Bluewood Cove. Then play everything else by ear," Rogue replies.

Titania looks back at Guariana. "She loves that place. She's not wrong, it is beautiful."

"Sound like you got something on your mind." Rogue cuts to the chase.

Titania chuckles. 'Yes. Uh, having some temporal alterations is an interesting experience. I can't imagine how you dealt with it for as long as you did." She holds up the Harbinger Weapon. "The Mistress can't have this; she would likely do some questionable things that humanity should not have to deal with."

"Thought you had a plan. Sounded solid to me" Rogue says.

"She will order me to stop before I can strike. And my body will stop, even if I don't want it to. She'll take this from me when I can't do anything and make me vanish," she replies, a cold tone.

Rogue nods. "Then I've got a plan, if you'll trust me."

The Mistress watches the osprey land outside the large eleven-tiered pagoda that makes up the Venator's headquarters. A layer of ash, burn damage, and smoke are all over the vehicle. She puts her hands behind her back as the engines cut off and the loading bay opens. Titania comes out, helping Guariana walk, and Rogue is helping Hunter hobble. No one else comes out.

"Where are Liliana and Formalia?" The Mistress asks.

"They did not make it," Titania replies. "The Gigas Archon, and the Archon's Wake, brought them down."

"I see." She looks over at Rogue. "It would seem you are expected in King Soto's court. Regarding the matter of Titania's arrest."

"It's null and void. The whole tundra turned into a

volcanic disaster area. We had no choice but to come this way. It was, in my professional opinion as a pilot, unfeasible to take any other route," Rogue says.

The Mistress nods and waves her hand at the pagoda with two fingers raised. "That is unfortunate for the Blooming Sandseas. Did any of their security detail survive?"

"Excluding the survivors on board the Pyrite Nest. There are no loose ends," Rogue replies.

"Better. I will have to send direct condolences to Empress Amenaza." The Mistress eyes Titania and Guariana, as if she's passing some sort of judgement on them. "No loose ends seems for the best."

Several soldiers, in all white armor, come out of the pagoda. Two are bringing medical gurneys. They're quick to help Hunter and Guariana. The Mistress looks over Guariana before she's wheeled away. "Halt this one. The other may be escorted."

Guariana's face turns pale, and she looks over at Rogue with fear. "No," she whimpers.

"Mr. Whip, the narrative will be that you stole that aircraft and Mr. Smith navigated you here. Juman fatalities are complete; there were no survivors." She places her hand on her katana.

Rogue tenses up. "Hang on."

"Don't interfere." The Mistress warns him. "Otherwise, the narrative will alter further."

Titania gulps and kneels. "I understand."

"Step back, Mr. Whip." The Mistress raises her voice.

Rogue steps to the side a bit and uses his hand out of the Mistresses' view to reach into the back of his shirt. *Titania was right, I'm not going to have much time to stop this.*

Titania looks the Mistress in the eye and lifts her chin up to expose her heck.

"Titania has died. Juman has no need for Tabatha Farsides, a girl who disappeared from the Suri Mountains." The Mistress places her hand on her katana.

Rogue aims the Harbinger Weapon at one of the hypnotized soldiers and fires, making him vanish, armor and all. "Kill either one of them and you're next."

The Mistress looks at him in shock, as he aims the weapon at her.

"Don't." Tabatha shakes her head no. "You don't want to challenge her."

The Mistress steps back, removes her hand from her katana, sidesteps directly in front of Rogue and calmly approaches him. "I see there is truth to the myth after all." She grips her katana and slashes at Rogue; her blade passes through him like he's not there.

"This can end only one way." Rogue's ready to shoot her.

The Mistress bows deeply upon realizing her circumstance. "I accept my fate."

"I killed Richtoff, because it was required for my survival. I'd like to think you're more sensible than he was. So, here's the deal: Yeraputs doesn't need to be destabilized further by your death. So, just between you and me, free these two of your hypnosis. They can choose to come with me as I make my way back home. That's what I want, in exchange for a de-escalation between us." Rogue lowers the Harbinger Weapon.

The Mistress stands up and meets Rogue's gaze. "Very well, Garnet and Tabatha will have their freedom."

Garnet? That's a pretty name. Rogue looks over at Guariana before returning his attention to the Mistress. "I'm curious about one thing. Did you know it was Isla who set the events of Camp Tor in motion?"

The Mistress is visibly taken aback. "Did she?"

"She's rather fearful of people who were invested in Richtoff's work. People like you. That's why she sought this thing." Rogue holds up the Harbinger Weapon. "Consider that knowledge a gesture of goodwill. And whatever you choose to do with that knowledge, I have no intention of interfering; as long as it doesn't involve me."

"I will have to reflect on this revelation. Thank you." The Mistress looks over to the soldiers that stepped away from Garnet's gurney and nods. "Take her to the infirmary. Mr. Whip, you are not to leave Tabatha's side for the duration of your stay, which will be permitted up until the point when Garnet has recovered. Consider yourself a welcome guest of Juman. Enjoy your stay."

Aftermath: The Lurking Shadow

One month later, King Soto of Hurlua and Empress Amenaza are standing at the side of a pyramid monument, made from airship scrap metal. Four obsidian pillars at the corners of the pyramids' base represent the four nations involved: Acinvar, Hurlua, Blooming Sandseas, and Juman. Each bears the names of the people lost on the Harbinger Tundra. The Ring storm rages in the far distance. And the pyramid reads a simple message on all four sides.

> THEY QUESTED FOR KNOWLEDGE.
> SCIENCE WILL FOREVER REMEMBER
> THEIR SACRIFICE.
>
> THEY ANSWERED THE CALL. PEOPLE
> WILL FOREVER REMEMBER THEIR
> HEROISM.

Jessie walks up with a bouquet of roses, tears streaming down her face; she lays the bouquet at the base of the pillar, where the names of the eleven heroes from Acinvar who perished on board Rogue's airship shine with gold lettering. The families of the Acinvar crew are coming up behind her to lay gifts and flowers and say goodbye. She steps aside for them and joins the empress and king.

"I am so sorry for your loss." Isla gives her a long hug. "And I thank you. If it wasn't for Rogue, all of us would have perished in that volcanic eruption. My people saw more than two hundred loved ones return because of him."

"I can't believe it happened. Rogue left right in the middle of a business meeting when Prince Cal came to him. It was so sudden." She turns to face King Soto. "My condolences to you; your son was a great man."

"My boy made me very proud. I want you to know that Rogue, and you, and your company, and the families of these fine men and women, will always be friends of Hurlua. You will always be welcome here," King Soto says.

Jessie moves along so the royals can speak to the other families and looks over at Rogue, who's kneeling at the pillar where four names are emblazoned in red marble. He and the two tall women with him are the only ones who visited that particular pillar. Rogue places four red lotuses in a small bowl of water, and the women with him do the same. Rogue lights the candle in the center of each bowl and crosses his arms over his chest, grabbing his shoulders, and tilting his head down. It is Lotus Island's traditional sendoff, and something he's only done twice before.

Jessie comes to them and looks at the names. "Formalia, Liliana, Guariana," she whispers to herself. The fourth name is barely legible, with less colorful marble. "Titania."

Rogue stands up when he's finished. "This is really nice of the king."

"I'm still having a hard time believing it happened." Jessie wipes the tears from her eyes and hugs Rogue tight. "We've never had anyone die on our watch before."

"Their bravery was without equal," Tabatha says, reassuringly.

"I know. It's not what I want to happen. And it won't be the last time either." Rogue hugs Jessie back. "Every day, people get their airships hijacked by governments and militaries to do dumb shit like what we did. Too many die, and they don't have monuments like this to remember them. That's why my project is so important."

"I get it now," Jessie says. "I'm sorry I tried to shut it down. Just, this is hard. And I'm sick about it." She lets go of him.

"It's going to take me a while to recover from what happened. Mentally and emotionally," Rogue says.

Garnet holds his hand. "It's never easy to lose friends or family."

Tabatha leans into Rogue's ear. "Have you told her the truth of what happened?" she whispers.

Rogue shakes his head. "She's got too much on her plate. She knows she doesn't know the whole truth, but I think she's ok with that. If she says otherwise, we'll tell her," he whispers back.

"You know what, this time I don't want to know. Really," Jessie mutters under her breath. "At least tell me they didn't die in vain."

"Our crew died trying to rescue people. That part is true. And our presence was the catalyst for two hundred and nineteen people to survive. That makes them heroes," Rogue replies in a normal voice.

Jessie wipes tears away from her eyes. "Yes, it does."

A beautiful woman with long red hair and perfect skin in a black dress walks up to them. I AM HAPPY YOUR NAME IS NOT ON HERE, ROGUE. She signs, using Lotus Island sign language.

Rogue gives her a tight hug. "Me too. Thank you for coming, Crystal. It means everything to me."

Crystal strokes his back then lets him go. IT IS IMPORTANT TO BE HERE. THIS IS BEAUTIFUL. YOUR PEOPLE DESERVE IT. ARE THESE THE NEW FRIENDS YOU TOLD ME ABOUT?

"Oh, yes. This is Garnet. A guardian like no other." He gestures to the woman wearing a stunning ash blue and mauve qi pao dress, meant to pair well with Rogue's sharp dress suit. "And this tall, titan of a woman here is Tabatha. Ladies, this is Crystal Whip. A strong friend of mine."

"It's a pleasure." Tabatha embraces her in a quick hug.

Garnet smiles. I WAS HOPING TO MEET YOU

Daniel Jones

UNDER BETTER CIRCUMSTANCES.

"Uh-oh, they can communicate silently. You're in serious trouble, man." Walker gives a half-hearted chuckle while coming over to them.

Crystal tightens the straps on her heels.

"Not here," Rogue whispers. "Please."

THEY WERE LOOSE. I WASN'T GOING TO KICK HIM, she replies. TOO HARD.

Garnet gives a small grin. "I like her. I see why you would too." She holds Rogue's hand.

Crystal holds Jessie's hand and leans on her shoulder.

"Excuse us. We'll meet you back at the accommodation?" Jessie looks over at Rogue.

"Yeah, we have a lot to go over," Rogue replies.

Jessie and Crystal link arms and walk around the rest of the monument.

"When did that happen?" Walker points at them when they're out of earshot.

"Don't ask," Rogue mumbles. "But it's for the best and they're happy. And I've got a bright future ahead of me too." He holds Garnet's waist as she smiles.

"Speaking of which... I'm used to seeing you both at least six inches taller in your armor. How's civilian life treating you?" Walker asks the Venators.

"It's an adjustment. Four-inch heels, versus the ten-inch slant foot weighted boots? Kinda miss being seven and a half feet tall," Tabatha replies, with a chuckle. "It's strange not seeing you in those gawdy BDU's. But you look sharp in a suit. If someone like you can adapt, so can I." She puts her arm around Walker's back.

"Once you get your residency sorted out, I can show you around the city," Walker says with a smile, and eyes her up and down in the elegant dark grey asymmetric dress she's wearing.

"I guess it's good you two get along so well," Rogue starts to say.

"We have some history." Walker holds Tabatha close to him.

Rogue reaches into his pocket. "Was saving this for tonight but might as well hand it over here." He hands Tabatha a letter. "Tabatha Farsides is now an official resident of Acinvar. Which means a position in the rescue division is yours, when you're ready. Garnet's should be in my hands in a few days."

Tabatha smiles. "Thank you, I've been a nervous wreck these past few weeks. Living without resources is strange. It will be good to have some routine and stability back."

"That was quick; it took Crystal and me a few months to get ours," Walker replies. "So, logistics? Not security?"

She stares at the Ring storm. "The Titan had her final spree out there. It's best she dies here on this pillar. Besides, I need to be part of something that can save lives; it won't atone for anything, but it can change the future," Tabatha replies.

"And you?" Walker looks at Garnet.

Garnet gives Rogue a peck on the cheek. "I'm focusing on my personal life for now. Losing my second family was tough, except for Tita... uh, erm... Tabatha. I'll get that right eventually. Rogue is proving to be all I need. Right, hon?"

Rogue and Tabatha turn and stare at the Ring Storm with deadpan serious expressions.

"You feel that?" Tabatha asks.

"Yeah" Rogue says.

Garnet tightens her grip on Rogue's arm. "I thought you got rid of it."

"It's gone," Rogue and Tabatha say, after exchanging glances.

Crystal runs up to them, while pointing at the storm. SOMETHING IS TRAPPED OUT THERE. SOMETHING REAL BAD!

Rogue nods. "Yes, there is, and it will stay that way. I should inform King Soto that anyone who survived the Hydra's Wake needs to stay away from this place."

Daniel Jones

UNTIL NEXT TIME

About the Author
Daniel Jones

Hi there, my name is Daniel Jones and I write action thrillers in the creature feature niche. I do both series and standalones that blend elements of the Fantasy, Horror, Science Fiction genres.

I have been writing ever since I was a kid, and I can remember "Dinotopia: A land Apart From Time" being what started it all. Then as time went by, I became a huge Michael Crichton fan. "Congo" and "Sphere" are my favorites from him, and I'll always cherish my signed copy of "The Lost World".

Growing up all over the world as an air force brat gave me a different view of the world, learning history and mythologies from a different perspective.

Creature features have always been a big part of my life. no matter where I moved there were always monster movies on TV, there were always dinosaurs in museums, there were always local legends with some sort of monster. Animals, nature, and Scouting are also a big part of my life, I started as a Tiger Cub Scout and went all the to Eagle w/ palms. I spend a lot of time in parks, zoos, aquariums, campgrounds... The outdoors rule!

All of that has influenced my storytelling, and what I want to do with my writing. I write stories that are entertaining, explore survival, and will break characters down to the very core of who they are when nothing else matters and the situation is life or death. The monsters/creatures I write about will feel alive, instinctual, and have their own way of doing what they do. They'll feel like wild animals doing what wild animals might do.

Stay awesome everyone!

The Wake Series

**It's time to bring back the Creature Feature!
Paranormal Kaiju Steampunk style!**

1. Hydra's Wake
2. Archon's Wake
3. Desert Wake (codenamed)
4. Island Wake (codenamed)
5. Swamp Wake (codenamed)

Other Books By Daniel Jones

Standalones

Hydra Tower

Fantasy – Swords and Sorcery

Trouble plagues the Kingdom of Grasen. Not only is King Edwards dealing with bandits, but he's helping distant relatives, including young Princess Lavina, escape a diphtheria outbreak. But shortly after Princess Lavina and her family arrive, a monster attacks — a fierce, acid-spitting hydra that even magic can't defeat.

As the island evacuates, King Edwards' son, Prince Malcolm, becomes trapped in the castle tower, unable to escape the hydra. His disappearance leaves Grasen vulnerable to political intrigue, and the hydra's appearance foreshadows a powerful evil growing in the land. When the king is poisoned, it's up to Princess Lavina to gather legendary warriors to kill the hydra, rescue the prince, and save the kingdom…before it's too late.

Toximaw Territory (Announced, coming 2025)

Horror – Military Science Fiction

Hi!
I'm **Ivan Zann** and I'm the guy behind the cover of this and other books by Daniel Jones. I'm a fiction book cover designer who has been working since the early 2000s and I specialize in all sorts of fiction.

In more than twenty years I have made over 1200 covers, and I just don't want to stop, because the next cover is always the most fun to do.
Need a cover? Want to see more?
Just scan the QR Code.

No Generative AI Content
(whole, partial, or altered)
Is in this work.

Thank you for your support!

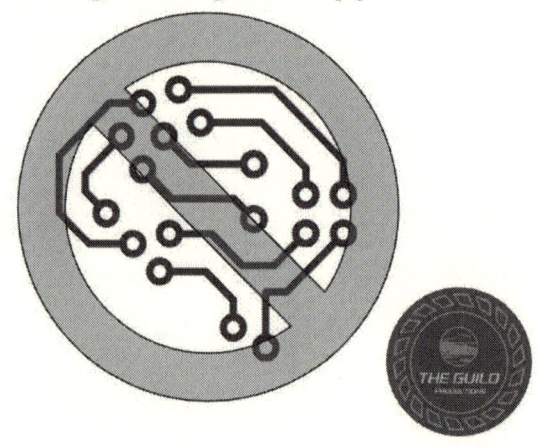